EMP LODGE

GRACE HAMILTON

BLURB

How far will a mother go to save her child in a dark new world?

In the post-apocalyptic aftermath, Megan Wolford is settling in with her makeshift family at the safe haven of their lodge. Despite her growing feelings for Wyatt Morris, the leader of the group, she still feels most secure on her own.

But when she becomes separated from her beloved daughter Caitlin in a storm, Megan is in danger of losing the one thing keeping her fighting to stay alive. Injured and desperate, she must fight every instinct within her to rely on the others for help when they find evidence that Caitlin has been kidnapped.

Can she put aside her stubborn need for independence and accept help from her newfound community before it's too late?

CONTENTS

1

Megan put her finger to her lips, shushing the group scurrying about gathering supplies. Everyone froze, nodded, and quietly took their designated positions. Megan's heart raced as she peeked out the window.

They were coming.

Wyatt had gone over the plan so often over the last few days, she thought she was prepared. She wasn't.

Rosie was crouched behind the center island in the kitchen with Willow right beside her. Wyatt stood sentry, flattened against the wall by the front door. When they came through the door, they wouldn't see him until they were practically on him. Albert was hiding in the bedroom, closest to the front door. Chase was crouched on the stairs where he couldn't be seen from the doorway, but would still be able to see Megan signal him.

Jack had chosen the closet where all of the guns and ammo were stashed to take cover in while Megan stood on the other side of the door. Her hiding spot allowed her to see the entire room. She was in charge of giving the signal to move. Megan held her breath and met Wyatt's cobalt blue eyes. She could stare at his dark blue eyes forever. His dark hair, which was a little too long, was falling around his face, making his eyes appear even darker.

He nodded calmly. The silent move was to settle her nerves enough for her to catch her breath. Over the past few months, she had come to rely on those looks to lift her spirits, calm her nerves or start a fire in the pit of her belly.

He was the perfect specimen of a man she had told him one night after they had enjoyed a romantic moonlit stroll around the property. He had laughed at that, but she'd been serious. Mostly. She probably could have worded it better when he'd started teasing her about it, so she'd shut him up with a kiss.

Megan looked around the room and thought about how much work had gone into making the lodge such a comfortable place to live. The Morris family had done all the work with Dale, Rosie's husband, at the helm, but he didn't survive to see all his hard work come to fruition. Dale's love and worry about the survival of his family was evident throughout the property and Megan was definitely appreciative of his foresight.

Over the past six months, she and her daughter had been made to feel like a real part of the family instead of outsiders, although there were times she still felt like an interloper because it all still felt so unreal.

Before the EMP, the world had been hectic and technology driven. Humans spent more time staring at their cell phones and tablets than they did enjoying each other's company. With no electrical power, the world had reverted to a much simpler life where family and friends were everything. Megan often wondered how she ever thought she'd survive on her own.

High stress situations always made her reflect on her life. People said their lives flashed before their eyes when they encountered near-death experiences. Now, she understood what they were talking about. Times like these always brought out little snapshots of the past flashing through her mind like a slideshow. She'd been lucky not to have too many negative ones.

This one made her smile.

Wyatt quietly coughed to get her attention. He'd caught her daydreaming. Megan brought her attention back to the situation at hand. This was it. It was the moment they had been waiting and planning for. Megan closed her eyes, adjusted the hat that was secured on her head, and waited.

"They're here," Wyatt whispered to no one in particular.

Duke barked; sounding the alarm that intruders were coming in.

"Now!" Wyatt shouted.

There was a flurry of motion as two people came through the doorway; causing everyone to spring into action at once, which sent Duke into a frantic state of barking and spinning around. He didn't know who to pounce on first.

"Surprise!"

Caitlin screamed as all of the adults jumped out of their hiding places. Her best friend and the only kid she knew, Ryland, hooted with laughter.

Megan rushed over to her daughter. Wrapping her arms around her, she squeezed her tight before kissing her forehead.

"Happy birthday, baby!"

Caitlin stood in the doorway, looking dumbfounded. Her blonde hair was still plastered against her face as she took in long, deep breaths.

The rest of the group circled around her, hugging her and affectionately rubbing her head.

"Oh my gosh," she exclaimed. "You guys scared me!"

Ryland was clearly proud of himself. "Gotcha!"

Everyone burst out laughing. Megan grabbed Caitlin's hand and pulled her to the center of the downstairs living area.

"Come see!"

Caitlin's eyes widened at the elaborate decorations that covered the kitchen table. There were paper chains made from magazine pages draped around the table and along the stair rail to the upstairs. Brightly colored cloths had been cut into strips and hung from the chandelier to resemble streamers. The table was covered with a pretty flowered tablecloth. Pinecones were arranged in a teepee on the table with bits of ribbon wrapped around the centerpiece.

Candles placed inside empty jars with rocks covering the bottom were scattered around the room. Two more jars sat on either side of the pinecone centerpiece. They were filled with flowers cut from cardboard and colored with crayons in a variety of pastel colors to look like bouquets.

Megan watched her daughter's face light up as she took in the elaborate display. They weren't able to find any of the traditional birthday party supplies, but together, they had come up with some creative ideas to make her day special.

"This is so cool!" Caitlin touched one of the cardboard flowers, "I love pink!"

"I made the flowers," Ryland piped up. "I told everyone we needed lots of flowers, even if the real ones were out of season." He smiled proudly.

Caitlin spun around. She stopped when she saw the cake on the kitchen counter. Megan watched as the emotions crossed her daughter's face. The cake was plain. They knew it but there was little they could do to make it look like a traditional birthday cake.

"Rosie made you a cake and we have a feast planned," Megan told her, gently turning her back to the table.

The eight-year-old girl smiled. The smile was forced. Megan knew her daughter was hoping for a chocolate cake, but they hadn't been able to find any chocolate on any of their scavenging runs. The baking chocolate they'd had in the pantry was long gone. There had been a few birthday celebrations since Megan and Caitlin had come to live at the lodge, which depleted the supply.

The last of the chocolate powder had been used for their harvest celebration. They had been splurging; celebrating small successes and were running out of the little luxuries like sugar, chocolate and even coffee. They all pretended like it didn't bother them but it was an adjustment. Chocolate made the world a little better but it was disappearing quickly and Megan didn't want to think about what would happen when the coffee finally ran out. Rosie had promised her that they could make different teas from some of the flowering plants that would taste just as good, but Megan had her doubts.

"Let's get your party hat on!" Megan exclaimed, hoping to lift Caitlin's spirits.

The cone-shaped hats looked like traditional birthday hats, but were made from magazine pages carefully folded together. At the top of each hat, wildflowers created a tassel of sorts. It was very comical and made everyone laugh. Each hat had a length of paracord attached to hold it secure on the head. Even Duke had a hat, which had slipped comically down to the side of his head.

Wyatt handed out half-sticks of gum and everyone hustled outside chewing and laughing. Megan had created a version of pin the tail on the donkey by using charcoal to draw a very crude donkey on the side of the cabin wall. They would use the gum to stick their "tails" on the donkey. Whoever came the closest won. Albert went first. Wyatt blindfolded him and Caitlin and Ryland spun him around three times as everyone cheered.

"One! Two! Three!" they shouted together.

The kids squealed and tried to run away as Albert chased them around attempting to pin the tail on one of them. Megan laughed and quickly covered her mouth when Albert turned his blindfolded head to look at her. Ducking behind Wyatt, she ran toward the side of the cabin where the donkey was while Albert stalked toward her, donkey tail in his outstretched hand. At the last second, she dropped to a squat and scooted out from under him as his fingers found the wall. Pressing the gum into it, he stepped back, whipping his blindfold off.

He'd pinned the tail to the donkey's nose. Putting his hands on his hips, he looked at what he'd done as if it were a piece of art.

"It could have been worse," Albert declared, as he spun around. "Like maybe one of you!" He took a step towards the kids, which had them shrieking and laughing as they danced out of his reach. He turned towards Megan with a grin and she quickly held her hands up in surrender.

There was a mix of booing and cheering and Chase clapped him on the back. "Well done, old man," Wyatt called out.

6

They took turns playing, each placement of a tail causing more and more laughter. When it was Megan's turn and Wyatt put the blindfold on her, she couldn't resist the chuckle. She could see through the blindfold. "Have fun," Wyatt whispered before he stepped back to spin her around as everyone counted out loud.

When Megan stopped spinning, she closed her eyes, wanting to give it a true shot. Walking toward the wall, she put her hand out and felt for the other tails. Mumbling to herself, she found Albert's, Chase's, Wyatt's. Rosie's had been the closest. Taking a guess, she pressed the tail to the wall and whipped off her blindfold.

"Wow, Mom. You did worse than Albert," Caitlin called out as she laughed.

Looking at what she had done, Megan realized that she'd visualized the donkey facing the other way in her mind. "Oops." She shrugged as she laughed with everyone else.

"Horseshoes next!" Ryland called out. Grabbing Caitlin's hand he dragged her over to the pitch area and handed out the horseshoes to see who would go first.

There was a lot of laughing, screaming, and groans as they played the first round of horseshoes. Ryland had become very good at the game and managed to win almost every time. Megan tossed her horseshoe and sighed when it missed the mark by several feet.

"Your aim is improving," Wyatt teased, wrapping his arms around her from behind. "At least it was better than your attempt with the donkey tail."

She turned and kissed him on the lips before pushing him away, scolding him for teasing her.

"Sore loser."

"You certainly aren't going to win," she shot back.

Caitlin threw her horseshoe. The clinking sound as the shoe hit the stake was cause for cheer as Ryland held her arm in the air declaring the birthday girl the winner.

Jack stepped forward, calling everyone to order. In as serious a ceremony as the happy group could muster, he held the golden horseshoe trophy up.

"Caitlin, you are hereby the winner of horseshoes. Please, take your trophy," he told her solemnly before winking.

The trophy had been making its way around the house for the past few months, but it was usually in Ryland's possession. Caitlin grabbed the shoe that had been painted gold with some spray paint they'd found a while back, hugging it to her chest.

"I'm going to put this on the wall in my room," she declared.

Her room was actually nothing more than a very small space walled off with blankets in a corner upstairs. Ryland and Caitlin had asked to have their own rooms halfway through the summer. Wyatt and Jack were still in the process of collecting wood and other materials to build another small addition on the cabin but it wasn't going to happen until after winter.

For now, they were all going to have to learn to live with each other in tight quarters. The open floor plan on the second floor allowed them to make each end of the U shape into small spaces for the kids. They had found cots on one of their supply runs at an old hotel and heavy blankets provided two of the walls and acted as a door. Ryland and Caitlin were free to decorate the two actual walls as they pleased. Ryland had plastered his side with pictures of video games he'd found in a magazine. Caitlin had asked permission to draw on the walls and had chosen to use chalk to draw pictures, washing it off when she got bored or wanted to change it out.

"Will you help me hang it, Ry?" Caitlin asked, still hugging the horseshoe.

"Ya, I'll grab the hammer."

Jack and Willow joined Megan walking into the cabin and together, they watched Ryland grab the toolbox from the hall closet and head up the stairs.

"I can't believe how much he's grown up right before our eyes," Willow murmured as Jack hugged her to his side.

"It's like he's a mini adult," Jack commented.

"Not so mini anymore," Willow replied. He's already taller than me and he's only twelve."

"They're forced to grow up so fast now," Megan commented as they turned to smile at her.

Jack wrapped his arms around his wife, his hands landing protectively on her belly. "Are you?" Megan wasn't sure how to ask because she knew they'd been talking about having another baby before the EMP, but now they were hesitant.

Shaking her head, Willow turned sideways to hug Jack. "Not yet, but this is a good thing. We've no idea what it will be like here once winter comes. Things could get rough fast," Jack told her as he hugged his wife tighter. "But it is nice to dream."

Winter was something they had all been thinking about as the fall weather rolled in. They knew there would be a lot of snow and it would be cold. They had planned and prepped and now had to hope for the best. It would be a true test. If they could make it through their first winter on the mountain, they knew they could survive anything.

2

From the moment Caitlin was up and around, Ryland had taken on the role of big brother; a position he took very seriously. It had only been a matter of weeks when the duo had approached all the adults for a "family meeting" complete with visuals.

"Mom. Dad," Ryland began. "I think it's time you had your own room and the same goes for you, Uncle Wyatt and Megan."

If it hadn't been for Albert warning everyone ahead of time, Megan wasn't sure how Willow and Jack were able to remain serious throughout the presentation. When Caitlin pulled out their sketches to show their plans for their own private spaces, Megan had to cover her mouth to hide her smiles.

The four of them excused themselves to go outside to discuss their thoughts before reaching a unanimous decision. They'd managed to make it as far as the orchard before laughing uncontrollably at the cuteness of it all.

Sobering, "It's a good idea. I certainly wouldn't mind some private time with my wife," Jack began.

"And it does solve some of our space issues," Wyatt offered between chuckles.

"Those two," Willow started to say as Megan nodded her head.

"Right?" Megan laughed. "So how much of this presentation was their idea or Albert's?"

"Oh no, that was all Ryland. The drawings might have been Albert's idea, but I'm guessing everything else was our son," Willow told them.

Coming to an agreement, the four went back into the house to give the good news to the kids, who were over the moon with excitement. They'd spent the rest of the evening moving things around up in the loft as they carved out their own personal spaces.

Even though Ryland was four years older, they found plenty of things to talk about. In six months, those two were closer than siblings right down to their squabbling. Granted, it wasn't as if they could complain about someone hogging the remote control or refusing to share a video game. No, their arguments were about the best way to trap rabbits or if it was better to flush wild turkeys or sneak up on them.

Both agreed that having Duke with them when hunting was usually a bad idea as the shepherd had fun barking and chasing after the game.

Megan couldn't be more pleased at how quickly her daughter bounced back after being poisoned and she seemed to be maturing quickly, leaving Megan to wonder if it was too much, too fast. She couldn't resist following them up the stairs and peeking over the rail to watch Ryland go into his "room" to retrieve the jar filled with finishing nails. As he parted the curtain, she could see the small shelf that he'd managed to build using scraps of wood and small branches. Albert had taught him how to cut tongue and groove joints using the hacksaw he liked to use so that he could piece the box shelf together without using the much-needed nails but not all the pieces had fit snugly together, so he ended up using a few nails to make sure it stayed together.

Ryland would collect rocks he found while on hunting expeditions. Caitlin contributed to his collection whenever she found a rock she thought was pretty including a trilobite, which Albert had recognized immediately. That had created a flurry of excitement as the kids began looking for other rocks with fossils in them.

His meager stack of clothing was neatly folded and sitting on the floor next to his display shelf. Willow allowed him to do as he wanted, but insisted he keep things tidy. Of course, it didn't always work that way.

Joining Caitlin in her room, Ryland helped her find the perfect spot for her trophy. They both knew it would probably be gone after the next game of horseshoes, but for now she clutched it to her chest while Ryland carefully picked out three nails to secure it to the wall.

"You wanted a chocolate cake, huh?" Ryland asked Caitlin as he stepped back to let her hang the horseshoe.

She shrugged. "Yea, I really did. Being able to buy chocolate at the store is one of the things I really miss but it's okay. Both Mom and Wyatt said that they won't stop looking when they go out scavenging, so I'm hoping they might find some. Your mom and grandma do make really good desserts even when they don't use chocolate. There, what do you think?" She stepped back, as Ryland crossed his arms over his chest and appeared to study the horseshoe. Megan clapped her hand over her mouth to keep from saying anything as she smiled broadly.

Nodding his head, "It looks good. I think it looks better in my room, but this is second best. Oww!" Ryland rubbed his arm where Caitlin had punched him. "Come on, we should get back."

Megan watched Caitlin adjust her party hat and barely made it back down the stairs before she heard her daughter shout, "I'll beat you down!"

Jumping down the last three steps, the kids joined the adults around the table where Rosie had placed the cake alongside a few gifts wrapped in an assortment of newspaper.

Caitlin beamed and clapped her hands.

A couple candles sat in a small jar next to the cake. Rosie had learned the hard way with Albert's birthday cake that the large candles they used for light destroyed the cake and made a huge waxy mess. When it happened, everyone had groaned and then laughed as Albert attempted to separate the cake from the wax. It didn't work, much to his dismay, but he didn't give up until Rosie had promised to make him another cake.

Megan started to sing Happy Birthday and the others joined in.

"Blow out the candles and make a wish," Megan instructed her daughter.

Caitlin squeezed her eyes shut, made a silent wish and blew. When Ryland asked her what she wished for, she looked at him in shock.

"I can't tell you or it won't come true!"

Everyone laughed. Megan loved that they could still have these moments. They were very fortunate. Most people didn't even know what day it was let alone have the luxury of being able to celebrate anything. Every birthday they celebrated meant so much more than it had before the collapse. Every year they survived would be a huge feat and it wasn't to be taken for granted. Wyatt had been insistent that they keep track of the days, partly as a means to track the time of year for plantings but also to give them a certain level of normalcy in a world gone dark.

When the solar flares came, causing the electromagnetic pulses to take out the power, chaos had instantly ensued. Megan had been witness to it in her own town. At first there'd been general looting and destruction as some folks treated it as an excuse to cause mayhem and destroy things. The larger big box stores had been the first to be invaded by people eager to take what wasn't theirs. The smaller business owners had tried to hold on to their inventory realizing that what they couldn't use, they could barter with, but that didn't last.

The world had quickly been divided into us and them. Those who were prepared, or had the means to take care of themselves, survived. Those who didn't quickly became fodder for those willing to take what they wanted in order to survive at any cost. Life had turned frightening fast.

Megan had done the best she could with her daughter but she wasn't sure they would have survived the last six months if it wasn't for the love and generosity of the Morris family. It had taken time, but everyone was slowly adjusting to the new way of life but there was always something coming up, or breaking, or needing replacement. Thankfully there was enough people around to help brainstorm ideas when necessary and they'd come up with some ingenious ideas thanks to the creativity and knowledge of everyone living there.

"Who wants cake?" Rosie asked, interrupting her thoughts.

Everyone raised their hand and Caitlin jumped up and down waving her hand shouting, "Me, me, me."

Megan wasn't exactly thrilled at the idea of eating what Rosie referred to as her spin on a cake from a scratch recipe without eggs or sugar. But Willow and Rosie were convinced that with a few tweaks, they could make it into a sweet treat that would satisfy everyone's sweet tooth.

Instead of using traditional cornmeal, they used one and three-quarters cup of whole-wheat flour and while they still had some brown sugar left, instead of the typical one cup, they only added enough to sweeten the dough. Two teaspoons baking powder gave the cake some fluffiness and a splash of vanilla, one-half teaspoon of salt and one teaspoon of cinnamon added to the flavor.

They had to use powdered milk for the binder instead of eggs, which would leave the cake a little flat, but it was all they had. They had used an additional cup of applesauce in place of a stick of butter and added some chopped hazelnuts they'd been able to forage to round out the treat. It wasn't a traditional cake by any means, but more of a sticky sweet-bread that reminded Megan of monkey bread.

Rosie quickly cut the cake and handed out the plates. While everyone ate, Caitlin unwrapped her gifts.

She whooped with glee when she opened the gift from Albert. It was a .22 caliber Crickett youth rifle. Albert had found the gun some months back and had carefully restored it. Wyatt had personalized the gun by carving a stylized "C.W." in the stock.

The rifle was a typical beginner rifle for a child. Megan remembered her own dad giving her a Crickett when she was Caitlin's age. She was so grateful that the tradition could be handed down, even in these difficult times.

Caitlin ran her hands over the carved lettering before hugging it like a doll.

"Can we go hunting?" she piped up as she bounced up and down on the balls of her feet.

Megan laughed. "Not at this very moment, but we can go first thing in the morning."

Caitlin clapped her hands excitedly.

The group had already decided it would be only Caitlin and Megan going. They needed some mother-daughter time. Living in such close quarters meant they were rarely alone. Jack and Willow would often take Ryland out hunting or scouting. It was a way for them to maintain their family unit and get a little privacy. It also gave them time to talk about things they'd prefer weren't made public just yet.

Wyatt and Megan had made it a point to spend time together both with Caitlin and without her. Starting a new relationship was never easy, but trying to do so under the watchful eyes of seven other people was difficult to say the least.

Megan watched as Caitlin took a bite of her cake. Her daughter swallowed without even chewing. The cake wasn't so bad Megan thought as she took a bite. Maybe a little too sticky. She wondered if it might taste better having been toasted a bit on the stove and decided she would mention it to Rosie later. Caitlin's hand kept disappearing under the table. Megan watched as she slowly tore off pieces of the cake and fed Duke who was patiently waiting below. Duke certainly liked the cake.

Caitlin noticed her mom watching her and quickly stopped feeding the dog under the table. Megan knew trips into town for supplies would probably stop as soon as the snow started to fall. It was unlikely they would find chocolate, sugar, or any of the other treats they were longing for. They were going to have to make do with what they had. Caitlin would learn to adjust.

The rest of the evening was spent playing Caitlin's favorite game, Twister. Each scouting trip had yielded another deck of cards or some new board game. Chase had come across an empty Twister box, so they decided to make their own using a patched tarp, some paint, and markers for the circles and they made the roulette using the box lid and an electric clock hand.

The group's matriarch, Rosie, along with Albert, declared themselves too old to play so they took turns spinning the dial and cheering everyone on while the rest of the group broke up into teams of four with Caitlin playing on both teams since it was her birthday.

"Left foot, red," Rosie called out.

"Hey, you aren't supposed to slide under me, Caitlin. What happens if I fall?" Chase demanded but Caitlin only giggled.

"You better not crush my daughter," Megan warned, as she laughed.

"Damn, my legs are shaking. Rosie, hurry up and call the next one," Chase called out.

"Right hand green," Rosie called out again, coughing to mask her laugh.

"Now, you did that on purpose! How am I supposed to reach that with Jack in my way?" Chase demanded.

"Well, considering you're the Jolly Green Giant, well... not so jolly, I believe you can manage just fine," Jack laughingly told him as he shifted into a position to make it harder for Chase to reach a green circle.

There was significant jostling and declarations of cheating if anyone shifted position. When Chase finally settled, his feet slipped out from under him and he went crashing down on top of Jack to a chorus of "Owws" from both men and much laughter.

Megan wiped her eyes, she'd been laughing so hard, before finally declaring it was time for bed, which Willow quickly seconded. Both kids grumbled about wanting to stay up later, until Megan reminded Caitlin about tomorrow.

"I can't wait to try out my new rifle," Caitlin said excitedly. Running over to Albert, she placed a kiss on his cheek and whispered something in his ear that had the older man blushing and clearing his throat. She then ran to each adult, handing out hugs and kisses along with whispered comments. When she got to Megan, she hugged her mom tight. "Thanks, Mom. I love you."

Ryland was waiting for her on the stairs. "Come on, Cait!"

Once the kids were upstairs, Megan headed to the bedroom she now shared with Wyatt. Crawling into bed, she nestled against Wyatt as he pulled her in close.

"You sure you don't want me to go with you guys tomorrow? I can hang back. You won't even know I'm there," Wyatt asked in the dark.

Megan sighed. "I would actually like you to go, but I think I need to spend some personal time with her."

He was silent for a while before answering. "She's been doing well with everything that's happened but there is a lot to adjust to. She is sharing her mom, inherited a brother, and a pretty big family all at once. Then, of course, all the other crap she's had to deal with at the hands of that monster who poisoned her."

The thought of what her life would have been like had Kyle Grice actually killed Caitlin six months back still gave Megan nightmares. They had managed to live through the EMP and the aftermath only to be nearly killed by some sort of serial killer intent on becoming a new world leader. If it hadn't been for Wyatt and his family, they would have been killed, and who knows what kind of damage Kyle could have done had he lived.

"She adores Ryland and I haven't figured out if it's part crush or mostly that he's the big brother she never knew she wanted."

"Maybe a bit of both."

"There must be something wrong with me because sometimes I miss the days when it was only the two of us. Don't get me wrong. I love it here. We both do but there are times where it all seems so overwhelming."

"You forget, I lived alone," Wyatt offered, squeezing her in a hug. "It can be overwhelming for me too because unless we're out hunting or scavenging, it always seems like we're part of a crowd here. Don't get me wrong, I love my family, but I miss the days where I had some privacy."

"Thank you for understanding." Megan kissed him before rolling over and closing her eyes.

3

Megan heard the annoying sound of her alarm clock and thought about smashing it against the floor. Why did they think it was a good idea to bring those horrible vintage style clocks home? Between the overly loud ticking and that hammer on the two bells…no, a hammer would be a better choice.

Wyatt poked her in the side. "Better get up. She'll never forgive you."

She groaned. "I am way too comfortable. Why did I suggest going this morning?"

She had grown accustomed to waking up next to Wyatt's big warm body every morning. She couldn't wait until winter when they could sleep in and cuddle under the warm blankets. With so many chores, and even more with winter approaching, they never got enough time to lie in bed doing nothing.

Wyatt was always up early, which got Megan up long before she wanted to. The days were getting shorter and Megan was secretly very thankful for that. The time in their room together was something she relished. She loved having him all to herself. She didn't have to be Caitlin's mom and he didn't have to be the leader of their group. It was just the two of them. They could let down their guards and simply be.

"Mom," Caitlin whispered through the door.

Megan knew there was no going back to sleep. She was surprised Caitlin was up. Usually she had to drag her out of bed. Clearly, the girl was excited to go hunting with her own gun.

"I'm coming, Cait. Give me a minute."

Wyatt rolled back to the other side. "Have fun. I'll be here all warm and toasty."

Megan stood, grabbed her pillow, and threw it at him. He laughed and hugged the pillow to his chest.

Dressing quickly in her beloved cargo pants with multiple pockets and a long-sleeved, green thermal shirt, she pulled a brush through her hair before sweeping it up into a ponytail. They had scored an entire wardrobe for everyone when they happened upon a warehouse. She would never forget that day.

She and Wyatt had gone on an extended scouting excursion and happened upon an industrial part of the city of Spokane that looked like it had already been scavenged. They hadn't had much success in their search for supplies, so decided to take a chance and they'd hit pay dirt. She wasn't sure which stores the warehouses supplied but they were all very well-dressed now.

The warm boot socks felt good on her feet. It was the one thing they didn't skimp on. They didn't completely wipe out the warehouse, not wanting to hoard it all, but they did grab more than one hundred pairs of socks in various weights and sizes. Their feet had to be taken care of. It was the one rule Wyatt enforced. They did far too much walking to let their feet be ignored.

Megan leaned over and gave Wyatt another kiss and he grabbed her hand. "Be sure to keep an eye on the weather. I know you weren't planning on going very far, but sometimes the weather can turn bad quickly and you don't want to get stuck out."

She squeezed his hand. "We'll be careful. If we get caught too far out, we'll find shelter."

Wyatt nodded before settling back under the covers and Megan headed out to join her daughter who was sitting on one of the barstools, swinging her legs back and forth impatiently.

"Finally! Mom, you said we had to go early."

Megan laughed. "It *is* early. We can't see when it is this dark anyway. Do you want some oatmeal or something before we go?"

Caitlin rolled her eyes. "I'm not hungry. I'm ready to go now."

Megan looked wistfully at the coffee pot. She wasn't going to get a cup this morning. Hopefully, Caitlin would grow tired and they would be back home by nine or ten.

"Okay, got your boots on?"

Waving her feet in front of the stool. "Yep, see?" Caitlin then jumped off the chair. "I'll grab my coat and gun."

Megan had been working with Caitlin all summer. She knew gun safety and was comfortable holding a gun and even firing one. She had been out with the others when they were hunting for birds and she'd become quite deft at setting both snare traps and, with some difficulty, deadfall traps, but this would be her first time hunting for larger game. With the fall rut season about to happen, she was ready.

They bundled up and put on the fanny packs they had packed the night before. The fanny packs were great for keeping things like their flashlights, knives, and whistle at hand. Each of the packs had twelve pockets, which allowed them to keep their gear organized and easy to find and their hands free.

A small pouch on the side held their plastic water bottles. Metal canteens were a huge no-no when hunting. The water jostling against the metal sides was too loud and would alert the game they were hunting to their presence. Ryland had learned that the hard way when he'd spooked a buck and sent it fleeing, taking the other deer along with it.

Megan planned to stick close to the cabin so she'd opted to leave her heavy pack behind since they had the basic survival gear in their fanny packs. Megan knew it wasn't the safest idea but she didn't plan to leave the property. The fifty acres Wyatt's family owned meant they rarely had to venture into other territories, and if something did happen, she knew that Albert would be up in the nest and would hear her whistle.

"Okay, you ready?" Megan asked, already knowing the answer. Caitlin was getting frustrated with Megan checking and rechecking gear.

"Yes, Mom. Can we go now?"

"I'm good. Let's go!"

They left out the back door. Today's goal was more about teaching Caitlin some of the basic skills needed to hunt successfully. She doubted they would find any game; much less do any actual hunting or shooting.

If they came across a flock of turkeys, that would be a good test of Caitlin's new rifle. Ryland had been out several times in the past couple months and had managed to harvest four turkeys on his own, plus what the guys were able to kill. They had been eating turkey regularly for the past three months or so and while it was nice to have fresh meat, it was getting a little boring, especially since they were running low on spices.

The wild turkeys were prolific in the area, which meant they had a reliable source of food and they were careful not to overhunt the population. Although they were a little tired of turkey soup, turkey pie or turkey-anything, it was food. They'd discussed possibly raising turkeys for both eggs and meat but they'd yet been able to spare the materials needed to build the coop, much less produce the crops needed to feed them.

As they walked towards the north mountain ridge, Megan kept her eyes open for any signs of bighorn sheep. She suspected they would be in the area, but she had yet to see one but both deer and moose would likely be seen in the area within the next month or so. Megan loved to watch the magnificent creatures and she knew that bringing down a bull moose could possibly feed everyone for up to a year if they only had the means to store it. There would be only so much jerky they could handle.

Wyatt had indicated interest in trading with others in the area and Megan would bet that they could find folks willing to trade for some of the fresh meat.

As they walked, Caitlin chatted about what she'd hoped to catch. "Wouldn't it be great if we could get a deer? Rosie has a meat grinder and she said we could make burgers. Doesn't that sound great?"

"It does sounds good. Steak sounds good too."

"Mmmm, with mashed potatoes and gravy." Caitlin made smacking noises and Megan wished they hadn't waited to eat, but it was too late now.

At the lodge, they had been working on how to lure in deer using antlers they had picked up. They didn't have the luxury of going to the outdoor store to buy an actual deer call and they hadn't found any on their scavenging trips. So they had to do it the old-fashioned way. Caitlin was pretty good at making the telltale grunting sound that mimicked a buck and they practiced as they walked.

It had been entertaining teaching the men how to grunt like a buck on the trail of a doe. There had been more laughter than actual grunting but they eventually got it worked out. Megan explained how important timing was. They were trying to imitate the sounds of two bucks fighting over a doe. There had to be grunting and then about twenty seconds of antler rattling.

When the full rut season was in swing, usually in early winter, the rattling would be more intense. An occasional snort followed by two loud exhales of breath was meant to sound like two bucks in a serious brawl. The sound would draw in another buck who was hoping to get in on the action.

Megan had stressed the importance of making the right sounds. There were plenty of black bears in the area. The bears would come running if the calls happened to sound like a wounded animal. While a bear would definitely provide a lot of meat, much like moose, Megan didn't like the risks that came with taking down a bear. So for now, they were going to stick with deer.

Caitlin had heard wolves one night and had been perfecting her wolf calls as well. The entire group marveled at how good she was mimicking the various animal sounds. She was a natural.

"You ready to try calling?" Megan asked, knowing Caitlin was dying to put her grunting sounds to the test.

"Yep."

They found some trees to hide in, in case they did actually manage to call in a buck. Megan reminded Caitlin how to hold her gun, with her finger on the stock and not on the trigger. If a buck came into sight, she needed to be ready to take the shot.

The shot had to be perfect. Caitlin knew to aim behind the elbow. Hitting the deer in the belly or backside would destroy the meat. It was a small target, but Caitlin had been practicing over the summer and had become quite proficient. Megan knew that a .22 LR wasn't the best choice for hunting especially if Caitlin missed the kill shot but truth be told, she was really hoping that they wouldn't find anything today. As much as she knew her daughter needed to grow up far more rapidly than she would like, she wasn't quite ready for her baby girl to kill a deer.

Caitlin stayed alert and did an excellent job of not talking. She scanned the tree line and listened for any sign that a buck was coming into the area. After about an hour of calling and waiting and calling again, Caitlin grew bored.

"I'm hungry," she said, pouting.

Megan sighed. "So am I. We should have eaten before we left."

She checked her watch. It was almost nine, which meant they had already been out for three hours. Caitlin lasted longer than she thought she would have.

Dark clouds were rolling in. Megan wanted to get back to the lodge before the storm hit but they were so close to the mountain ridge, she wanted to peek first.

"Let's go see if we can find any deer trails that way." She pointed toward the ridge.

As they were walking, the first raindrops started to fall.

"That was fast," Megan grumbled. She thought they had more time.

"Mom, we better go back. We can look tomorrow."

They were so close. Megan could see the clearing indicating they were close to the cliff's edge. She had never been to this area before and wanted to see if there was a stream or meadow that would attract the deer.

"Look," Megan said with excitement, calling Caitlin over.

Down below, there was a meadow. Megan looked around to see if there was a way to climb down the hill. She just knew that would be an excellent place to hunt.

The rain started to fall harder and the wind picked up.

"Mom, let's go."

The fear in Caitlin's voice brought Megan back to the situation at hand. She had gotten so excited about the meadow she had ignored the weather warnings and Wyatt had reminded her of exactly that this morning. She should have paid more attention to the weather signs as both Wyatt and Chase had been instructing her.

"You're right, we need to go, but we are going to come back up here tomorrow. We'll bring Wyatt and find a way down."

Megan pulled her hood over her head and made sure Caitlin's was up as well.

"Wow, this storm came out of nowhere, huh?" she said to her daughter, hoping to lighten the mood a bit.

The wind was gusting strong enough that it made it difficult for them to move forward.

"Let's get back into the trees." Megan had to shout to be heard over the howling wind. The rain was slamming into the ground, making a loud drumming sound. How had it come on so fast?

Caitlin nodded and struggled to move against the wind and into the trees. Just as they reached the shelter of the trees, they heard a horrible cracking noise. Megan looked up in time to see a large tree branch falling through the thick trees.

"Caitlin!" she screamed, grabbing her daughter and pulling her back out of the trees.

More cracking and a loud boom. Megan knew a tree had just fallen. The trees were no safer than the exposed ledge. They would need to push through to get down the mountain. She was counting on the wind not being quite as strong farther down.

The rain was coming down in sheets now, making it impossible for them to see anything. Megan grabbed Caitlin, doing what she could to shelter her with her own body.

"Just hang tight, baby! It will be over soon!" Megan didn't know if her daughter heard her. She could barely hear herself.

The wind blew the rain sideways; soaking them both and making the ground quickly turn to mud. Megan knew the walk back to the lodge would be difficult. She hoped they could manage without twisting an ankle.

"Mom, I'm scared," Caitlin wailed and clutched her tighter, her little body shaking.

"I know. I am too. Hold on to me."

As she stood there with her arms wrapped around her daughter, pushing her head into her belly, she couldn't help but get angry with herself. She should have been paying better attention to the weather. She knew it could change within minutes. She should have known better. Wyatt had drilled into her the cardinal rules of survival. Being aware of your environment was at the top of the list.

The rain began to subside a little.

"Let's go, Cait," she said, untangling her daughter's arms from around her waist. "The rain is slowing down; we can make it back now."

They started walking along the ledge, with Megan walking on the outside. The wind was still gusting and she didn't want to risk a strong gust blowing her daughter over the edge.

Just when she thought the rain had stopped, it picked up with a force she wasn't prepared for, blinding her. Puddles formed all over the ground. It was so loud she couldn't hear anything but the rain beating the earth and then, suddenly, she was sliding.

Megan screamed as the ground beneath her disappeared and she landed on her back. She reached up to grab Caitlin but her daughter wasn't there. She heard a faint scream and saw a blur of pink whip by her.

Caitlin was sliding down the face of the ridge with Megan right behind her. Megan's descent down was brutal. Her right leg had been bent behind her and her left leg seemed to be smashing into every rock on the way down. She desperately grabbed at the ground, hoping to slow her fall. She could feel her fingernails breaking as she clawed at the rocks.

Her body rolled and her forehead smacked into a jagged rock. She could feel the rock slice into her skin and prayed it was only a shallow cut. Worried that she might break her leg, or worse, she managed to pull both her knees toward her chest but hadn't quite succeeded when she made contact with a large boulder. The landing sucked the wind out of her as she took gasping breaths.

At least she was no longer sliding down the hill, she thought vaguely as she tried to take inventory of her body without moving. Megan opened her eyes and tried to focus. Blood was pouring down her nose and into her eyes. She used the back of her hand to wipe the blood away but it did little to help her see. She was definitely at the bottom of the ravine.

Using her elbows to prop herself up, she looked around the area yelling for Caitlin. Nothing. The rain had come to a sudden stop as if a faucet had been turned off and the wind wasn't nearly as bad at the bottom, which made her thankful.

"Caitlin!" she yelled again.

Her head was spinning from what she was sure was a concussion and her left foot was swelling. She tried to move her injured leg. A powerful, shooting pain tore through her body. Rolling to her side, Megan vomited before collapsing back down. The world was spinning. Taking a few deep breaths, she waited for the pain to subside.

She called for Caitlin again and waited. Nothing. Deafening silence.

Megan had to find her daughter. She took another deep breath and shifted slowly into a sitting position. The agony in her leg radiated from her toes to her hip. She had no idea where the actual injury was. *Maybe it was just a badly sprained ankle.* She'd torn ligaments before and knew the pain could be excruciating. In fact, the doctor told her a torn ligament could be more painful than a broken bone.

"Please, please don't be broken. Not now."

She moved her right leg and was relieved to feel no intense pain so she could still support the majority of her weight on that leg. Megan slowly tried to stand but even moving the injured leg was brutally painful.

"You're not walking out of here, Megan. Time to sit back down."

She collapsed on the ground and screamed as loud as she could, putting all her anguish into her cry. She couldn't believe she had been so foolish as to not keep track of the weather when Wyatt had reminded her this morning. Now her daughter was out there some-where, possibly injured or unconscious. There was no way she was going to sit here with Caitlin out there all alone.

Megan took a deep breath and rolled onto her stomach. The move jarred her foot and sent shooting anguish throughout her entire body. She gave herself a few seconds to breathe through the pain before pulling her body across the rocky ground in a low crawl.

She needed to look around the bottom before she made her way back up that rocky incline. She had no idea how she was going to do that, but she had to. Megan pulled herself at a slightly upward angle that would give her a better vantage point to see the area.

Caitlin's bright pink coat would stand out. She hadn't been too worried about her daughter wearing camo on their hunting expedition. Her dad had insisted she wear the bright orange vests whenever they went out hunting so he could always see her. It was a safety thing that had been drilled into her brain from an early age.

Megan had to stop every few minutes. She knew she was on the verge of passing out from the pain. Or maybe it was the concussion; at least her head had stopped bleeding. She refused to succumb until she knew her daughter was safe.

She made it back to the tree line that led up the hill. A thick branch lying on the ground gave her an idea. She could make crutches. They wouldn't exactly be comfortable, but sliding her body across the rocks and wet ground wasn't exactly a walk in the park.

The branch was strong enough to hold her body weight. She used a tree and the branch as a crutch to get to a standing position. Her injured leg felt as if it was heavy as a rock and as thick as a tree trunk. She looked down to make sure it hadn't tripled in size.

Nothing. It looked perfectly normal, minus the tears and mud. *That was a good thing, right?*

"Move, Megan," she said aloud. Caitlin was out there somewhere, waiting for her mom to find her.

It was a slow, painful climb back up the slippery slope. Thankfully, the trees actually provided something to hold on to. This was the path she had been looking for. This is where they would climb down the hill to get to the meadow; that is, if she ever went hunting again.

Megan collapsed at the base of a large pine tree and propped herself up using the large trunk as support. Staring out at the meadow below and the area where she had crawled up from, she lost her breath. It was a long fall. Her daughter was so much smaller than her and Caitlin had flown past her when the ground had washed away under their feet as if she was on a sled. She didn't know whether to be relieved or terrified Caitlin was not down there. With her view of the entire meadow, she took a relieved breath. There was no pink coat and definitely no body of a broken little girl.

Caitlin must have been able to stop her fall. She had to have run for help. *Did she know the way back to the cabin?*

It was becoming increasingly difficult to stay awake and Megan shook her head trying to clear the increasing fuzziness that was wrapping around her vision. She had no idea how much time had passed. It could have been an hour or more. If Caitlin knew her way back to the cabin, it would take her about an hour to get there from here. Help could be arriving at any minute. As her vision blackened, she sent out a heartfelt prayer that her daughter was safe.

4

W yatt finished splitting another cord of wood, stacking it neatly next to the woodshed on the platform they'd built. This would make ten, but he wasn't convinced it would be enough. As the old adage said, better safe than sorry.

Sweat dripped from his brow even though the temperature hovered around fifty degrees. He grabbed the bottom of his shirt and wiped his face. A cool breeze whipped through, cooling his skin. Looking up at the sky, he wasn't very surprised to see dark clouds building up in the north. He expected Caitlin and Megan would return anytime. She knew to watch the weather and get back home before it hit.

Rosie stuck her head out the back door. "You want something to eat, hon?"

"No, Mom, I'm good, thanks. Is Albert still in there?"

"Yep, just gave him some ointment for his knee. His arthritis is really acting up. I would say we are in for a good storm," Rosie said matter-of-factly.

Wyatt used to question her theory about arthritis pain and incoming rain, but she was usually right. The clouds confirmed it. Megan better get her butt home.

He tried to stay busy but the nagging feeling in his gut wouldn't be ignored. Megan and Caitlin hadn't taken any gear with them besides the basics. She should be back by now. He had been fighting back the desire to go with her, knowing that the two of them needed some mother-daughter time, but it wasn't easy. He was so used to protecting those he loved, and he loved Megan and Caitlin.

His mother had lectured him repeatedly about his overprotective nature but it was like trying to tell him not to breathe. He'd been like that since he was a teen and his time in the SEALs only reinforced it for him. The thought of not being there when a loved one needed him filled him with dread. When he had seen Kyle holding the gun on Megan, rage and terror gave him superhuman strength. The only thing he thought of as he fought against the man who threatened Megan was her. Her safety. Her well-being. Her life.

Wyatt helped his mom carry in a basket of laundry and hang it by the fire. The rain was starting and the wind was picking up. If Megan didn't come walking through that door in the next minute he was going to lose his mind.

Suddenly, the door swung open slamming against the wall with a loud thunk. Looking up in relief, he frowned to see it was only Jack and Chase.

"Wow, that wind came out of nowhere!" Chase said, brushing crushed bits of leaves and pine needles from his hair.

Wyatt went to the back door to check out what was happening outside. This was the downside of not having any large windows on the ground floor. He pulled open the back door and was nearly blown off his feet. The wind gusted through the open door, blowing the clothes that were hanging near the stove.

"Oh my," Rosie said, quickly grabbing a sock that had been ripped from the clothespin holding it on the rope.

"You should see what it looks like from up here," Willow called out from upstairs

Wyatt slammed the door shut and took the stairs two at a time. He stared out the huge windows. It was the middle of the morning but the sun had been blocked out. He could see the tops of the trees bending sideways with the force of the wind.

"Give her some time," Jack said from below. "She probably saw the storm and took shelter somewhere to wait it out since there's no way they could walk back in this wind."

Wyatt slowly walked down the stairs.

"She better have," he grumbled. "I need to secure the root cellar."

"I'll help you," his brother said, grabbing a rain jacket from the hall closet. He grabbed another and handed it to Wyatt.

The brothers struggled against the wind and the rain beating them with tiny, sharp pellets. They heard a loud crashing sound and watched as a tree fell onto the cabin. Jack raced inside to make sure everyone was okay.

Wyatt struggled to walk against the wind. The tree was resting on the metal roof of the lodge, but there didn't appear to be any serious damage. It was a fairly small tree and the cabin was well-built. It wouldn't be a problem.

Another cracking sound had him frantically looking around to see where it was coming from. He couldn't see any falling trees, but he could hear it happening all around him.

Jack slapped him on the shoulder, pulling him back into the house. He was shouting something, but Wyatt couldn't make it out.

When he walked through the door, everyone was huddling in the kitchen, terrified. Megan and Caitlin were in this storm, exposed and alone.

"The heart of the storm will pass within minutes," Chase assured Wyatt. "Then we'll go."

The small kitchen window shattered as a tree limb burst through, spraying glass all over the counter. Duke started barking as Rosie gave an involuntary scream.

Wyatt looked at Jack. His little brother was worried about his own family. This storm was a wild one. The lodge was sturdy, but he wasn't sure it could take a larger tree coming down on it. One was more than enough.

"Ry, Mom, Willow, you guys need to move away from the windows. They are small, but I don't want anyone getting hurt. You can sit at the table for now but if the wind gets much worse, I'd feel more comfortable if you sat next to the staircase, which would provide some additional protection and support." Wyatt tried to remain calm but inside, he was panicked. If he could barely stand in this wind, how were Megan and Caitlin supposed to manage?

"Chase, help me put together some go bags, would you?" The severity of the storm caught everyone by surprise and he knew his friend was worried about them too.

Jack started to go help Chase but Wyatt put his hand on his brother's shoulder. "You'll need to stay here with Albert and take care of any damage from the storm."

The two brothers looked at each other and communicated without words. Jack needed to stay behind and protect his family.

They packed quickly, hoping to leave the second the storm started to subside. Wyatt threw in extra first aid supplies, just in case the worst had happened. He added some bread that had been left over from yesterday's batch. A pack of dried apple slices from this year's harvest was also added.

He dug through the other bugout bags they kept at the ready, pulling out a couple of ponchos, Mylar blankets and more paracord. Wyatt wasn't sure what they would find, but he wanted to be ready for anything. They were planning a rescue mission, not a survival mission. If Megan and Caitlin had been caught in the storm, they would be cold, wet and likely injured. Their first goal would be to assess any injuries and then get them warmed up in a hurry.

Wyatt was praying they could walk but if not, he was prepared to carry them home. He added in a pair of leather gloves for himself and Chase. Wyatt stared into the open backpack and went over a mental checklist. He hoped this would be enough.

Ryland stood up. "Dad, you have to go with them. I will take care of Mom and Grandma."

Jack looked at Wyatt, who was about to say no.

"I would appreciate that, Ry."

"Jack," Wyatt started, but was cut off by his mother.

"I think he's right. The three of you can cover more ground. Ryland and Albert can hold the fort down."

Willow laughed. "We aren't exactly incapable here, guys. Thanks for the confidence, but we aren't a bunch of wilting flowers."

Wyatt knew they were right. His mom, and especially Willow, hated being treated as if they were fragile.

"Fine, get your bag together, Jack. I'm gonna check the weather."

When Wyatt opened the door again, the wind was still howling but the rain had subsided a bit. It was still pouring but it wasn't that violent rain that drove into your skin like nails.

He looked up at the sky, which had shifted from black to a dark, smoky gray. *Good enough.*

"Let's go," he said, grabbing his bag and heading out the door.

Jack and Chase rushed to catch up to him.

His brother asked the obvious. "Where are we going, Wyatt?"

Wyatt pointed. "She told me they were heading up the mountain. She wanted to check out the area and look for good places to hunt in the coming weeks."

"The way this storm came on, they could have easily gotten turned around. There's no telling where she might have ended up," Chase muttered. "Please tell me she has a compass with her?"

"She promised never to leave home without it," Wyatt told them as they trudged through the wet leaves and mud, which had become slippery, making their trek that much more difficult.

They all knew that Megan was an excellent hunter and trapper. Her father had made his living leading hunting expeditions into both the Cascades and the Rocky Mountains. While she'd readily taught the others what she knew, this season would be the first time they would put it all to the test. The group was hoping to get several deer. With the makeshift freezer they'd built, they were hoping to have fresh meat throughout the winter, as well as make jerky.

Wyatt and Megan had talked extensively about hunting and the best place to find deer. With their food supply dwindling quickly, deer, bear, elk or whatever else they could hunt would be fair game. Megan had explained cougars could be an issue while they stalked their prey. Cougars were also on the menu if they happened to come across one, although Megan had warned that they needed to be careful and make sure the meat was thoroughly cooked so as not to get trichinella. Meat-eating animals could carry it, unlike deer and elk, which were herbivores.

His mind was hung up on the predators. If Megan and Caitlin had been hurt in the storm, it could be an open invitation for a hungry animal.

"We'll find her, Wyatt," Chase assured him. "She'll be okay."

"She better be," he growled.

5

Megan couldn't stop the tears from flowing. The pain in her ankle was excruciating, but the idea of Caitlin out there all alone nearly killed her. She cursed herself for letting it happen. She'd been so intent on finding feeding grounds for the deer she knew lived in the area that she hadn't been paying attention to the rapid shift in the weather. Rain this time of year was normal and expected and while she'd been in some extremely windy weather from their precarious perch on the mountain, they were lucky the wind hadn't blown them clear off the mountain.

Granted, a mudslide wasn't much better and she let out a groan both from pain and despair.

"Wyatt, I should have asked you to come with us." She knew he would have said yes. Megan knew her daughter had been looking forward to their mom-daughter time together, and chances were that if the weather hadn't turned, they would have been fine, but in hindsight, would having Wyatt with them have helped?

At the very least, he would have been more attuned to the weather and insisted they turn around sooner. But then again, he might have also been injured in the mudslide. Or worse.

She didn't want to contemplate what could be worse. Not with her daughter missing.

"Stop the pity party, Megan," she scolded herself aloud, partly to wake herself up and partly because she needed to hear the words.

"Get up. Get moving. Get help."

She used the tree and her makeshift crutch to stand up again. Her leg was completely useless now. She knew if she removed her boot, she wouldn't be able to get it back on. It was already feeling tight. Megan couldn't deal with the idea of it being broken. How would a broken bone heal without a cast? It wasn't as if a surgeon could go in and put the bones back together. It would heal on its own, but if it didn't heal correctly, she could be crippled for the rest of her life.

"Well that's dismal."

She sat back down and dug in her fanny pack. Walking on a broken leg or ankle would make it worse.

Her fingers wrapped around the whistle she'd added to both hers and Caitlin's packs, just in case they were separated. Megan couldn't believe she hadn't thought about it sooner. She put the whistle to her lips and started to blow. After several loud bursts, she stopped and waited to hear if Caitlin would return her call.

She strained to try to catch any manmade noises.

Nothing. Nothing but the wind and the rain answered her.

She scanned the area, looking for any sign of movement. The wind blew the fall leaves from the birch trees in the area, but she couldn't see much else. The putrid smell of wet, decaying leaves made her nauseated. Usually, she liked the smell of the damp earth and the fresh smell of rain. But being on the ground in agony and sick with worry was a completely different story.

Caitlin was gone. She had vanished. The only thing Megan could think happened is her daughter had gone for help. That had to be it. "Hold onto that thought, Megan. Caitlin, stay safe. I'll find you."

Megan continued to blow the whistle every few minutes. She didn't dare try to walk but she couldn't just sit on the ground doing nothing. She shivered as the cold seeped into her bones. The ground was wet and cold, which wasn't helping her already soaked clothes from her slide down the mountain. She knew hypothermia could be an issue if she didn't get out of her wet clothes soon but with everything drenched as it was, there was no way she could make a fire even if she wasn't injured.

The pain was a constant throb shooting up her leg every time she shifted, which made it hard for her to focus on much else. She wasn't sure how long she had been sitting there but it was time to move. She was going to have to drag herself back to the lodge and get help. She assumed Wyatt would be out looking for her but with her own clothing green and beige, he could walk right by her and not see her. Megan once again became frustrated with her own poor decisions. She should have worn a bright color like Caitlin but the only bright clothes they had were made from synthetic fabrics and just in case they did spot some deer, she didn't want to give their position away by flashing white. Her dad had always been insistent on wearing natural fabrics while hunting. The harder synthetic fabrics could reflect light in the blue spectrum, making it easier for deer to see them. So while it was bad for deer hunting, it would have made her easier for humans to find.

Wyatt bit back his panic. Even on SEAL missions, he'd always remained calm and clearheaded, but those missions didn't involve someone close to him. It was easier to be objective when it wasn't someone you cared about. He stopped the feeling of dread that unfurled inside his stomach. Something was very wrong. He could feel it in his gut. There was no way Megan would stay out in this weather. Even if she had been caught in the storm, they would have heard or seen her by now.

He thought about Evan Grice, who had sworn revenge on them for killing his brother, Kyle. Maybe he had found Megan and Caitlin and hurt, or killed, them. They hadn't seen or heard from him in months but they knew there were still people in the region. They suspected it was Evan's group and had kept to their side of the mountain to avoid any confrontations.

Now, Wyatt questioned their decision to ignore them and hope they simply went away. The thought of Megan and Caitlin being harmed at the hands of someone intent on doing harm made him physically ill. He *had* to find them.

"Let's split up," Chase said, interrupting Wyatt's thoughts of tracking down Evan Grice.

Wyatt nodded. "Stay close. Look for tracks or any sign of trouble."

He didn't have to say to look for blood or a body. They had all expected to find Megan and Caitlin quickly and easily. The sense of foreboding weighed heavy on them all.

They fanned out and spent another forty-five minutes walking in a semicircle up the mountain.

"Stop!" Wyatt shouted.

They all froze, looking around.

The noise that alerted Wyatt cut through the silence. A whistle. They all moved at once, following the sound coming from the mountain ridge. Wyatt's heart raced. He knew what that meant. They had fallen off the ledge.

"Dammit! No!"

Before he could take another step, Chase put a heavy hand on his shoulder. "The ground's a mess. Let's take it slow. We'll find them."

Wyatt could only nod his head. They had to stop every few minutes to wait for the whistle to guide them in the right direction.

Wyatt started shouting Megan's name and then Caitlin's when he didn't get a response. A short blast from the whistle led them into the trees on the sloped hill that led to the meadow below. Wyatt was familiar with the area and knew a little of what to expect. He wasn't prepared for the mud that made walking downhill almost as slippery as leather-soled shoes on ice.

"Megan!" he shouted, waiting to hear the sweet sound of her voice.

It floated through the trees, "Wyatt? Wyatt! Wyatt, I'm down here!"

Wyatt slipped and slid halfway down the hillside. When he saw her muddy, bloody face, he couldn't stop the tears from welling in his eyes. She was alone. His eyes instantly looked down the hill and into the rocky bottom below.

Chase quickly realized the situation and took off running down the hill in search of Caitlin.

"She's gone, I don't know what happened. She just vanished." Megan was crying.

Jack dropped to his knees, pulling off his pack. He quickly pulled out the emergency blanket and covered her. Wyatt was digging through his bag and pulled out a pack of wet wipes.

"What happened, baby?" Wyatt asked in a soothing tone, hoping to calm Megan down.

She shook her head, "I don't know. We fell. When I came to, she was gone. I hit my head," she said as if she just remembered the injury.

He grabbed her hand to stop her from touching the bloody gash. It had stopped bleeding, but judging by the blood dried on her face and the bloody trail he could see leading up the hill, it had bled a lot. Head wounds always did but it never made it any less shocking to see how much blood a small cut could produce.

Wyatt gently cleaned her face, unsure if there were more cuts under the mud and blood. It appeared to be only the one nasty gash on her forehead.

"My leg," she mumbled. "I think my ankle is broken."

Wyatt quickly stopped cleaning her face and looked at her legs stretched out in front of her. He didn't have to ask which one. He could see the ankle of her left leg was swollen.

Jack looked incredulous, "You were at the bottom and climbed up here?"

She nodded. "More like crawled."

Wyatt had broken a leg before. He didn't think he would have been able to climb a steep, muddy hillside. The fact that she did said a lot about her determination.

"Wyatt, you have to find her. When we fell, I saw a glimpse of her go by, but—" Her voice cracked.

"It's okay, we'll find her. Chase is looking now. We need to get your leg splinted and get you back to the house."

Jack was already on it. He came back with a couple of branches, about an inch in diameter. Wyatt grabbed the Ace bandage and duct tape he always carried from his bag. The two of them carefully placed the branches against either side of her leg, all the way down to the sole of her boot. Wyatt wrapped the Ace bandage around the leg to hold the branches in place. He paused when Megan cried out in pain. She was shaking and he wasn't sure how much of that was cold or pain.

"I need to secure the bandage with this." He held up the duct tape. "Do you think you can handle it?" At her nod, he worked as carefully as he could but he could feel her tremble and she didn't hold back the small gasps.

"This will help keep your leg and ankle braced. The stretcher ride back home may get a little bumpy. We don't want to jostle your leg any more than we have to."

She nodded but her face was pale and perspiration lined her brow. Wyatt could tell she was fading fast.

"Megan, I need you to stay with me, okay?"

She nodded again, indicating she heard him but she wasn't doing well.

He grabbed the bottle of water and put it to her lips, making her take a few small sips. Pulling the bread out of his pack, he fed her a few small bites.

"Concussion," she mumbled. "My head." She put her hand to the wound on her head, wincing when her fingers brushed her hair.

"Probably, which is why I need you to try to stay awake. I still need to check you for other injuries."

He quickly bandaged the gash on her head before checking her over. She had a lot of bruises from her slide down, but it didn't look as if anything else was broken.

"I think I'm okay. Other than my ankle. Where's Chase? Has he found Caitlin?" Megan started to move, but Wyatt quickly stopped her.

Jack had been scouting the surrounding area for the material needed to make a stretcher. They would use the tarp Chase had in his pack, but they still needed a couple long branches to secure the tarp and hold Megan's weight.

Hearing Megan's question, Jack handed Wyatt two branches about two inches in diameter and eight feet long.

"I'll go get the tarp from Chase and see if there's anything I can do," he told them before rushing off down the hill.

Wyatt sat next to Megan on the muddy ground. Grabbing her hand he rubbed his thumb over her palm.

"You're gonna be okay and so will Caitlin," he told her in a soft voice.

She squeezed his hand. "I can't lose her, Wyatt. I can't believe I was so stupid. I wasn't paying attention to the weather. That wind came on so fast, we couldn't move. Then came the rain. Before we could find shelter, the ground gave way and we were falling. Oh Wyatt, we have to find her."

"Stop. The weather did shift quickly; even we were caught by surprise. You couldn't have known any of this would happen. I am so glad you had that whistle. That was a very smart move."

"I was hoping Caitlin would hear it and respond. I'm glad you heard me, but I'm so worried. How could she have just disappeared? Is she lying somewhere injured?" Megan closed her eyes, her head rocking slightly as if she was about to fall asleep. Snapping her head back, she opened her eyes and winced. "Oh, I really don't feel well. My head hurts and I feel sick."

Wyatt wanted to assure her that everything would be okay but he couldn't truthfully. Not when a broken bone could mean death and a little girl lost in an area known for predators could get killed. If this had been in the BT, as Megan had called it. The before times before the EMP, at least this side of the mountain had cellular service and he could have called for emergency assistance.

Now?

Megan was clearly suffering from a head injury. The leg injury should heal but her head? He prayed it was simply a mild concussion combined with a little hypothermia. The trees provided some shelter from the rain, but it was still wet and the temperature was dropping. With the wind blowing across their wet clothing, it was dropping their body temperature and with everything so wet, a fire wasn't an option.

Wyatt estimated that she'd been out here at least three hours and was at serious risk of her core body temperature lowering to the point where it could threaten her life. Her hands were cold. She was still sweating, which would be drying cold to her skin. Megan was in danger. They had to get her back now!

Jack came back up the hill carrying the green tarp.

"We need to move now," Wyatt said forcefully.

Jack looked at Megan and nodded in understanding. He pointed behind him. "Chase is right behind me."

Megan's eyes popped open. "Caitlin?"

Jack gave Wyatt a slight shake of the head before he opened up the tarp.

"Wyatt?" Megan called out.

Wyatt didn't want to tell her they had to leave without Caitlin. Megan's life might well depend on getting her back to the lodge as quickly as possible.

Chase rushed back up the hill to help Jack make the stretcher while Wyatt talked to Megan. He was trying to keep her awake and conscious even though passing out would provide her escape from the pain in her leg but she needed to stay alert. While he suspected she had no other extensive injuries, he was afraid to move her if she was unconscious. If something happened and she couldn't tell him what was wrong. He shook his head. He wasn't going to think about that.

He had Megan drink a bit more water but she pushed it away. "Caitlin? Where is she?"

Wyatt looked to Chase who gave him a negative head shake. Taking both her hands, he tried to rub some warmth into them, but he was cold too. "We don't know yet." Before he could say more, Megan began to cry.

"Wyatt, we need to find her."

Wrapping his arm around her, he held her tight. "We will. I promise. But first we have to get you back."

. . .

He watched Chase and Jack lay the unfolded tarp on the ground. As Chase instructed, Jack placed a pole in the middle of the tarp folding the tarp over the pole to fold it perfectly in half. Chase grabbed the other pole and placed it a few inches from the edge. He then folded the top layer of the tarp over the second branch and began to roll it in the tarp several times until it was about two feet from the first pole.

Grabbing the bottom layer of the tarp, he placed it over the space, reaching the first branch. He then used paracord to tie the branches together at the top, center and bottom of the tarp. Chase left about a foot of branches exposed at both ends so it would be easy to hold when they carried her or if needed, they could drag her across the muddy terrain like a sled.

Jack and Chase tested the stretcher. It would work just fine with Megan's light weight.

Wyatt lifted Megan and placed her on the stretcher, wrapping the blanket around her. She was fading fast. He knew she would be unconscious before Chase and Jack got her back to the cabin. He also knew his mom would know what to do.

"I'll be back by dark," he said, closing his pack and putting it back on.

"Be careful," Jack cautioned him.

The rain was slowing and he suspected it would clear up by the end of the day but the damage was done. Trees were weakened and the ground was a muddy mess. It wouldn't take more than a small breeze to knock more limbs and trees to the ground.

"I will. Take care of her." Before Wyatt could head back down the hill, Megan reached her hand out.

"Wyatt. Find my daughter."

Clutching her hand, Wyatt bent down to kiss her forehead. "I promise."

Wyatt was a man of his word and that wasn't going to change. Especially, now.

6

Megan tried her best to keep her eyes open but the motion while lying on the stretcher was testing her resolve. When it became evident that wasn't going to be an option, she conceded and closed her eyes, but vowed to stay awake. The bouncing of the stretcher jostled her leg to the point she couldn't hold back the grunts of pain.

The splint minimized some of the movement, but it was still pure agony. She couldn't tell if it was her ankle or lower leg or both that was injured. The pain radiated up and down, masking the true source. A sudden urge to vomit came over her.

"Stop!" she croaked.

Chase and Jack came to an instant halt to see what was wrong.

Megan leaned over the side of the stretcher and vomited. Since she hadn't had breakfast, there was very little to throw up. Dry heaves shook her whole body, jerking her leg. The wave of pain with each jerk made her vomit more.

Her moan turned into a choked sob.

Setting her gently down, Jack bent down to soothe Megan.

"I know, sweetie, I know. Try to take deep breaths through your nose. We will go slower, okay? Would you like some water?"

Megan squeezed her eyes shut, giving her head a brief shake. She had to get through this. There was no other way. She could do it.

Jack stayed next to her for a couple minutes as she gained control of her revolting stomach.

"I'm good," she whispered.

Jack resumed his position and nodded to Chase. "We better slow it down."

Chase agreed. No matter how slow and careful they were, the stretcher bounced with every step forward.

Megan moaned. The need to give in was too much. She finally quit trying and let the blissfulness of unconsciousness take her.

When Megan awoke next, she was lying in the bed she shared with Wyatt. It took her a few seconds to remember what had happened. She propped herself up on her elbows and looked around the room. It was dark.

How long had she been out?

"Take it easy." Rosie's soothing voice came out of the corner.

She was sitting in the same chair Megan had sat in so often when Caitlin had been ill and confined to bed.

"Caitlin?"

"Wyatt is still out looking. He'll be home soon."

Megan's head was pounding and a wave of nausea swept over her as she groaned and collapsed back on the bed.

"That's probably going to happen a few more times. You have a concussion. Try to relax and let your body heal," Rosie said, getting up to grab another pillow. "I'll put this behind you so you can sit up a bit more."

Megan blinked several times. There was a blanket over her. She wanted to see her leg. She hadn't let herself look when she had been out in the forest.

"My leg?"

She looked down to see she had been put into a pair of shorts. Her leg was wrapped from toe to mid-thigh and propped up on a few pillows.

Rosie winced. "Your ankle is three times the size of the other but I don't think it's broken. Probably badly sprained. Did you hit it against something? There is a nasty bruise on your shin."

Megan nodded. "I think I hit a few rocks on my way down but it was my landing that probably did it. At least that is when it really started to hurt."

"Your leg is wrapped, but I didn't splint it, yet. We need to leave it elevated and wait for the swelling to go down a bit. I also want to keep a close watch on your circulation to make sure there is no trouble. That means I need to be able to see your toes to make sure they stay a nice pretty pink." Rosie winked.

Megan reached up and felt her forehead. There was a bandage on it. She remembered Wyatt carefully cleaning and bandaging the area.

"I put in a couple of stitches to get it to heal quicker and hopefully with less scarring. You got a pretty good knock there and it's going to make you feel a bit loopy until things settle down."

Megan leaned back against the pillow and sighed.

Willow came in and smiled when she saw Megan was awake.

"Hey! How're you feeling? You gave us all a good scare!"

Willow sat at the foot of the bed, being very careful not to jostle Megan's leg.

"I'm okay," Megan replied, feeling uncomfortable with all the attention. Especially since she wouldn't need it if she'd paid attention to the weather shifts.

"Well, you just sit back and relax. I made some homemade soup stock with the leftover rabbit Ryland trapped. Rosie says you can start with broth and we will see how you hold it down."

Megan didn't think she could hold anything down. How could she eat when her daughter was out in the woods starving, freezing, and possibly injured?

"No, thank you, maybe later."

Rosie shook her head. "Megan, you need to get some broth down. I have some lovely nettle tea waiting for you as well. It is rich in calcium and iron, which your body needs. I also added some pine needles to give you a healthy dose of vitamin C as well. Unfortunately, we don't have any echinacea available, as it's already late in the season, so I had to make do. I would love to find some goldenseal seeds to try to grow in the greenhouse because it will definitely come in handy."

Megan knew Rosie was right. She wasn't going to be of any use if she was laid up in bed and she certainly didn't want her ankle to take its sweet time healing. She hoped that Rosie was also right in that nothing was broken. Well, other than her pride, which was still at the bottom of that ravine.

"I also put together an herbal mix that we will make into a poultice to put on your leg. It is a combination of peppermint leaves and plantain to help bring down some of the inflammation. The peppermint will help soothe the leg and the plantain has its own magical healing properties," Rosie explained. "Comfrey would be my first choice, but we don't have it around here and I'm all out of pine resin. The next time the boys plan to cut down any pine trees, I will make sure we collect as much as we can before we use the wood."

Megan remembered Rosie cautioning about not cutting into pine trees for their resin because of the long-term damage to the trees. As another wave of vertigo swept through her, Megan closed her eyes until it passed. "Thank you, Rosie. Whatever it takes to get me out of this bed," Megan mumbled as her stomach lurched.

Rosie patted her leg while Megan took slow breaths. "I'll get the tea. You rest."

"Thank you."

Willow sat with her as Duke paced back and forth. He definitely knew something was wrong. He jumped up onto the bed to sniff at Megan's leg, freezing when she winced. Giving her his most sympathetic look, he settled at the foot of the bed with a groan. Lifting his head, he rested it on her good leg.

"Well, it looks like you have a nurse," Willow quipped with a smile.

Megan reached down to pet the dog but couldn't quite reach him. When she tried to sit up more, the room went for a spin, so she settled back down again. "Sorry, big guy, but the belly rubs will have to wait."

Rosie brought her the tea and Willow helped Megan roll to her side and up onto her forearm. She winced at what she was sure were more bruises from her fall. Megan had witnessed Rosie's healing teas work in the past but this was her first time drinking one. Sniffing at the light-colored tea, she took a tentative sip.

"Wow, um, that tastes terrible." She laughed at her own comment then went for it and gulped it down, which made Rosie and Willow laugh.

"That's how the boys used to get it down," Rosie told her as Willow nodded.

"Ryland too."

Megan gave a sheepish smile. "Sorry, but that really does taste bad."

Wyatt's mother reached out and patted her on the leg, "I know, dear. I did add a bit of honey but it clearly didn't help."

Before she could respond, Duke got off the bed and left the room. Willow looked out to see where the dog went. "He's at the door. Someone must be coming this way."

As Wyatt approached the lodge, he tried to think of what he would say to Megan, assuming she was conscious. The whole time he searched for Caitlin, he worried about Megan. She had been in bad shape when they found her. His initial reaction was to go with her and leave Chase or Jack behind to look for the little girl, but realistically, he was the most qualified.

Not that he was successful. He'd followed the devastation left behind by the mudslide, but the little girl was nowhere to be found. The intense storm had managed to obliterate what, if any, traces the little girl might have left from her fall. He'd searched around for hours hoping to find footprints but everything was a swirling, muddy mess.

On the positive side, not finding her could mean that she'd survived the fall and had wandered off in search of help. While he worried that any help she might find wouldn't be friendly, he had to hope that there wasn't anyone else around eager to harm a child. Then again, he might be pushing too hard to be optimistic.

Wyatt looked down at himself. He was covered in mud, which had started to dry in places while the rest of him was a soggy mess. He stopped at the outhouse to clean up as best as he could with the cold water. He would need to heat water to get some of the stickiness off and he was looking forward to changing his clothes, but first....

He walked through the door, not sure what to expect. The house was silent. Duke came over to him, his tail at half mast, as though he knew he had bad news. Albert stepped out of his room and Jack, Chase and Ryland appeared at the top of the stairs. Both of the men had cleaned up from their muddy ordeal. They all looked at him, waiting for news.

Wyatt's breath hitched as he saw the look of concern and hope. He gave a quick jerk of his head, indicating he hadn't found her. The looks of shock and grief nearly killed him. Duke bumped his body against his leg as if to tell him that he understood and he reached down to pet the dog in thanks.

Willow was standing in the doorway to his bedroom and saw him silently tell the group he hadn't found Caitlin. Her mouth fell open.

She went to Wyatt, wrapped her arms around him and reassured him it wasn't his fault and they would find her.

"You need to go talk to her," she encouraged him.

His voice was barely a whisper. "How? How do I tell her?"

Willow didn't offer any words of advice. Instead, she walked him to the room, gave him a quick hug and walked away. Everyone else headed upstairs to give Wyatt and Megan the privacy they needed. This was probably going to be the most difficult conversation they ever had.

Megan held her breath, waiting to hear Caitlin's voice. Instead, there was silence. She heard the door close. No excited chatter. Her heart started to race as she realized what the lack of celebration meant. If Wyatt had found Caitlin, she would have been talking a mile a minute. Unless she was unconscious!

"I have to see!" Megan pleaded with Rosie, who gently pushed her back down on the pillow.

"He'll be right in. Just sit tight. I'll go check."

Megan waited impatiently, straining to hear something. There were murmured voices, but she couldn't tell who was speaking. The suspense was killing her.

Wyatt came through the door. He looked exhausted and he was almost as dirty as she was after her fall.

"Megan—"

"Where is she, Wyatt?"

The panic in her voice was obvious. She turned slightly when a wave of nausea rolled through her. She knew it had nothing to do with her concussion.

Wyatt shook his head. Clearly, he didn't know what to say.

She attempted to take a deep breath, but it ended on a sob. "Did you...? Is she...? Was there...?" Megan couldn't force herself to finish any of those sentences because the very idea of her baby girl's body laying crumpled and broken somewhere was just too much.

Wyatt seemed to realize what she was asking and his eyes got big as he rapidly shook his head. "No, it's not that."

He sat down next to her on the bed and squeezed her hand and she reached over to clutch his arm.

"So, there was no...sign of her?"

Wyatt shook his head again. "No. Nothing. I followed the mudslide and couldn't find any trace of her. The rain was relentless and it wiped out any chance of following her footprints, or anyone else's for that matter."

Megan tried to sit up but the vertigo was too much and she lay back gasping.

Wyatt squeezed her hand. "Where do you think you're going?"

"To go find my daughter?" She'd meant to sound more certain but her head was swimming and her leg was throbbing. "But that's wishful thinking. Oh, Wyatt, what are we going to do? She's just a little girl."

"She's also smart and resourceful, just like her mom. We drilled all summer with the kids on what to do if they get caught out by themselves and they both did great." Wyatt's tone was soothing, as though he was trying to calm a skittish animal.

"But what if she's injured and can't? Wyatt!" She couldn't stop the tears as all the different worst-case scenarios went through her head.

This was so very bad. She hiccupped and reached up to wipe the tears away but Wyatt beat her too it.

Gently wiping her face, "It's getting dark, Megan. It isn't smart for anyone to be out there in the dark, especially alone. We'll work out a search pattern and start again tomorrow when we can see where we're walking. We won't stop until we find her."

She knew he was right, but it only drove home the point that Caitlin was alone, in the dark. She was a little girl; how would she ever survive?

7

Wyatt wanted to stay with Megan and offer comfort but she shooed him out the door, telling him he needed to eat and get cleaned up.

He agreed with her. While he would like nothing better than to wrap his arms around her and hold her tight, neither of them would appreciate the level of mud he'd add to the already dirty blanket. "I'm gonna talk with the guys and we'll plan our search for tomorrow. We will head out at first light and we'll cover more ground with more of us looking in some sort of grid pattern."

Megan nodded and gave him a wan smile. "Thank you, Wyatt. I'm sorry I can't be out there helping you. What am I going to do if you can't find her? What, Wyatt?" Her body began to shake as more tears fell.

"Megan, she is a smart kid. She'll know to seek shelter and get warm. We could search all night and not even see her. You taught her well. She'll be okay."

"I want to believe you and I think a part of me does. This was the exact thing we've been teaching the kids, but teaching it and doing it are two very different things. She's only eight, Wyatt. I just want to protect her from all the bad in the world and I can't even get out of bed without the room spinning rapidly in circles."

He had considered staying out looking until he found her but it was too risky. With the heavy cloud cover, it was too dark to see and his headlamp could only provide a limited range of light. It would be much too dangerous for him to search the woods alone after dark.

Wyatt had to weigh the needs of the group as well. If he were injured, or worse, they would have to waste more time and resources tracking him down. They couldn't afford to have two of them laid up going into winter. He was confident Caitlin would know what to do. The temperature at night this time of year was well above freezing, which was still cold, but not life-threatening if she found shelter.

Over the summer, Caitlin had surprised everyone at how quickly she took to navigating in the woods. She definitely did not inherit her mom's navigational challenges. While Megan was getting better at it, Caitlin was already a pro. On some of the warmer evenings, Ryland and Caitlin had asked to camp outside and the little girl was far more proficient at putting together a shelter and building a fire than Willow and his mom. The kid was a natural in the woods.

He leaned over and pressed a kiss to her cheek, which was about the only part of her that didn't look to be bruised. "I'll let you rest. If you need anything, just holler. We'll be right out here."

Megan settled back with a sigh. "Thank you Wyatt."

Wyatt walked out of the room and took a seat on one of the barstools. He needed to compose himself. He felt horrible having to return home without Caitlin and felt even worse to see the devastation on Megan's face when he had to tell her. He froze when he could hear her crying and he contemplated heading back out to search all night.

"You'll be of no use to anyone, especially yourself, if you go back out," his mom told him as she came down the stairs.

Wyatt looked up at her. "How did you know?"

Smiling, she leaned in to hug him and kissed his head. "Because I know you. She'll be okay."

"Are you sure? Because I'm not." He whispered the words, not wanting Megan to hear his fear.

"I am." She went to the stove and stirred the pot that was on there. Picking up a large spoon, she ladled some soup into a bowl and handed it to him along with some bread.

Wyatt took a bite of the soup and his stomach felt like it was contracting in pain. He hadn't eaten anything all day and with all the activity, his body was desperate for some calories. He stopped talking as he shoveled food into his mouth. It was made from the leftover rabbit and was delicious.

The rest of the group trickled down the stairs. Each passed by and patted his shoulder or offered some words of encouragement. It didn't help. The woman he loved was heartbroken that her daughter was missing.

Chase dropped several maps on the counter and pulled up a stool to sit next to Wyatt.

"We start with this. We make a grid and do it the right way." Chase was all business. This was an area in which he excelled.

Wyatt nodded. He stuffed the last piece of bread in his mouth and set the mug aside. The idea of actually doing something instead of sitting and waiting, doing nothing, made him feel useful.

"I'm gonna have a chat with her," Albert said, grabbing a piece of paper from the notebook.

Wyatt looked at him. "Probably not a good idea, man. Maybe let her rest."

Albert waved him off. "Megan might not be able to get out of bed, but she can be useful too. So I'm going to see what she remembers." He winked before leaving the room.

Megan wiped the tears off her face when she heard someone come through the door. She wasn't in the mood to talk to anyone. She simply wanted to wallow in her own pain and misery. This was all her fault and she was feeling way too powerless for her own comfort and she really didn't want to have to talk anyone right now.

"Hey, hon." Albert's voice cut through the silence.

Megan turned her head to make sure it was actually Albert. He was the last person she expected to come in. While the two of them had grown closer in the past six months, they really didn't interact too much. He was always so grumbly.

"Hi."

"Pretty crappy deal, isn't it?"

He limped to the chair and sat down.

"I know what it feels like to want to get out of that bed and help out. It sucks when your body fails you."

Megan nodded. Albert couldn't possibly understand what she was going through, but he would know the pain of not being able to move about freely.

Albert looked wistful.

"I do understand what it feels like to be helpless when a loved one is in danger or hurting."

Megan turned to look at him. He sat in the chair for several minutes without saying a word.

"You know how I got this bad knee?"

Albert had been dealing with arthritis for several years, from what Rosie had shared when she was making different salves for him, but she had never thought to ask him what happened. Truth be told, she'd been cautious around him ever since they first met. They'd slowly been growing on each other over the past few months, but they'd been so busy, unless they were working on a project together, they didn't sit around chatting.

He took a deep breath. "I was driving my wife home from church one beautiful Sunday afternoon. We were talking about the potluck and what she had planned to bring. She wanted to make her usual corn-bread casserole. I hated that stuff." He smiled. "I would kill for some of it right now, though."

Megan didn't speak. Albert had never opened up to her, let alone talked to her for more than a few minutes about anything more important than household chores.

"I had just told her she needed to get some new recipes when an eighteen-wheeler blew through a stop sign, hitting us on her side. Back then, we didn't wear seatbelts. She was ejected from the car. When everything stopped moving, I realized I was trapped. My legs were smashed."

He choked as he spoke and had to pause to regain his composure. Megan had a feeling she knew how the story ended. She didn't want to hear it. It was too much for her emotions.

"Well, that man in the truck jumped out of his rig and took off. I could see my wife, lying on that old two-lane highway. I was trapped. I couldn't help her. It felt like an eternity before another car came along. The whole time I was in that mangled car, I grew madder and madder. I was furious at the truck driver and myself for allowing the guy to hit us."

"You couldn't have known, Al," Megan quickly assured him. She wanted to reach out to him as he seemed to relive that accident over in his mind.

He shrugged. "No, I couldn't have, could I?"

Megan understood what he was saying. He was trying to tell her that accidents happen. He knew her pain of being trapped and unable to help.

"Anyway," he continued, "she had been killed instantly. There was nothing I could have done, even if I had been able to get out of that car. It happened and I had to figure out how to keep living."

"She's not dead!" Megan said with more force than she had meant to.

Albert shook his head. "No, she isn't. You know that. We all know that. Maybe not the best story, but then again, I'm not exactly great at boosting morale." He cleared his throat. "I hope you see what I am trying to say. Some things are out of our control. Like that storm and the mudslide."

Megan stayed quiet.

"You also know that little girl is one smart, tough, cookie. You can't jump out of this bed and go drag her back home, but—" He pointed out the door. "Those guys can and you better believe they will. Let them do their job while you do yours by staying in bed and resting."

"You're right, Albert. Thank you and I am sorry for your loss."

He waved his hand dismissively but she could see the tears glistening in his eyes.

Pointing to the other room, "They are out there going over maps of the area and planning the search. I need some information from you to help them."

Megan tried to sit up a little straighter and froze when the nausea rolled through. Moving slowly, she inched herself up so she was fully upright. She paused, waiting for the nausea to subside.

"What do you need?"

"First, I need you to tell me what she is wearing?"

Megan realized he used the present tense. He wasn't accepting anything other than she was out there huddled in some fort either. That was reassuring.

She quickly described what Caitlin had on, including the blue fanny pack.

"Can you tell me the last moment you saw her?"

Megan winced. The last moment had been nothing more than a blur. She told Albert all she saw was a flash of pink pass by her as she tumbled down the steep slope. She flashed back to her daughter's cry as she fell and prayed that wouldn't be the last thing she ever heard from her.

He nodded. "You tell me what you think she would have done. Imagine she reaches the bottom or manages to catch her balance and stop the slide. Where would she have gone?"

"I had assumed she would come back here to get help. After I hit my head, my vision was swimming and I was having trouble keeping my eyes open. I'm sure I passed out, but I've no idea for how long. Minutes? Hours?"

Albert scribbled on the paper. "That makes sense and quite frankly, I think that is exactly what she would have done. I'm guessing she got turned around and couldn't find her way back. That gives us a better idea of where to start looking."

It gave them a place to start. She only wished she could go with them. She vowed to find a way to help, even if she couldn't get out there and physically search. She would do everything she could around the lodge to free up more time for them to look.

She looked at her leg. Albert must have known what she was thinking.

"You can use the crutches. I'm good for now," he told her, slowly getting out of the chair and leaving the room.

With her mind made up and something to focus on, she felt a little better. At least she didn't feel completely useless.

Albert stood to the side to allow Willow to come in. She was carrying a tray with a bowl of soup and a chunk of bread on it. Duke slipped in behind her to stand at the edge of the bed, silently asking to jump on again. Willow managed to block him and told him to go lay down somewhere else. With a grumble, he settled on the floor.

"Rosie says you need to eat so that tea doesn't give you an upset stomach."

Smelling the soup, Megan realized she was hungry.

"Thank you. It smells great."

Her friend smiled. "I can't even imagine what you must be going through. We are here for you. If you need anything, just say the word."

Megan finished her soup and tried to get comfortable. Her ankle was throbbing, her head ached and her heart was broken. She started to feel groggy and knew Rosie had dosed her with some kind of sleeping herb. At first, Megan was a little irritated, but she was exhausted and she knew she wouldn't be able to sleep. Her worry for Caitlin combined with the pain would make sleep impossible.

The low murmur of voices in the kitchen area was soothing. She could hear Wyatt's voice from time to time, which gave her a little comfort. He was near. She knew he wouldn't leave her and he wouldn't give up on finding her little girl.

She sank back into the pillows and let the herbs work their magic. It felt good to let it all go.

8

The guys were at it for hours, mapping out a plan based on the direction of the mudslide and what little info Albert was able to get from Megan. When he'd repeated himself for the third time, Chase had called it quits for the night. Everyone needed their rest.

His mom had left a large pot of water on the stove and he'd used it to clean the day's mud and grime off his body. His clothes looked like a lost cause, but he knew his mom and Willow could perform miracles at getting their clothes looking presentable and he didn't doubt they could do it again.

It felt good to be clean.

Wyatt crept into the bedroom to find Megan sound asleep. His mom had cautioned him against jostling her leg when he got into bed.

He watched her sleep for several minutes, trying to think of a way to crawl into bed and hold her tight without waking her or disturbing her leg. He couldn't. He wouldn't risk waking her up. She was in so much physical and emotional pain, it would be cruel.

Instead, he made a bed on the floor next to her in case she woke up in the middle of the night and needed to use the bathroom. He was so glad they had the composting toilet in the cabin functional again. They only used it in emergencies, which limited how often the bucket needed to be emptied, making life a little easier for them all.

The hardwood floors throughout the cabin were easy to keep clean, but they were not fun to sleep on. He did what he could to make the bed as comfortable as possible but he knew he wasn't going to get much rest.

He'd been floating somewhere around exhaustion when Wyatt heard her moan and quickly sat up.

"What's wrong? You okay?" he whispered in the dark.

He didn't turn on the small battery-powered touch light they kept in the room in case she was still asleep and just restless.

"My leg fell off the pillow."

The pain in her voice had him bolting up, turning on the light.

"Hold on, don't move. Let me do it."

He gently put her leg back on the pillow, being careful not to put too much pressure on the ankle area.

Tears streamed down her face.

"I'm so sorry you're hurting like this," he said, leaning down to gently wipe the tears from her face.

He couldn't imagine the pain. She had been adamant she didn't want any pain meds, but his mom had ground some up and put them in her soup. They had a very limited supply but this injury was worthy of a couple Percocets they'd found on one of their scavenging trips.

He couldn't stay away from her. He carefully sat and then slowly laid down next to her, pulling her in close. She didn't say a word, but he could feel the tears soaking his bare chest.

"Honey, I'm going to get you a pain pill. You don't have to suffer."

"No, I'll be okay."

He sighed. "Yes, you will, but a pain pill will help you be okay sooner."

He got out of bed and went to the kitchen where Rosie had left the bottle of pills. She had suspected Megan was going to have a rough night and would need them to take the edge off.

Wyatt took the pill and a small cup of water back in the room. Megan tried to refuse, repeating that she would be okay, but he insisted. In the end, she took the pill. He grabbed the pillow off the floor and made a small wall around her leg to keep it from sliding off again.

Lying down next to her, he held her close as she drifted off to sleep again. He knew she would heal and within a couple of days the pain would subside. At least the physical pain.

The only thing he could do to help her was to get Caitlin home safely. He'd made her a promise.

Wyatt woke with a start, quickly looking down to make sure he didn't wake Megan but she was still asleep and softly snoring. Thank God. Carefully extracting his arm from around her, he gave her a quick kiss on her temple, careful to avoid the bandage as she mumbled some-thing in her sleep.

Pulling his t-shirt on, he headed into the kitchen to find Chase and Jack had already put their packs by the back door and were quietly sipping coffee. Albert, who'd insisted on being included in the search, came out of his room wearing a brightly colored shirt that looked like it came from the seventies.

Chase raised an eyebrow in question.

"Hey, if I get lost, I want to make sure you guys can find me. I am too old to be lying around out in the woods waiting for rescue."

That got a chuckle out of all of them, which helped lighten the mood, but Albert did have a point. They all needed to be hyper-vigilant.

No one said it but they had to wonder if someone had found Caitlin. Would they keep her safe? Was she injured? There were so many possibilities. They couldn't ignore the fact that Evan and his group were somewhere out there.

In a very convoluted way, Caitlin played a role in Kyle's death and Evan had sworn to get revenge. Kidnapping the little girl was certainly an effective way to bring his family to their knees. Although Evan was a possibility, they were operating under the assumption she had gotten lost in the forest. The night before, they'd pored over the map of the area, creating a grid pattern that they would follow.

Albert was given the quadrant closest to the lodge. His knee was on the mend but after walking around on rough terrain for a day, he would be laid up in bed tomorrow.

Chase, Jack and Wyatt were all going to fan out over the mountain and cover as much territory as possible. With a plan in place, they all felt a little better.

Rosie had come downstairs to make sure everyone had something to eat and insisted they stay positive. No one wanted to accept the possibility that she could be seriously injured or captured.

Everyone was outfitted with a whistle and a flare gun. If they found her, they were to start with the whistle but if they didn't get a response, then shooting a flare into the air would be the next option. They didn't want to risk anyone staying out longer than they had to but they were prepared.

Ryland came bounding down the stairs, dressed and ready to go. He would be teaming up with Albert. Jack had made him put on a bright orange hunting vest that had belonged to Dale Morris, the family patriarch who had died trying to protect his family. It was much too big, but it would do the trick and it fit over his jacket. None of them wanted to take the chance of anyone else getting lost in the woods. It was the middle of September and a winter storm could strike at any time as they already found out.

They quickly went over their plans for their specific search grid. Each of them would be carrying a well-stocked backpack that would see them through up to three nights out in the woods if the worst happened, as well as additional supplies to support Caitlin should they find her.

Jack insisted they keep the packs under twenty-five pounds. Ryland's was about fifteen pounds.

"In a typical bugout survival situation, we could be expected to carry as much as forty pounds of gear, which would be a bit too much for you, Ry," Wyatt explained. The formula was no more than twenty percent of their body weight. Since all the men were at least two hundred pounds, twenty-five pounds was very light.

"We want to be fast on our feet and every pound in the pack is going to make you that much more tired," Chase added.

"Yep. So be sure to conserve your strength. Albert and Ryland should be okay since you're sticking close to the lodge. The rest of us," Wyatt gestured to his brother and Chase, "In order to cover the miles in our respective search grid, we need to be careful. If our packs are too heavy, it could throw any one of us off-balance, which would only make the situation far worse."

Ryland nodded his head, taking it all in. They had spent an hour the night before carefully packing the most essential gear. Water was an absolute necessity. Caitlin would need water when they found her. Jack, Wyatt, and Chase were going to be the farthest from the lodge and from safe drinking water. They intended to carry a gallon each just in case one of them found Caitlin, but after a lot of debate, realized it was simply too heavy.

A single gallon of water weighed eight pounds. Even distributing it in several water bottles was too much weight. They opted to carry half a gallon each along with purification tablets they could use since there was plenty of water to be found on the mountain; especially after the rainstorm last night. Old tree stumps were plentiful in the forest, which often served as natural water basins. There would also be plenty of little creeks around the area to draw water from.

They ate quickly and drank plenty of water. They needed to be hydrated and fueled. The oats Rosie had cooked provided plenty of B vitamins that would give them the energy they needed and like his mom always said, it stuck to the ribs.

Wyatt went upstairs to find his mom sitting with Willow. They were busy looking at her medical books again.

"You headed out?" Rosie asked, looking up from her book.

"Yep. I gave Megan a pill about one this morning. Please make her take another one."

Rosie smiled. "Oh, she will get a pill one way or another."

Megan was as stubborn as he was when it came to the people she loved. But he knew his mom would do everything she could to keep Megan in bed and comfortable.

"Thanks, Mom."

She stood and gave him a quick, tight hug.

"Be careful, please. You will find her."

"Damn straight I will."

9

Caitlin cracked her eyes open before quickly shutting them again. Her arms weren't moving so well but she managed to lift her left hand so she could rub at her face before opening her eyes again to a dark room. Rolling to her side, she sat up slowly, only to end up leaning against the wall gasping for breath as pain shot through her.

"Mom!" she cried out, hoping her mom would make it better.

She cried out when she tried to shift her feet. Pulling the blanket back, she saw that her right foot was wrapped in a bandage. She reached to touch it, but her right arm still wouldn't move.

Her head felt fuzzy but she managed to look down at her arm and saw it was handcuffed to a small metal ring attached to the floor. Tugging uselessly at the cuff, she panicked, calling out for her mom as the tears fell.

Where was she? Where was Wyatt? Or Ryland?

In an instant, everything came flooding back. She and her mom had been hunting. When the storm came, they both fell and her mom was hurt bad. Caitlin remembered the blood on her mom's face, which started a new round of crying.

She remembered trying to walk back toward the lodge when something snapped around her ankle. It had felt like a hundred knives were cutting into her skin and she couldn't move. Falling to the ground, she tried to pry open the steel jaws that had snapped around her foot. Caitlin knew what it was. She had helped her mom set traps in the summer but this wasn't one of them.

The trap that had her was much bigger than anything her mom used. Caitlin knew there was a trick to opening it, but the pain had made it hard for her to remember. The memory triggered another memory. Her stomach had been cut and bleeding.

Caitlin lifted her shirt and gasped when she saw the neat little row of stitches that stretched from her chest to her belly. She remembered landing on a tree stump during her fall down the hill. The cut had hurt, but her mom's bloody face had scared her too much to think about it.

She knew she had to find Wyatt. Rosie would fix the cut on her stomach. While she was walking, she had stepped in the trap. She had been on the ground, trying to free her foot when she heard a voice.

Someone had bent down and opened the trap. Who? It wasn't her mom or anyone else from her family. That person must have taken her here.

She struggled, tugging on the handcuff. She knew her family would be looking for her, but she had no idea where she was or how long she had been here. She had no way to help them find her if she didn't even know where she was. She shook her wrist, making the handcuff rattle. Her growing panic was making it hard to breathe and she gasped when a shooting pain from her stomach shot through her.

She needed to get out of here!

Caitlin froze when she heard a noise at the door. Someone was coming! She quickly lay back down on the bed, using her free hand to pull the covers up around her. Caitlin didn't move a muscle when she heard the door open.

Footsteps crossed the tiny room. Caitlin could hear someone breathing. The person didn't say a word. Her curiosity got the best of her and she barely opened her right eye to get a peek. It was a woman with a tray of food in her hand, which she placed on the floor.

When the woman turned to get something out of the drawer of the bedside table, Caitlin got a good look. She was tall and skinny and she could see glasses on her face. She also noticed the gun holstered at her waist. At home, they always put the guns away; no one wore them in the house.

The woman stood and turned back to Caitlin.

Caitlin squeezed her eyes shut and feigned sleep again.

"I know you're awake, I can tell by your breathing. You need to try to eat something so you can get better," the woman told her.

Caitlin didn't answer or move.

"I'm going to take off the handcuff, okay? It's very important you stay still. You don't want to rip those stitches out."

The woman undid the cuff that held Caitlin's wrist and gently rubbed the area where the cuff had been.

"Stay put and I won't have to put the cuff back on."

Caitlin laid perfectly still for several minutes after the woman left. Her mom had warned her in the past about kidnappers and what to do if someone tried to snatch her. But this was different. She was injured and she didn't remember much of anything, including how she got here. She didn't get to use any of the things her mom had taught her like paying attention to her surroundings and the people kidnapping her.

The reality of her situation started to sink in. She was kidnapped in the woods. Her mom wouldn't be able to call the police and no one would find her. Caitlin wondered what would happen to her. Horrible images flashed through her mind.

All she could do was cry.

"Please, Mom, come get me," she whispered into the room. "I'm so scared. Please don't leave me here."

10

Chase and Jack set out to their designated section. Wyatt walked with Ryland and Albert to the far end of their section.

"Now, we went over this last night. Do you know what to do?" He was talking to Ryland, but he was also directing his questions to Albert. The man had a soft spot for both of the kids and he didn't want him getting hurt if he tried to do too much.

"Yes, Uncle Wyatt." Ryland rolled his eyes and Wyatt bit back a smile.

"Humor me, little man, and tell me anyway."

Ryland sighed loudly. "Since there's two of us, Albert and I are going to walk a grid pattern making sure to keep each other in sight. That way, we can cover more ground. If we find her, we're to use our whistles to get everyone's attention and if that doesn't work, Albert has a flare gun."

Wyatt rubbed his nephew's head and grinned when the boy scowled at him. "Good job. I'll leave you to it."

As he walked away, he could hear them talking as Ryland suggested he take the side farther from the lodge.

Right now would have been a great time to have two-way radios. Unfortunately, while the ones they had still worked, the batteries were dead. They had been scouring every house, store and shop on their trips into town, but had yet to find batteries to fit.

He knew they would be hard to come by but he thought for sure they would find some by now. Next spring, they were planning to head east to see what they could find. They had pretty much searched all the small towns in the area and had made it into the outskirts of Spokane on several occasions. They were all now picked clean, which he suspected was going to be the norm all over, but you never knew what you might find. Someone's trash being another's treasure, or however the saying went. In times like this, nothing was really trash if it was reusable.

Wyatt's mind wandered as he walked along, looking down at the ground. He was looking for footprints but it was impossible to make anything out. The rain had washed everything away in yesterday's storm. He swore he wouldn't lose hope. They'd only just started.

He didn't care how long it took, how cold it got or how much it rained; he was going to find her. She was going to be just fine. There was a cool breeze whipping through the trees as the sun came over the horizon. The weather was getting much colder the closer they got to winter. If Caitlin was in the woods on her own, she wouldn't survive the cold temperatures much longer. And if she was injured?

His mind flashed to finding Megan and how quickly her stats were dropping as shock kicked in. Unable to make a fire or get dry, she would have struggled to make it through the night.

He worried that Caitlin might be in a similar situation and he picked up the pace. They needed to find her *now*.

Megan woke up when she heard the men leave. When she tried to move, the pain shot through her body, reminding her what had happened the day before and an involuntary groan escaped her lips.

Rosie appeared at the doorway as if she had been hovering nearby. "I thought you would be up soon. Do you need to use the bathroom?"

Megan did, but was not looking forward to getting out of bed. This was going to hurt.

Rosie left and came right back carrying Albert's crutches. "I adjusted them so they should work perfect for you. I know it's going to hurt, but getting up and moving will actually help you a little."

Megan wished she could jump out of bed and be her normal self. Her ankle was preventing her from looking for Caitlin and it was seriously ticking her off.

Rosie helped her to the bathroom and then back to bed. By the time she laid down, she was breathing heavy and covered in sweat, but at least the vertigo was mostly gone. The pain was severe, but there was no way she was giving in. Mind over matter is what her dad always said.

After a quick check of her toes, Rosie declared all was well.

"I'm going to get you another Percocet."

When Megan tried to refuse, Rosie held up her hand.

"You need the rest, Megan. One more pill and then we will see how you are doing. The guys are out looking. There is nothing you can do but sit here and heal. Caitlin will not be happy to see you injured and miserable."

Megan wanted to argue, to tell her to save the pills for when they had a real emergency but the pain really was brutal. She figured she would take a pill, sleep a few hours and when she woke up again, Caitlin would be waiting to talk her ear off.

"Thank you, Rosie. I'm sorry I'm being difficult."

The older woman smiled. "No, Wyatt was difficult when he was injured. You are just fine. I'll get the pill and something for you to take it with."

Megan ate a few bites of the oatmeal Rosie delivered and swallowed her pill like a good patient. She closed her eyes and imagined holding Caitlin in her arms. She drifted off to sleep knowing Caitlin would be there when she woke up.

Wyatt was so frustrated he wanted to punch something. The sun was setting and no one had shot a flare up. No Caitlin. He couldn't believe this was happening. How did an eight-year-old simply disappear without a trace in an area they were familiar with?

He heard Chase coming before he saw him.

"What the hell, Wyatt?"

Wyatt shook his head. "I don't know."

"We have scoured this area and she isn't here. She couldn't have disappeared. Are we dealing with a kidnapping? Who would do that?"

Based on what little they knew about Kyle Grice, Wyatt didn't want to think about why a kidnapper might want to take a little girl. He'd managed to avoid those thoughts all day, but now that Chase mentioned it, something was definitely going on. Given how much of a mess Megan made in the mudslide, it was too suspicious that there was no sign of Caitlin anywhere. While the rain could have washed away some of the tracks, there would still be something.

He was not going to jump to any conclusions. They simply had to widen their search. Caitlin could have wandered away and kept going in the wrong direction. It wouldn't be the first time something like that happened to an accident victim; especially if they hit their head.

The two men continued walking with no particular direction in mind. They were lost in their own thoughts when Wyatt focused on a Grand Fir tree that was surrounded by a group of Douglas firs. It stood out because of its height but what drew Wyatt's attention was the shelter it created underneath its boughs.

"Chase, look."

Chase followed Wyatt's stare and quickly understood.

Both men jogged to the spot. They found a length of gauze with blood on it.

"This could be from Caitlin," Wyatt said, picking it up and scanning the area expecting to see Caitlin. Nothing.

Chase seemed confused. "I thought Megan said she didn't have a first aid kit with her?"

Wyatt shook his head. "She didn't."

Both men took a moment to process what the bloody bandage meant. It could have nothing to do with Caitlin and had been left behind by someone else, or possibly blown this way in the wind and gotten stuck. Wyatt hoped it was simply a coincidence.

"This could be from anyone." Chase stated the obvious.

What were the chances of someone being out here, bleeding, without anyone from their group knowing? He thought about that for a few seconds; it was actually very plausible. They had seen others around in search of food and shelter, but had chosen to keep their distance and no one had made it as far as their property line. It was possible someone else had gotten injured.

Wyatt squatted and carefully studied the area under the tree. He finally found what he was looking for. Footprints. Walking to the prints, being careful not to disturb them, he dropped to his knees like Megan had taught him to do when he was tracking an animal.

From his SEAL training, he knew it was best to get as close to the print as possible to identify all of the details and it was the same when hunting. When tracking animals, the smallest detail mattered. Megan had told him to put the track between him and the sun. Unfortunately, the sun was going down and the trees made it difficult for the sunlight to filter through.

The track was nothing more than a heel with a light impression of the toe. It was too big to be Caitlin's. He tried to find the trail by following the direction of the print. He was rewarded with another print that was barely noticeable in the mud. Wyatt stayed low to the ground, envisioning where the next footprint would be.

There was only one set of obviously adult footprints leading out from under the tree. The trail was lost once the shield of the heavy branches was gone. Whoever it was had boots on. It could have been male or female. The print was small, suggesting that it was a woman, but there was no way to tell for sure.

"Those are pretty small. I'm thinking female," Chase said, confirming Wyatt's own conclusion.

He walked beside the tracks he found to get a sense of the person's walking pattern. The strides were much smaller than his own were. "It could be a woman or possibly a shorter man. See the strides?" Wyatt pointed. "Maybe the strides are closer together because the person is carrying something heavy."

"Like Caitlin," Chase finished for him.

"Yep." Wyatt kept looking. When he could find no more tracks, he imitated the mystery person's stride and headed in the general direction the prints went. Chase followed, keeping an eye to either side of the track. There was nothing but more trees and the setting sun made it difficult to see too far around them.

Wyatt stood still and did what Megan told him to do; he used his senses. Closing his eyes, he took a deep breath through his nose. He couldn't smell any smoke that would indicate someone had a fire nearby and he didn't hear anyone, besides Chase walking on dried leaves and snapping twigs. He held his hand up for Chase to freeze and closed his eyes again.

They were alone.

He opened his eyes and scanned the area. Nothing. This part of the forest looked like every other part of the forest.

"We better head back," Chase said, breaking through the quiet.

It was almost five and the sun was well on its way out of the sky. It would be dark by the time they got back to the lodge.

As they walked, they hashed out the various possibilities.

"Assuming it was Caitlin who was injured, someone obviously took the time to take care of whatever injury she had before moving her. That has to be a good sign, right?" Chase asked.

Wyatt nodded. "Yeah, but why wouldn't they bring her home? Caitlin would have a general idea of where home was."

"Maybe she was unconscious or disoriented?" Chase offered.

That thought didn't sit any better with Wyatt. He wasn't sure how Megan was going to take the news. On the one hand the bandage could mean Caitlin was alive. Injured but alive and being cared for. On the other hand someone took the injured little girl instead of trying to bring her home. Of course, there was the very real possibility it wasn't Caitlin's blood or bandage at all. The tree was quite a bit away from where the accident happened but if she had been disoriented from her fall, she might have headed the wrong way.

The tracks led to the east, which was where they assumed Evan's people camped. They had no idea if the other group had left for the winter or had found shelter to ride it out up on the mountain.

Ever since the situation with Kyle had gone down, they had been waiting for Evan to make good on his promise to avenge his brother's death. Could this be it? Would they actually stoop so low to kidnap an injured little girl?

Wyatt realized he had voiced his concerns aloud when Chase answered.

"I don't know, man. I think we need to find Evan. There is only one way to know if we can rule him out."

Megan would come unglued. Injured ankle or not, she would storm Evan's camp to get her daughter back. She would die trying to rescue her daughter.

Wyatt flipped on the headlamp he put on his forehead.

"Let's not assume the worst yet," Wyatt said aloud, trying to calm his own fears as well as his friend's.

Chase nodded. "Got it. If Caitlin was here, she'd come farther east than we anticipated. We need to go over the maps again and come up with another search plan for this area. At least we have a general idea of where to go."

Wyatt saw the lodge looming through the trees. There was a faint glow in the windows on the second floor. He imagined his mom working on her puzzle by candlelight, waiting for everyone to come home. It looked so peaceful and welcoming.

He dreaded walking through that door empty-handed again. He felt like a complete failure. Megan was so upset yesterday when he couldn't find her daughter. He could only imagine how she would feel the second time.

11

Megan felt like she was on pins and needles she was so restless. It was a struggle to stay in bed where she had been ordered to spend the day.

To say she was uncomfortable was an understatement. She had refused to take any more pain pills and her ankle actually did feel as if it were being stabbed with a million pins. She was either sleeping or complaining about being stuck in bed. Rosie had been very patient with her, but Megan knew she was being a serious pain in the butt.

And impatient.

She couldn't help it. Being laid up in bed while everyone else searched for her daughter had her wanting to wear a groove in the hardwood floors pacing, but she couldn't even do that. Every time the door opened, she held her breath, waiting to hear Caitlin's voice only to be disappointed each time. Duke had been in and out of the room to check up on her but even he couldn't help her feel better.

He'd tried hopping up on the bed a couple times, but without the pain pills, the jostling was too much for Megan and she had to tell him no. Instead, she invited him to stand next to the bed so she could rub his head. She quietly talked to Duke, telling him not to worry; Caitlin would be home soon.

Duke was a very intelligent dog. His ears always stood straight up when someone was talking to him. He would tilt his head to the side and maintain eye contact. The dog was an excellent listener and Megan took comfort in being able to say what was on her mind without worrying about hurting anyone's feelings. Duke wasn't going to repeat a word she said.

Albert and Ryland were the first to return.

"Hey," Albert said, popping his head into the room.

"Nothing?"

"Sorry hon, we searched our area, but the others are still out there. Don't you worry, she'll be home by dinner," Albert assured her before leaving her to her own thoughts again.

Jack came in just before the sun started to set. Again, Megan got her hopes up only to be let down again.

She wanted to pace, clean, do anything to take her mind off her missing daughter!

Chase and Wyatt had yet to come home. Megan didn't know what that meant but she was staying hopeful.

When she heard the stomping of boots, she tried to sit up in bed but it pulled her foot, causing her to wince in pain.

She waited. Not breathing. Not moving a muscle.

Rosie's sigh of disappointment nearly made her vomit. They hadn't found her.

"Wyatt!" she called out. She was furious at herself over everything that had happened and absolutely terrified. Where was Caitlin and why wasn't there any sign of her?

Wyatt's large frame appeared in the doorway. Megan took a second to look at him. He was pale under the mud he was covered in and she could see dark circles under his eyes.

The man looked exhausted and defeated. She could see it on his face, by the way his shoulders drooped and the look in his eyes.

"Wyatt?" she said softly.

He shook his head.

"I'm sorry."

She leaned against the pillows holding her up. Wyatt slowly walked to the bed and dropped to his knees on the floor beside her. He reached out and grabbed her hand.

"We'll go back out tomorrow," he promised. "We will find her, Megan."

She looked at him. There was no stopping the tears streaming down her face. The thought of Caitlin alone in the forest for a second night was too much to bear. She remembered hearing miracle stories of kids surviving in the forest alone before all this EMP stuff happened; she hoped Caitlin would be one of those miracle stories.

She had to. Megan refused to believe her daughter wouldn't be okay.

"Megan?" Wyatt started softly.

She jerked her eyes back to his. "What?"

"We found something."

Megan's heart raced. It didn't sound like this was something she wanted to hear. She started shaking her head.

"Don't you dare tell me anything bad, Wyatt Morris!"

"No, no. I don't think it's bad. It may be nothing at all."

"What?" she said louder than she had meant to.

He took a deep breath. "We found a bloody bandage underneath the canopy of a big fir tree. There were some footprints but it looked like it was only one person."

Megan processed the information. "And?"

Wyatt squeezed her hand.

"We followed one set of tracks, but they disappeared once we got out from the protection of the trees. They were too big to be Caitlin's. It could mean the bandage didn't come from her or it could mean someone found her, cared for an injury, and then carried her out of there."

"Carried her where, Wyatt?"

The hysteria in Megan's voice was hard to miss and she didn't think she could swallow it down. It was bubbling up and up, threatening to consume her.

"We don't know yet."

Megan pulled her hand away so she could shift positions. "Did you follow the tracks?"

He nodded. "Yes and we have a good idea of where to look, but it was already dark. We couldn't see anything under the canopy. Chase is going over the maps and we are going to focus our search in that area tomorrow. We'll find her, Megan. I promise."

Megan pressed her head against the pillows and closed her eyes, willing her frustration and terror to calm down. She knew they were doing the best they could but a part of her was convinced that if *she* were out there looking, she would find her!

It was wishful thinking on her part and she knew that, but laying around doing nothing was not helping her rampant thoughts.

"Thanks. Why don't you go get cleaned up before dinner. I'm sure you'll feel better"

Wyatt could tell that Megan needed some time to herself. His mom had told him how antsy she'd been all day and he had no good news for her. He knew her well enough to understand that she was beating herself up over all of this and he was doing the same. The more time passed, the colder Caitlin's trail would get and he didn't even want to contemplate not finding her. That wasn't an option.

Going into the bathroom, he quickly cleaned up. They had found his dad's camp shower and had been using it the past few months, which had improved morale tremendously. He longed for a hot shower but he was too tired to go through the process of heating water and filling the bag.

Jack and Albert had hung a tarp to create a nice little shower stall. A rubber mat, the kind used in restaurants where the cooks would stand for hours, made a perfect floor to stand on.

It was the highlight of the summer in Wyatt's eyes. An outdoor heated shower was luxurious, even in their old world. When the weather turned cold, they had moved it inside the house, but that meant he had to heat the water on the stove. He would go without for now.

Exiting the bathroom, Wyatt felt better but exhaustion was creeping around him. He sat down at the table and gratefully took the stew his mother placed in front of him. She squeezed his shoulder, but he didn't want to talk.

The rest of the night passed in relative silence. No one was up for idle chitchat. Caitlin's absence left a huge hole in their blended family unit. Even Duke was having a hard time. The German shepherd paced the floor, continuously looking for his friend.

Ryland had the idea that Duke should go out with them tomorrow. Wyatt wasn't about to turn down any ideas and agreed to take the dog. Chase, Jack and Wyatt once again went over the maps and planned a new search grid that covered the area where they found the tracks and east.

Albert was going to stay behind. His knee was swollen and they couldn't risk him being injured out there. There was still plenty to do around the house to get ready for the rapidly approaching winter and their to-do list was long.

It was nearly ten o'clock when Wyatt crept back into the bedroom. His mom had folded the blankets and left them on the floor next to his dresser. He didn't want to disturb Megan, who was moaning and restless in her sleep, and quickly made his bed on the floor again.

As he lay there, wide awake staring into the darkness, he could tell by the change in Megan's breathing that she had settled into a deep sleep. He lay there quietly listening to her even breaths, which eventually lulled him into a fitful sleep.

The sound of footsteps woke him up. He blinked several times trying to orientate himself. Lifting his head to make sure Megan was still asleep, he rose and folded the blanket over, pushing it out of the way before heading out to meet whoever was up. It was Jack.

He stretched and arched his back, trying to work the kinks out. That floor was way too hard to sleep on every night, which meant he needed an alternative. Given how much pain she was in, he didn't want to make things worse trying to sleep with her if he was restless. He worried that he might roll over and jostle her. It might be better if he slept on a couch tonight to give her more room without worry of bumping her leg.

They quickly went over their plans for the search. Ryland and Duke were joining Jack while Wyatt and Chase split up again. They wanted to cover as much ground as possible. He walked outside, appreciating how peaceful it felt. Taking a deep breath, he could feel the moisture in the air. Fluffy gray clouds had rolled in, which could mean rain or even snow. That would be a very bad thing.

"We better get moving," Chase said, coming up behind him and handing him his pack.

The men headed out in silence once again.

The tree where they had found the bloody bandage was more than two miles from the lodge. The men covered the ground in no time and went their separate ways. Wyatt was determined to bring Caitlin home today.

12

Megan woke up feeling better than she had the day before. She hated taking pain pills. They always left her feeling foggy and drained. Her last pill had been yesterday afternoon and she felt much clearer today. The pain was still in her ankle and lower leg, but it wasn't nearly as bad and Rosie had pointed out that her toes still looked okay.

She vaguely heard Wyatt leave, but trying to swim through the thick fog of sleep had proven to be too much and she'd fallen back asleep. She wished she'd been awake enough to wish them luck. Not that they needed it. They were doing everything they could to find her daughter and yesterday was their first potential clue. It was killing her that she couldn't be out there too. Under normal circumstances, they'd have to tie her down to keep her from searching for her daughter and Megan's frustration had her feeling like an absolute grouch but she couldn't seem to get it under control.

The crutches were leaning against the wall next to the bed. Megan didn't want to ask Rosie for help and figured she could manage on her own. She used her hands to lift her leg gently off the pillow. The moment she let it hang off the side of the bed, she hissed through her teeth. The pressure of the hanging limb was always painful for the first few seconds.

She breathed through the pain, grabbed the crutches, and stood up. It felt good to do something without anyone helping. Megan slowly moved out the door and to the bathroom. She would use the outhouse once the ankle healed a bit more, but for now she wasn't going to risk falling and possibly breaking the ankle or even her leg.

When she came out of the bathroom, Rosie was standing there, hands on her hips, looking very displeased.

"I could have helped you," she scolded.

"I needed to do it on my own. I feel a lot better today and if I don't get out of that bed and that room, things are going to get ugly."

Rosie smiled. "Thank God. I was hoping you would be back to your fighting self!"

Megan grinned and then wiped it away as quick as it appeared. She shouldn't be smiling when her daughter was alone and scared.

"Since you are feeling better, why don't you have breakfast at the table today?"

Megan tried to turn down the offer of food, but Rosie wouldn't listen. She had lost her appetite. The stress over her daughter missing made her stomach churn at the very thought of eating.

Rosie insisted she eat a little to help keep up her strength and to drink more of that horrible tea.

Megan sat at the table for a long time, watching as Rosie went about doing her typical chores. Willow was upstairs, cleaning she imagined.

The woman liked a tidy home and was constantly dusting, rearranging, and tidying up. Even before the EMP hit, Megan didn't spend that much time cleaning but she could understand how it'd help pass the time; not to mention how helpful it was with so many people living under one roof.

"What can I do to help, Rosie?"

Her adopted mother didn't answer right away.

"Well, I do need to darn the socks. If you could do that, it would help me out."

Even though they had hit the motherlode on warm socks, they couldn't afford to throw any away simply because they had a small hole in a toe. It was an old-fashioned trick that most people didn't even know how to do but since Rosie's mom was old school, it was something that had been passed down to her and Megan had been eager to learn.

"Anything to take my mind off what's happening out there in the forest." She waved her hand dramatically.

Normally, Megan wouldn't have thought much about holes, but with all the time they spent walking and working with boots on, socks with holes could have them run the risk of blisters or worse. Wyatt constantly stressed the need for healthy feet and everyone listened.

Rosie brought her the small basket of socks that had been building up over the summer. Every time someone got a snag or small hole, they dropped it in the basket for mending. The little wood chunk they used to stretch the sock was on top along with a little package that contained a needle and thread. They weren't picky about what color thread was used. It was about being functional, not pretty.

Megan got to work, sticking the wood block in a sock, making a few stitches to close the hole, and moving on to the next one. It was tedious work but the time was mercifully flying by and it gave her something else to concentrate on.

"You feel like helping me with dinner?" Rosie asked.

Megan had finished her sock duty and was sitting at the table, staring off into space.

"Sure."

Megan peeled the potatoes they had dug from the garden. They had an excellent potato crop. Willow had planted a variety of red and yellow potatoes and while both did well, it was the red potatoes that really produced the best and they were juicy.

The potatoes they harvested earlier in the season were already forming eyes, which meant they would be in good shape for planting in early spring.

They had plenty of corn as well. That had been another successful crop. Their tomatoes and peppers had not fared quite as well. The growing season was too short and they didn't get the heat needed to make the plants thrive.

Rosie and Jack had talked about it and if they could find the supplies to build a larger greenhouse, it would be warm enough to extend the growing time for heat-loving fruits and vegetables.

Their dinner tonight would be a combination of fried potatoes with some freeze-dried beef cubes and some freeze-dried pepper slices. It was essentially a fajita without all the flare.

"It you'd like to make the dough for the tortillas, I can then cook them," Rosie offered as she set ingredients down in front of Megan.

Megan sat forward. "I've never made them before, what do I need to do?"

"I've already ground the wheat for the flour, so it's just a matter of mixing the ingredients into a workable dough. Are you ready?"

The idea of eating homemade tortillas was making Megan's mouth water as she eagerly nodded her head. Rosie handed her a large bowl with the flour already in it.

"How much flour is in here?" Megan asked, looking down at the bowl.

"That's only about a one-third of what we'll need to make all the tortillas, but since we can't use a standing mixer, I've found it's easier to mix the dough in smaller batches." Rosie went to the stove and brought a pan back that looked like bubbling water. "I've found that the tortillas tend to taste better if I dissolve the salt in the water first." Rosie explained how to mix the salted water, the flour and the oil and what the dough should look like.

Working the dough was tiring and Megan was finding more bruises and aches as she worked, but it felt really good to be busy and she was working out some of her angst.

"How's this?" Megan pointed to the neat rows of similarly sized balls of dough.

"That's great, hon." Rosie bent down in front of one of the cabinets and pulled out a heavy, cast-iron press. Setting it on the counter, she showed Megan how to press the balls. "I have the skillet heating. As soon as it's hot enough, I'll get started on cooking the tortillas while you finish up."

Megan continued to work, carefully pressing each ball and setting the flattened future tortilla aside. She found the repetition almost meditative. She jumped when Rosie set a plate down next to her.

"I thought you might like to taste what you're making," Rosie told her with a smile. She was holding one up before she took a big bite.

Megan grabbed the tortilla and bit into it. It was warm and soft and just a little chewy. "Oh, that's delicious. Can we make these more often? I'm happy to help."

"To make enough tortillas for this large group takes a lot of flour. I need to start experimenting on using different types of flour to see how they will taste, but assuming we can spare the supplies, then definitely," Rosie told her as she handed Megan another tortilla to eat.

"What else can we use?" Megan knew about corn, almonds, even acorns.

"If it's edible and has seeds, chances are we could grind it into a flour, but it will take a lot of seeds. There's amaranth and curly dock, both of which grow around here. We could use rice, but that seems like a waste since the rice will fill us up." Rosie continued to cook the tortillas as she talked. "Years ago, I remember seeing a Swedish recipe for bark bread that was made from pine bark. I've always wanted to try it."

"Wait. Pine? Really? So do we just peel the bark off the trees?" Megan was constantly in awe about how much the Morris family seemed to know about surviving.

"Oh goodness, no. That would be too damaging to the trees. No, the boys have all been told that if they have plans to cut down any pine trees to let me know so that we can get as much from the trees as possible. The pine needles are wonderful and healthy, and then there's the pine nuts. Most every part of the tree is useful to us in some way or another but we don't want to waste any of it."

While Megan's strengths were in hunting and trapping, she always seemed to feel like a student around Rosie. The older woman had so much to teach her.

Megan knew Rosie was keeping her busy for a reason. Each of the jobs she was assigned allowed her to remain sitting and keep her leg up.

They'd been so busy that both women looked up in surprise when the door opened and the guys came trudging in looking downtrodden. Even Duke had hung his head low. They'd all hoped that bringing Duke to the area they thought Caitlin had gone would make finding her easier but that wasn't the case.

Megan excused herself and went back to the bedroom. She couldn't deal with seeing them back without her daughter. How could life be so cruel?

Wyatt was quietly talking to Rosie in the corner of the great room as Megan strained to overhear what they were saying.

"I can't believe you didn't find her. Someone has to have taken her," Rosie told him.

"I agree. Whether she's being held against her will, or doesn't know how to get back home, I just don't know but I'm not giving up. She's family and we don't give up on family."

Rosie prepared a plate and took it into Megan.

When she came out of the bedroom, Wyatt looked at her, silently asking how Megan was doing.

"She's heartbroken, dear, and she's struggling," she told him.

"I don't know how to help her except to find Caitlin and I'm failing at that."

"It is one of those things that each one of us has to get through on our own. Be there for her. Support her. Encourage her."

Wyatt felt helpless.

"I don't know what else I can do. We've looked everywhere. I just don't know where she could be. Either we're missing something or," he paused, not wanting to say it, "someone doesn't want her found."

Chase slapped him on the shoulder. "We'll go over the map tonight and set up a new search plan for tomorrow. We will find her. That's not even a question in my mind. She is holed up with someone who is keeping her safe. We find them, we find her. We need to refocus our search. We aren't looking for Caitlin. We are looking for Evan and his band of misfits."

"That's assuming it's Evan that has her."

Wyatt wasn't sure they could assume that was the case. There were many variables. For now, they would work that theory until they found her or determined he didn't have her.

"Come on, let's start with the maps," Chase started. "If there is a group of people living up here, we should be able to find them on the map. They will need to grow food, be near water, and have easy access to hunting. Or at least you would hope they would know they needed that."

"We've been all over this side of the mountain and there aren't any new groups. Where did Kyle say he was from originally? I'm thinking they're probably in town or close to it, not that it will do them much good as supplies become scarce."

"We'll search this entire mountain until we find her, Wyatt. Let's start at the top and work our way down."

With tomorrow's search grid laid out, they all sat down to dinner. It was another quiet meal with very little conversation and no Megan.

Wyatt didn't bother going into the bedroom. He felt like a coward, but he had no idea what to say to her. He knew she was worried, but it felt like each unsuccessful search was only making things worse. He went straight upstairs and collapsed on one of the couches, exhausted. They must have walked close to sixty miles in the past two days. He felt every one of those miles.

13

The next morning, Megan woke up as Wyatt was grabbing something from the bedroom.

"Wyatt? You didn't come to bed last night." She tried to sit up, but Wyatt stopped her.

Dropping to one knee beside the bed, he kissed her cheek and covered her back up with the blanket. "You were so upset last night and with the pain you've been in, I didn't want to disturb you. Go back to sleep. I hope to have good news for you later."

She squeezed his hand. "Find my baby, Wyatt. Please."

When Megan emerged from the bedroom a couple hours later, the sun was out. As she hobbled out toward the kitchen, Rosie gave her a big smile.

"Good morning, sleepyhead. Are you feeling any better today?" Rosie set a cup of coffee down on the counter for her as Megan sat down.

"The pain is better. Thank you, Rosie." She took a sip of coffee. "I just feel so useless. I want to be out there with them looking for my daughter."

Rosie came over to give her a hug. "I know, dear. I used to worry every time Wyatt went out on a mission as a SEAL." Sitting down next to her, Rosie took her hand. "Wyatt, Jack and Chase left early this morning and will continue their search. The boys won't stop until they find her."

Megan squeezed her hand in thanks. She knew Rosie was right, but it didn't help the growing sense of dread in her stomach or that she was feeling so useless. If only they had ATVs or some other way for her to help in the search without having to use her legs. "What about Albert and Ryland? Is Albert's knee okay?"

"Don't let Albert hear you worrying about him. That man is worse than you and Wyatt combined and does not want a fuss made about him. He and Ryland are sticking around the lodge to catch up on some of the chores that we're falling behind on."

Megan cringed, knowing that this was all her fault, but Rosie patted her arm before getting back up.

"If you're looking to keep busy, I've made a list of chores for you too," Rosie told her with a smile.

Taking another sip of coffee, Megan rubbed her hands together. "Bring it."

They'd gotten a decent crop of apples and there were still some on the trees. Willow had asked Ryland and Albert to pull the remaining apples off that were still good, leaving the rest for the birds and the local animals.

Albert had wanted to try his hand at making hard cider, but needed some additional supplies, so was hoping to give it a try next year. He'd been successful making moonshine, if you could stomach the taste, and he hoped this would be better. They all did.

They'd had so many apples that Willow and Rosie had managed to make several gallons of applesauce. Willow had tried her hand at making apple bread using modified ingredients, and everyone had agreed that it was tasty, and they'd even managed to make a boiled apple cider syrup that didn't take the place of regular sugar, but it was plenty sweet enough and they'd been using it in the desserts.

Rosie had been disappointed that her attempt at making apple sugar had failed. While it certainly looked like a brown sugar, it was anything but sweet. Everyone had a good laugh over it, but Megan could tell from the look on her face that it wasn't over yet. With apples so readily available in season, the older woman was determined to make full use of everything they grew.

The door opened and Megan looked up, thinking it was Wyatt coming back with Caitlin. She hid her disappointment when Ryland and Albert walked in carrying a large tub of apples.

"Here you go, Grandma," Ryland called out. "Here's most of the apples minus the ones that were too far gone. We threw most of those in the compost."

There was a crunching noise and everyone looked to see Albert munching on an apple. He raised his eyebrow. "An apple a day keeps the doctor away," he told everyone.

Ryland bumped his arm with his elbow. "So, since you just ate five, does that make you invincible?"

Albert stared Ryland down before he answered him. "Keep mouthing off like that and you might not live to thirteen."

Willow clapped her hands. "All right you two, back to work." Albert and Ryland went back outside as Willow shook her head laughing. "Those two. You would think they were both twelve."

Megan got to work washing and peeling each of the apples before carefully cutting them into thin slices. She spread them out on one of the window screens they were using for this and drizzled some of the lemon juice they had over the top. Willow then carried the screens to the rack they'd built by the stove.

The rack was a dehydrator of sorts that would rely on the heat from the wood stove to dry the food. The contraption stood about four feet high and two feet deep. There were four legs made from thick tree limbs. Smaller two-foot long branches were lashed to the legs to create a ledge, similar to what was inside an oven. The ledges were just wide enough to hold the window screens where the food was laid out.

It looked like a bread rack and actually served multiple purposes. They dried fruit and veggies on it and when it wasn't being used for that, they hung clothes on it to dry. They'd come a long way from the initial frames she had made with Wyatt her very first day here at the lodge.

"Penny for your thoughts," Willow asked her and Megan smiled.

"I was just thinking about my first day here. Wyatt had brought me outside to help build racks for the planned dehydrator to try to take my mind off Caitlin and well…" She gestured to what they were doing. "I seem to be doing it again."

"Is it working?"

Shaking her head, "Unfortunately no. Between my throbbing ankle and constantly fearing the worst about Caitlin, I'm surprised I haven't cut any fingers off." Holding her hands up, Megan counted her fingers. "Yep, all still there."

Willow reached out to her. "You do know that what happened isn't your fault, right?"

Megan shook her head. "But it *is* my fault. I'd gotten so excited at maybe finding better feeding grounds for deer that I'd ignored the weather. If I had.... If I had just looked at the sky, I might have gotten us to safety faster."

That intense feeling of powerlessness completely overwhelmed her and she couldn't stop the tears. "What if they don't find her? What am I going to do?"

Both Willow and Rosie stopped what they were doing, came over to her, and Megan found herself wrapped in a giant hug. Clutching both women, she let the tears flow as she mumbled incoherently all the worries she'd been holding back since the mudslide.

Willow rubbed her back while Rosie patted her arm. "It might take some time, but they will find her. You just need to hold onto your hope. You hear me?"

Megan nodded her head and took the hankie that Rosie handed her. "Thank you. I know they won't give up, but I just feel so helpless."

"I know you do, but you have us to lean on and there's plenty of things to do around here to keep you busy," Willow offered, which made Megan chuckle.

"You're right, there is. So I guess that means I need to stop wallowing and get back to work?"

"That's the right idea." Willow gave her another hug. "But if you need to talk, we're here for you."

Once the screens had been filled, Megan started prepping the remaining apples to make more applesauce. They'd come across a bunch of canning jars on one of their scavenging runs and had more than enough for whatever they might need. Megan didn't help the last time Willow and Rosie made applesauce, so she was curious to see how they did it.

Willow had explained that fruit was safe to preserve in a boiling water bath because of the high acidity levels. They didn't need a pressure cooker like they would if they were trying to can vegetables or meat.

The actual canning would be done on the stove where they could reach a good rolling boil. They wanted to preserve as much fuel as possible and used the water that was already heated on the woodstove. Putting a lid over the pot would also help trap the heat and bring the water to a boil in no time at all.

"Be sure to put all the peels and cores in this big pot," Rosie reminded her. "We have so much now, I can make a big batch of apple cider vinegar. I miss having that stuff around!"

Before the EMP, Megan had heard about ACV as it was called, as an excellent weight loss remedy. Rosie laughed when Megan told her that. She said it probably did help, but she liked it for other reasons.

"I use it to treat colds, sinus infections, and for relieving the pain of a bee sting. It's one of those all-purpose things you want to have around."

Spotting the apples Megan had prepared, Rosie beamed. "Wow! Look at all those slices! This is great. You ready?" she asked, wiping her hands on the flowery apron she was wearing.

"Yep, show me how to make your magic potion." Megan appreciated everything she was learning and she was always in awe at how Rosie always managed to use up every aspect of their food. If it couldn't be eaten or used for something else, it ended up in the compost heap to be used in the garden. Unless it was meat, in which case, she'd dry it and Megan and the others could use the dried bits in their traps rather than using the meat meant to be eaten.

Megan remembered reading about product lifecycles in a marketing class and how recycled products were an attempt at expanding the lifespan of products that would normally be thrown away. Unfortunately, in some cases, the cost to create these more sustainable products often made the products too costly for many consumers.

Rosie and the Morris family took that to a whole new level, reminding Megan of how much she'd thrown away over the years when she thought whatever she was using was no longer useful. Even in the short time she'd been here, Megan learned that most everything had multiple uses if you were willing to think outside the box.

Rosie grabbed the bucket of raw honey. The honey was a staple around the house and used in meal preparations all the time. While chopping wood last month, Jack had sliced his finger nearly clean off. Rosie stitched it, slapped some honey on it, and it healed in record time with no sign of infection. She always joked that if she could only have one thing in this world, it would be her raw honey.

"So, we are going to put all these peels and cores in this big pickle jar. I'll go get some water; can you spoon about eight tablespoons of honey into the jar. Just put it on top of the slices."

Rosie came back in carrying a pitcher of fresh water from the potable water supply. She poured it over the slices until all were covered. Then she grabbed a pair of old pantyhose, stretched a piece over the opening of the jar and tied a string around the edge to keep it in place.

"There. That's it. Now, we let nature take its course. In two weeks, we'll strain it, saving the liquid. It will be time to pull out all the chunky stuff, which we'll add to the compost, and let the liquid ferment for about four weeks. One of us will need to give it a good stir every day."

"That's it?" Megan was incredulous. "All these years I've been throwing away apple peels and cores, when I could have been making my own magic potions?"

Rosie chuckled. "It really is that easy. Now, since we didn't use all the apple slices, we will make us some nice potpourri. We'll just let them dry and put them in a bowl on the table. I love the way they smell for the first week or two. After that, into the compost heap they go."

Willow chimed in. "Those bad boys are super high in nitrogen. That is going to get that compost heap cooking!"

Megan had to laugh. Willow got very excited about her compost heap. At times it stunk so bad it made Megan want to vomit but Willow said that was a good sign things were really cooking. She would give it a good stir and the smell would die down after a day or so.

There was so much to learn and Megan enjoyed every minute of it.

14

The steady rain and dropping temperature added to Wyatt's diminishing confidence in finding Caitlin. Under normal circumstances, the first forty-eight hours were critical but this was the new normal and he was at a loss. Sighing, a puff of steam in front of his face reminded him of just how cold it was, as he'd gone numb hours ago. Numb to the miserable cold, wet and the blister that had decided to show up on his heel earlier that day.

Over the last five days, they'd covered more miles than they had in the six months they'd been living on the mountain full-time and each new day dawned with hope only to end in failure. Caitlin simply wasn't out there. Maybe the person who found her was on the move, which could mean that they were sixty miles away by now. He had no idea which direction to look.

Before the EMP, the police would have used social media and Crime Stoppers to help find a missing child. Out here in the woods, there weren't enough people out here to make putting up signs worth it, plus it would draw unwanted attention. Their only option was to keep searching, but deep down Wyatt knew that when the weather did turn, that would become impossible.

As it was, the chores around the house were being ignored. They still needed to finish the preparations for winter. He had wanted to get another storage bin built to hold the potatoes and carrots. They had also planned to attach a mudroom of sorts onto the back door.

A mudroom would allow them to keep their snowy boots and other gear out of the house. It would also cut down on the drafts and bursts of cold air that came in every time the back door was opened. He had no idea what this winter would hold, but he knew it would be a struggle to keep the entire cabin warm. They were already burning through their wood supply quickly.

Wyatt felt as if he was stuck in a horrible repeating pattern. Every morning he went out with the intention of bringing Caitlin home and every night he returned empty-handed.

He couldn't stand the look of disappointment on Megan's face when he came through the door without her daughter. There was a very good possibility Megan would leave the group if Caitlin weren't found. He knew what it was like to run away from the place where there were so many reminders of what had been lost.

It was one of the reasons why he joined the Navy. The loss of his little sister was too much to cope with and while his parents never blamed him, he should have been able to stop her from running in front of that car. He was the big brother. He should have known better.

Wyatt walked through the door, hoping everyone was busy so he wouldn't have to see the disappointed looks on their faces, again.

He wasn't so lucky. Chase and Jack had already returned and were sitting at the kitchen table with Megan. The maps were spread out in front of them showing Megan where they had already searched.

No one looked at him. They all knew he hadn't found her. Their focus was on the maps. His mom and Willow were busy folding laundry and quietly talking. Duke gave out a bark in welcome. He was under the table, lying next to Megan's one good foot.

Ryland looked over the railing from upstairs. When he saw it was only Wyatt, he shook his head, apparently telling Albert, who was also upstairs, that he had failed again.

It was a relief not to say anything and he went about cleaning up and repacking his gear to leave by the door for when he went back out in the morning.

After another quiet dinner, they had to have a conversation about the search for tomorrow. Megan understood their concerns. While she was certainly trying to pick up the slack, she wasn't exactly mobile. She couldn't haul wood or help remove the plastic from the greenhouse without risking her own injury. She appreciated that no one wanted to make her feel any worse about the situation but they had to think of the needs of everyone in the house and with winter coming, while they needed to find Caitlin, they also had to make sure they were prepared for the long cold days. Their survival depended on it.

It was decided Wyatt and Chase would continue the search. Willow insisted she go along. Jack was at first hesitant, but her eyes and ears were as good as anyone else. Jack would stay behind to work on the mudroom. Albert would split wood while Ryland stacked it.

The following morning, everyone got to work, including Megan. She was down to using only one crutch and was moving around much better so long as she didn't overdo it. Placed on laundry duty, the women worked as a team. Rosie took care of dumping the bucket of water and hauling the clothes to the woodstove for Megan to hang on the rack.

Then it was more candlemaking, before it was time to show Megan another new skill—how to make soap. This one intrigued Megan the most. Prior to the EMP, she knew people who made all kinds of pretty soaps and sold them at a high price in specialty shops and craft fairs.

Apparently, Rosie had done that kind of thing too, but didn't see the cost effectiveness of buying all the expensive ingredients and going through the hassle of making her own. Today, it was a necessity.

They'd been saving the fat from the animals they'd harvested and Megan knew that some of it was being used in their cooking since they were running low on cooking oil and couldn't just go to the market.

She appreciated all the knowledge and skills Rosie had when it came to survival and it was thanks to her that everyone was alive and well, but she couldn't help feeling appalled when Rosie set the large container of animal fat on the counter.

Despite her initial reaction, Rosie promised her she would never know she was washing her body with the fat of an animal by the time they were done. Megan wasn't convinced, but she was ready to learn.

"Grab that big stainless steel pot," Rosie instructed.

Megan hopped over on one foot and grabbed the large pot. Turning around, she used the counter for balance and swung the pot up to set it down. As she moved, she set her foot down and hissed in pain. Clutching the counter, she took several deep breaths while she waited for the pain to subside.

Rosie tapped her arm lightly. "Are you okay, dear? Do you need to take a break?"

Megan kept her eyes tightly closed, but held up her hand. A few more breaths and the shooting pains had settled down to a throb. Opening her eyes, "I'm okay. We have work to do."

Rosie looked like she was going to disagree but she must have seen something on Megan's face because she merely nodded her head.

Handing her a knife, "Here, you cut the fat chunks into small pieces while I check on the ash I have heating on the stove."

Sitting down on the stool, she lifted her foot onto the chair. She then chopped the fat, trying not to think of rubbing it all over her body or in her hair, while watching Rosie. Wyatt's mother had turned one of the old freeze-dried food buckets into a strainer of sorts. There were tiny holes punched through the bottom to allow for drainage.

Earlier, Rosie had heated ash mixed with fresh rainwater on the wood-stove in an old enamel cookpot. Now that it was cool, she poured it into a big glass bowl covered in a square of cloth cut from a cotton t-shirt. Since they didn't have cheesecloth to use, the t-shirt would have to do, she told her.

"What is that for?" Megan asked as she watched Rosie work.

"This is lye," Rosie said, holding up the smaller bowl of liquid that had just been strained through the shirt.

"Really?"

Megan had heard of lye of course. It was the stuff they used in soaps and detergents but she had no idea it was so easy to make.

Rosie nodded. "Yep. If we were making larger batches, I would let the ash water sit overnight but considering how much ash we end up with and will have by the end of winter; I'm not worried about having enough to make soap."

"I'm all done with this part." Megan pointed to the pot that contained the chunks of fat.

"Great." Picking up the pot, she set it on the stove. "Now for the fat to melt down. It will probably take an hour or so. Once it's melted, we can strain it through another cloth so we only have the clear liquid left. Once everything is ready, we can then marry the two together and start to make soap. Do you have anything else you wanted to do while we wait?" Rosie asked her, covering the pot with a lid to trap in the heat.

Other than joining Wyatt, Chase and Willow in the search for her daughter, Megan couldn't think of anything. "Not really. I'll go see if Jack needs any help. Holler when it's time to do the next step. I want to see how you are going to make that into soap."

"I will, dear. Be careful. You just found out how much your ankle still hurts, so don't overdo it."

"I won't. I promise."

Megan was able to walk around inside the lodge without the crutches, but she still used them when she went outside. Navigating over the bumpy ground was becoming easier and she couldn't wait until she was back to normal. Thankfully, her leg didn't feel like a lead ball dragging her down. Rosie had been checking it daily and was pleased that the swelling was going down. The key was keeping it elevated as much as she could. Standing upright still made it throb.

"Hey, Jack," she said when she saw him standing outside the back door.

He was staring at the ground, which was littered with wood and various construction supplies.

"Hey," he said without looking up.

Megan waited. She knew that look. He was thinking.

"Okay," he said, looking up and clapping his hands together, "Got it!"

She smiled. "Got what?"

"I was trying to do a little math to figure out how many of these branches I would need to frame the walls."

She nodded. Jack was an intelligent guy and was always working out problems in his head. He rarely had to sit down and use pen and paper to get through an equation. Megan was not quite so blessed in the math department. All that arithmetic to come up with spacing made her head hurt. She usually left it to Jack and then happily followed his direction.

"Can I help with anything?" she asked, hoping he would say yes.

He thought for a moment. She knew building was typically something a person did while standing on both feet, but figured she could hold the wood while he nailed or something.

"Sure," he finally said. "I'm going to lay out the frame. As I move along, it would be great if you could hold the wood up while I nail it to the bottom board."

Megan nodded her head. She was still wrestling with her guilt over what happened and anything she could do to help around the lodge, she happily jumped, or limped, on.

They worked together in silence until Rosie popped her head out the back door.

"Megan, are you ready for the next step in our soap making?"

Megan was secretly thrilled to be getting back inside and, hopefully, into a chair. The throbbing had become a little too much to bear and she knew she'd been on her injured leg too much today. It didn't matter how good she felt, she still needed time to heal.

Rosie gave her a knowing look as she hobbled by, trying not to wince. Rosie quickly pulled out a chair, ordered her to sit, and disappeared into the bedroom.

"You have to take it easy for a few more days," she lectured, gently lifting Megan's wrapped ankle and placing it on another chair with the pillow she'd retrieved from the bedroom.

Megan sighed in relief. Rosie pulled off the sock that was stretched over her foot.

"You see this, Megan Wolford?" she said angrily. "Your toes are very red, turning purple. When you feel your heartbeat in your toes, sit down!"

Megan winced as the woman fussed over her. Rosie took her doctoring duties seriously and did not tolerate uncooperative patients. She didn't want to lose a foot or a leg and promised to obey.

Rosie brought the pot to the table. "Since you were busy outside, I went ahead and mixed the lye with the tallow, which is what's left after melting and straining the animal fat." Megan peered inside; it was a creamy color and thick.

"It reminds me of Crisco only not as white."

"That's the consistency we want."

Rosie brought two old bread pans to the table. They didn't use the bread pans for baking because they were too thin to handle the heat of the woodstove.

"Use the ladle and spoon the soap into the pans," Rosie instructed.

Megan did as she was told. The pans slowly filled and she gave them a bit of a tap to get the bubbles out even though she wasn't sure that was necessary.

"Now, we will let them sit overnight. Tomorrow, we will take them out of the pans and cut them up to make bars."

Once again, Megan was thoroughly impressed.

"That is amazing." She sniffed at the soon-to-be soap. "It doesn't smell very strong."

"No, it shouldn't. I would have loved to add some frankincense oil to the soap to help with our dry skin, but I didn't want to use it all up, so we'll have to settle for unscented this time around," Rosie told her.

"Next spring, we need to collect some lavender and other fragrant flowers. We can mix it into the soap to get some nice, pretty colors and smells, and the lavender will also be good for dry skin."

"Oh, that would be awesome. And some mint," Megan added. She loved the refreshing smell of mint and it always made her skin feel so alive.

"Definitely. If we do end up getting a couple of dairy goats, a little milk goes a long way for making soap. The goat's milk will leave your skin nice and soft. I imagine after another long summer in the sun working in the garden, we could all use a little skin pampering."

Megan was excited. The group had talked a lot about getting some goats. It was the next step in their sustainable living. They had to keep moving forward and chickens and goats were definitely on the list.

"Oh! What about some sort of an exfoliant? I think all our skins could use some of that."

Rosie agreed. "If we have some old pumice stones, we can grind it down into a powder to add to the soap. We could also use peach and cherry pits. I must say, I actually hadn't thought about that. What a wonderful idea, Megan."

Megan beamed. In a family where everyone was so knowledgeable about survival, it felt so good knowing that she was contributing.

Wyatt stopped and stared out over the area that stretched out below him. He was back at the very spot where Caitlin had vanished. The steep, rocky hillside that led to the meadow below was inches from his feet. He imagined Megan standing in this same spot, captivated by the beauty below.

She had told him she knew deer would be down there. He looked to the left. The slope was a little easier to navigate, but it would still be a difficult climb down. He couldn't believe Megan had managed to climb up that hillside with a seriously sprained ankle. The woman was tough.

Wyatt took a few moments to try to see beyond the tree line in the distance that surrounded the meadow. That is where he needed to go. It wasn't on his search grid, but the maps didn't give them too many details about the land itself. If he were living off the land up here, he would want to be close to the meadow. There was likely a camp on the other side.

Checking his watch, it was already after noon. Leaning back, he looked at the sky; it was cloudy, but the weather was mild. He could make it across the meadow. He needed to see what was beyond those trees.

The journey down the hill was slow. Wyatt spent a long time looking for any signs of Caitlin. Megan had told them she saw Caitlin tumble down past her.

Wyatt stayed close to the tree line on the left. This is where Megan had climbed up the hill, using the trees to gain support. He looked at the trunks to see if there were any signs of blood that would indicate Caitlin had hit one of them on her way down. Nothing. With all the rain they'd had, he wasn't particularly hopeful that there were any physical signs, but he wasn't ready to give up yet.

He kept moving, keeping his eyes on the ground and scanning the area for a sign Caitlin had been there. He heard a noise and whipped his head to the right. Two beautiful deer were in the meadow. One was looking around while the other one grazed.

As he watched the deer, his subconscious started nagging. He had seen something. What was it? He slowly turned his head back to the left.

There! Up ahead he saw pink. He ran towards it and whooped with glee when he discovered it was a piece of pink material. Snatching it off the branch, he looked at it, recognizing the material from Caitlin's coat. Tucking it in his pocket, he took a moment to orientate himself. The tree with the bloody bandage was through the trees on his left. Caitlin may have been a little confused and headed in the wrong direction. Someone found her, bandaged her and then where?

"Where are you, Caitlin?"

Wyatt slowed down, searching for more clues about what happened to Caitlin on that fateful morning. Walking in a semicircle back and forth, widening his search, he searched for any sign of where the little girl might have been taken.

It was the most frustrating thing he had ever encountered. A little girl didn't simply walk into the forest and disappear. Not without help from someone intentionally hiding their tracks.

Wyatt checked his watch; it had taken him two hours to search this one area. Now he didn't have enough time to get to that far tree line and back home before dark. He would take Chase with him tomorrow and head east. It was about a two-hour walk from the lodge. With the days growing shorter that only gave them about eight hours of daylight.

If they left at dawn that would give them about four hours search time plus travel to and from the location before it got too dark to see. Walking through the forest with a flashlight was tough business. He couldn't afford to trip over a root or log and hurt himself nor did he want to come upon a predator. They were already down one person. Wyatt couldn't risk him getting injured or worse.

Wyatt started the trek back, alone with his thoughts. He missed the normally bubbly Megan. He knew she was in a lot of pain—both physically and emotionally—and every day Caitlin remained missing made it that much worse. Once again, he was going to have to return home without her little girl and he had no idea how much more she could take.

15

With Chase already back for close to an hour, Megan anxiously waited for Wyatt's return. She no longer expected him to walk through the door with Caitlin, but a part of her remained hopeful that her daughter would be found safe. It had been four long days since the mudslide and while she was healing, she still had a long way to go.

Wyatt hadn't complained once. Every day, he was out from dawn to dusk, working himself to the bone to find her. Her injury and feelings of helplessness were tearing her up inside. If she were able, she would have been out there side by side with the guys searching for her daughter and probably forcibly returned home in the evenings but at least she would be doing something.

While the Morris family had welcomed both her and Caitlin into the family and she'd slowly come to accept that working as a team was far more beneficial than going it alone, at times like this, it killed her to rely on others. Not that they weren't trying, but the listlessness she was feeling at not being part of the search was weighing on her.

Her heart skipped a beat when she heard his footsteps. Maybe today he would have good news.

He came through the door, looking like a man with the weight of the world on his shoulders. Megan waited for him to look at her.

When he finally lifted his eyes, he scanned the room. She knew he was looking for her.

Rosie and Willow had been standing in the kitchen, preparing dinner, but suddenly decided they heard Ryland calling them from upstairs. Albert decided he was in need of some time outside and needed Jack and Chase to help him as the men quickly left the room.

Megan stood up with the help of her crutches. When Wyatt finally looked at her, she gently tilted her head, motioning for him to go in their bedroom. At first, she thought he was going to say no, but instead he crossed the room, stopping in front of her. She stood there, unsure what to expect, when he kissed her.

Instead of waiting for her to hobble into the room, he picked her up and carried her, knocking the crutches to the floor, breaking the silence that had settled over the house.

Striding into the room, he kicked the door shut and carefully laid her on the bed. Joining her, they laid together, not saying a word for several long minutes.

"I should have taken my boots off," he finally said.

Megan laughed, propping up on her elbows and looking down at their feet. There was dirt all over the pretty yellow bedspread she had hand-picked on one of their outings to town.

"Oh well, it will wash."

They both started to talk at the same time. Megan held up a hand to silence him.

"Me first. I know things have been strained between us. You've been amazing these last few days searching for Caitlin with no complaints. It's been killing me not being able to go with you and I want you to know how much I appreciate everything you've been doing."

Wyatt hugged her. "I would do the same for anyone here but Caitlin is special because you're special to me."

She rested her head on his shoulder. "She's my little girl. I don't know what I'll do if we don't find her." Megan couldn't hold back the sob and Wyatt pulled her tighter against him.

"We're doing everything we can to find her and you're helping with all the chores here," he assured her.

"I know, it's just, I hate being stuck here. I hate that she isn't here. I hate that I feel so helpless!" She swiped at her tears but they wouldn't stop.

"Your strength and determination are part of what I love about you. Now, don't get too excited but I wanted to show you this." Reaching into his pocket, Wyatt pulled out the bit of pink material.

Reaching for it excitedly. "This is from Caitlin's jacket, I'm sure of it," Megan exclaimed. "Where did you find it?"

"Where we think she landed after the slide. I realize it isn't much but at least we know we're looking in the right area," Wyatt told her as she hugged him.

"Oh, this is good news. Thank you, Wyatt."

Not bothering to hide his yawn, he looked at her in surprise. "For what?"

"Giving me a little more hope."

They lay together on the bed for close to an hour. She missed being held. He was her rock. Megan could hear the others in the kitchen and figured they better get up for dinner. Hopefully, they hadn't held up the meal, waiting on the two of them to emerge from the bedroom.

Megan started to ask Wyatt if he was hungry when she realized he was asleep. The man was clearly exhausted. She considered taking his boots off for him, but didn't want to disturb him. Instead, she lay perfectly still with her face pressed against his chest. The soothing sound of his heartbeat lulled her to sleep.

She didn't know how much time had passed when Megan felt the change in Wyatt's breathing. He was awake. She knew he couldn't be comfortable wearing those heavy boots.

"Go ahead. Get comfortable," Megan said in the darkness.

"Okay."

He quickly shed his boots and clothes and climbed back under the covers. She leaned over, kissed him and settled back in against his bare chest.

Wyatt woke early, feeling refreshed and energized. His night with Megan had restored him and given him the hope he needed to keep going. He was positive today would be the day he would find Caitlin and return her to her mother's arms.

Chase clearly hadn't had such a good night's rest. He stumbled down the stairs, his hair sticking up in various places around his head. The glow from the candle he was carrying gave his face a yellow pallor and highlighted the heavy bags under his eyes.

No one was sleeping well. Chase had been going just as hard as Wyatt had the past week and was clearly exhausted. Wyatt considered telling him to stay home, but knew his suggestion would be ignored. Chase would be insulted.

They didn't say a word as they grabbed their gear and prepared to set out. Today was going to be a long hike. With only the two of them, they could move fast, but it was still going to take a couple hours to get there. It was hard to say for sure what was beyond the tree line. He had vague memories of his father exploring the area before they built the lodge but Wyatt had yet to make it that far on his own.

There had been no need. He knew it was more forestland that stretched into Idaho. The maps indicated there was nothing out there, but given that their own lodge wasn't on any maps, he knew that could be wrong. The nearest town was at least twenty miles away. It would be very easy for someone who was disoriented or didn't have a compass to get lost. Once you were that deep into the forest, it all tended to look the same no matter which way you went.

Because there was a very strong possibility they would encounter other people, Wyatt and Chase were each carrying a handgun in a holster. The last time they had seen Evan, it hadn't been a friendly occasion. Guns had been drawn and Wyatt had been shot. They weren't taking any chances.

The two men made good time, only stopping for a few minutes here and there to drink water. Wyatt had skipped dinner the night before and was pretty hungry. He should have made time to eat something before they left, but he was too excited to get out there.

"Here. Eat up." Chase handed him a Ziploc bag filled with turkey jerky and a biscuit from last night's dinner.

"Thanks!" He put two pieces of jerky in his mouth and began to chew. His stomach clenched as his mouth salivated. He wasn't a huge fan of turkey jerky but it was calories and he needed to eat in order to have the strength to make it back home with Caitlin.

Megan woke up, stretched, and felt beside the bed for Duke's head.

"Good morning, buddy. What do you think? Is today the day we get our girl back?"

Duke's tail started to thump against the wood floor.

"I know. I'm excited too. She is going to be so happy to be home and to see you, of course."

Duke carefully put his front paws on the bed to give Megan better access to his head. He lifted a paw, indicating he wanted a belly scratch as well.

"Fine, one quick belly rub, and then I have to get up. Not all of us get to lie around and be fed all day."

Megan made her way out to the kitchen. The house was still very quiet. She used the peace and quiet to go over the maps. Wyatt had made a small X on the spot where the bloody bandage had been found. From there, she slid her finger in the direction Wyatt said he saw the footprints go in.

It was all forestland owned by the government. She doubted there would be any cabins in the area where a person, or even Evan's group, could take shelter. She grabbed another map of the same area and compared the two. The second map was a little more detailed and appeared to be more recent.

As she studied the map, she saw a small area that appeared to be privately owned land. It was surrounded on three sides by forest, but it was not designated as managed by the Bureau of Land Management.

She got excited and turned to Duke. "That has to be it. That has to be where Evan and his group are. I bet you Caitlin is there!"

Duke jumped up, excited. His tongue hung out of his mouth as he rapidly wagged his tail. She turned back to the map and then back to Duke. He gave her a big lick to show his own excitement.

"I know, buddy. I can't wait to tell Wyatt. We have to get over there."

She continued to study the map. It was going to be quite a hike. She used the key to determine how far the area was from the lodge. She was guessing fifteen, possibly twenty, miles. Carrying a backpack and walking through the forest would mean a person would travel about two miles per hour. It looked to be about the same elevation as the lodge but they would have to go up and then down, which would slow them down a bit more.

Using the hiker formula of one hour for three miles, she figured on the high side of about seven hours. That was assuming the hiker didn't stop to eat or didn't have to climb any steep cliffs. The idea of her daughter being that far away from her was frightening.

Megan grabbed the pencil and circled the area on the map. She was certain this was where Evan or another group would have set up camp. This had to be where Caitlin was being held. Megan was convinced more than ever that her daughter was kidnapped and not simply missing.

The rest of the day Megan tried to keep busy but her mind was elsewhere. She helped Jack with the mudroom as much as she could before Rosie demanded she sit down. Dragging a chair outside, she rested her bad leg on it while she held the wood for Chase to pound in the nails. Her leg was feeling much better so she felt more comfortable standing with her weight on her good leg. She handed Chase nails and let him know when the boards were straight.

As dusk fell, Megan waited for Wyatt. She knew in her heart he wouldn't be bringing Caitlin home, but she was okay with that. She was certain she knew right where her daughter was. Now, it was figuring out how to get her back. She hadn't shared what she believed with Jack or anyone else. She wanted to wait for Wyatt.

She knew they would all be hesitant to storm into an enemy camp and demand Caitlin be returned. They might be cautious, but Megan would walk right through the front door and take her daughter. She didn't care what might happen. Caitlin was hers!

Wyatt and Chase were famished when they finally came home. Dropping their packs, they both stumbled over to the table to inhale the dinner Rosie had set before them. Stew had never tasted so good. Conversation at the table was minimal as the two men rapidly spooned food into their mouths.

After dinner, Wyatt went outside to use the bathroom and grab some water to clean up. He felt her before he heard or saw her.

"What are you doing out here?" he asked before turning around.

"I need to talk to you. About Caitlin," Megan said softly.

Wyatt put down the water, turned and wrapped his arms around her.

"I'm trying, Megan. I swear to God I am doing everything I can to find her."

She pushed back. "I know. I have an idea. Will you give me ten minutes to explain?"

"Of course. Let me clean up and I would love to hear what you have to say."

Megan kissed him and hobbled back inside.

Wyatt took his time cleaning up. It wasn't that he didn't want to hear what she had to say, but he was so exhausted, all he wanted to do was collapse in bed. When he got back inside, she was sitting at the table, waiting for him. Jack, Albert and Chase all sat down as well. They knew something was up and it was probably easiest for Megan to talk to everyone at once.

Wyatt sat down in the chair next to Megan, stretched his arm out behind her and nodded his head, giving her the go ahead to share her plan.

Megan unfolded the two maps, putting the one where she had drawn the circle on top.

"I think she is here."

Wyatt raised an eyebrow.

"Why there?"

She excitedly explained how she came up with the idea. The rest of the men nodded, seeming to agree with her.

"You think Evan's group has her?"

Megan shrugged. "I think *someone* has her. It seems logical that others would be living up here. That area is where I would set up a camp. It's close to hunting, water, and would provide plenty of shelter. I'm guessing there are some cabins already in that area, and like the lodge, the owners managed to keep that info off any records."

Wyatt nodded. "I think you're right. The problem is the distance we'd have to travel on foot."

Nodding her head, Megan pulled out a scrap of paper with a bunch of numbers and calculations on it.

"I think it will take six to seven hours depending on how fast you can move."

Chase whistled. "One way?"

Megan grimaced. "Yeah. It's far, I know, but in terms of location, it's the best place to find others. What I don't understand is if Caitlin was disoriented after our fall, it's a long way for her to have wandered. So someone must have found her and I think they're over there or close to it. Otherwise, wouldn't you have found her by now?"

Wyatt agreed with her reasoning. He looked at each of the men. Albert couldn't make the hike. There was no way. Jack and Chase would insist on going. If they did this, that would mean they would have to spend the night in the woods, leaving the others behind for at least two full days.

Leaving the others alone bothered him. What if Evan was like his brother and was using this as a way to get them away from the cabin? Of course, he would need to have someone watching the lodge to know when they left and there hadn't been anyone else around.

Chase was the first to object to the plan. Jack and Albert had their own concerns.

"She's right. This is probably where Evan is set up. It would be smart for us to know where our enemies are. We've been waiting all summer for the other shoe to drop," Wyatt explained.

Albert wasn't convinced. "So, you think it is better to walk into enemy territory and ask nicely? Do you really think that is going to end well?"

Wyatt shrugged. "I don't really see any other options. We are wasting time scouting the same areas day in and day out. No one here is willing to give up on finding Caitlin, right?"

The silence was telling.

Wyatt could feel the frustration radiating off Megan. He put his hand on her back to calm her down.

"Guys, we need to do something. I would rather know my enemy. Sitting here waiting and hoping isn't doing anyone any good."

Albert stood up. "Wyatt, you aren't being objective. You aren't thinking clearly because you are thinking with your heart rather than your brain."

Wyatt stood up so fast his chair went flying behind him, making everyone jump.

"Don't even question my motives, Albert. This is about a little girl. This is about making sure we are all safe. How can we be prepared to defend against something that we don't know? What if they aren't even there at all? I'm tired of waiting for them to follow through on their threats."

Jack grabbed Albert's arm, pulling him back down to the table. He looked at Wyatt, waiting for him to grab his chair and sit back down as well.

Chase came up with a compromise.

"How about we continue searching around this area first." He used his finger to cover areas to the east and south that hadn't been searched yet. "While we are searching, Megan, Rosie and Willow can put together some things that we could use to barter with Evan's group."

"What?" Megan asked. "Are you serious? You want me to trade a can of corn for my daughter?"

Chase held up a hand. "No, I'm saying if we don't find her, we go to their camp under the guise of wanting to trade goods before winter. It will appear neighborly. If they are innocent, this will give us a chance to mend fences between our groups. If they aren't, then we'll be able to check the place out and look for Caitlin while we are there."

"Why are we waiting? If Caitlin is there, we need to get my daughter back."

Megan was practically vibrating with anger so Wyatt put his hand on the small of her back to calm her down.

"This is a good plan, Megan. We need some time to put stuff together," Wyatt said in a soothing voice.

She rolled her eyes. "It won't take a week to do that."

"I'll get the distiller fired up and make some moonshine. That stuff will have them begging for more and giving us whatever we want," Albert stated.

Albert's moonshine was stout. The group had been thrilled when he made the first few batches, but had quickly realized it was very potent. After a particularly painful hangover, Chase had suggested reducing the proof by adding more fresh water but Albert wouldn't hear of it. So, it was decided the moonshine would only be brought out for really special occasions.

The group talked a bit more about what they could feasibly carry that far and what would earn them the most points with the other group. Megan was quiet for the rest of the conversation. She excused herself from the table and went to bed without saying another word. Wyatt knew she was frustrated and a little hurt that the others weren't willing to rush over there.

He could see both sides of the argument. Heading out without being fully prepared wasn't smart. He would try to push up the timeline. A week was a little too long, but he didn't want to get Megan's hopes up. He would talk to Chase tomorrow when they went out on their next search.

For now, he would do his best to assure Megan it would all work out. It had to.

16

Megan's patience was wearing thin and she wasn't happy having to wait for the cavalry to rescue her daughter. Rosie could sense her growing frustration and kept her busy digging through boxes, looking for things that would make good trades.

"We probably should have done something like this sooner," Rosie murmured as they went through their supplies. "We are bound to run into other groups and having things to trade makes good sense."

Megan agreed with her. If Caitlin was with them, then they needed to give up some of their valuable items in order to get the other group's attention. If they walked in there with a bunch of stuff that could be easily found elsewhere, they would never get information on Caitlin.

The sock warehouse was proving to be a very valuable find. They had chosen twenty pairs of wool socks to offer for trade. Socks were a big deal, especially during winter in the mountains. People had to walk; often in snow and frigid temperatures. Keeping their feet warm and dry at all times would be a priority. Having extra socks to change into once one pair got wet was just common sense.

"What about these?" Rosie said, holding up a couple pairs of worn, but still functional boots.

They were her husband's and didn't fit anyone, but could be another invaluable trade item. Megan was tasked with putting in new laces and cleaning them up. Ryland pulled together some books that he and Caitlin no longer read for any kids that may be in the camp, as well as some old magazines.

Even though the magazines were outdated, they were entertaining to read and once they had been read, they could be used for other purposes.

Willow and Rosie put together some dried apples, Ziploc bags of applesauce and a bag of the potatoes they harvested from the garden. The applesauce had been removed from the jars and stored in the Ziploc bags to make it easier and lighter to transport. While they really couldn't afford to part with the food, they were willing to if it meant getting Caitlin back.

The items were distributed into piles to try to balance the weight. No matter how they did it, the backpacks were going to be very heavy. The heavier the bag, the slower the trip would be. They also had to account for the extra supplies the guys would need to stay out in the woods overnight.

Going back through the items they were willing to part with, they pulled out the heavier or harder to carry items and set them aside, only going with those they thought would be of most value.

Megan grew restless. Every passing hour could be jeopardizing her daughter's life. She hobbled outside, needing a few minutes to herself. Duke followed.

"They sure are taking their sweet time," she told the dog, knowing he would never betray her confidence. "I don't think I can wait another day, buddy. What about you?"

Duke sat down and leaned into her one good leg, nearly toppling her over. She took that as a sign he was on her side.

Caitlin had witnessed Kyle Grice murder a young man and had inadvertently become a target. The man had gone to great lengths to try to kill her and Megan. At the time, Evan didn't seem any more stable when he'd sworn to avenge his brother's death. Caitlin being stuck alone in that group could not be a good thing.

Wyatt had done his best to calm her fears, but it wasn't helping. He reasoned if they took the time to bandage an injury, assuming the bloody bandage was Caitlin's, then they wouldn't hurt her. Maybe there were other mothers in the group and they were taking care of her.

Megan always had the same question. "Why won't they let her come home?"

Duke tilted his head to the side.

"You are pretty much the only one willing to listen to me, big guy. You know I'm right, don't you?"

She rubbed his ears. "Maybe we should go get her ourselves? What do you think about that?"

Duke thumped his tail and turned to lick the hand that was petting him.

Megan took that as a yes and contemplated taking matters into her own hands and what that would mean. Her ankle was definitely better and while it wasn't one hundred percent, she was able to walk around without using the crutches.

She chewed on her lower lip, agonizing over what her heart was telling her to do. Whenever there was a missing person report on television, law enforcement always stressed how important the first twenty-four to forty-eight hours were and they were beyond that. Way beyond that and okay, she reasoned, these were different times, but that didn't diminish the urgency.

The big question was, could she do it on her own? It wasn't as though she'd never walked that kind of a distance before. She'd managed to walk much farther carrying Caitlin when she'd fallen ill. At least now, she'd have both her hands even if she only had one good leg.

Megan was tired of waiting. Tired of watching the guys come through the door each night exhausted and without her daughter. It was too much pressure on them, which wasn't fair to everyone. Something needed to change.

She was ready for action.

The next morning, she made her move.

It was early Tuesday morning. Wyatt and Chase had set out to follow their plan to search another area closer to where they fell. They were leaving no stone unturned. While Megan appreciated their efforts, she knew they wouldn't find her. Her gut told her Evan had her and they were nowhere near where Chase and Wyatt were searching.

Rosie was upstairs, making beds. Willow was busy organizing the root cellar. Ryland and Jack were finishing the mudroom. Megan looked around and thought about her plan. Could she do it on her own?

Time here had taught her that things worked better with a team, but this team was searching in the wrong place.

She couldn't wait. Megan hobbled back to the bedroom as fast as she could move and tossed her emergency gear into her pack. Planning to stay the night in the woods meant she would need to be able to start a fire, need a way to clean water, some sort of shelter and food. She threw in extra socks and a couple Mylar blankets. While she would have liked to take an actual blanket, she didn't think she could handle the weight and bulk. Her leg was going to slow her down even if she was able to walk around the cabin now without crutches.

The one thing she knew she needed was the gun Wyatt kept in the top drawer of the dresser. It was the same gun he had left for her in the bag hanging in the tree. The same gun that saved her life and took the life of Kyle Grice. Checking it for ammunition, she vowed that if she had to, she was willing to kill again if it meant saving her daughter. She grabbed a handful of the .45 cartridges out of the drawer and put them in the pocket of her backpack. Making sure the safety was on; she put the gun in her bag. A holster would have helped lighten the load, but she would make do.

She wished there was a cane to help her across the terrain but they didn't have one. She knew walking would be slow but she was done with sitting around waiting for others.

"You want to go with me, Duke?"

The dog had followed her into the bedroom and was watching her. Megan figured he would not only provide her with companionship, but could also help protect her. He would hopefully be able to sniff out Caitlin should she be at the camp.

Megan considered the dog's needs. She would need water for him as well as food. She went back to the kitchen and grabbed some more of the jerky and some leftover bread. It wasn't much, but it would keep them going until they could get back.

With her mind made up and a goal set, Megan felt a sense of relief. She was finally doing something to bring her daughter back. It gave her strength and a burst of energy. She was going to need both to make the long trek.

When she opened the door to go outside, she took in a long, deep breath. The air was slightly chilly and damp. She looked towards the forest. The mist gave the trees a sinister, yet beautiful look.

"You ready?" she asked Duke who, for the first time, seemed a little apprehensive.

Megan ruffled the fur on the back of his neck and started forward. The pack on her back was light, but she could already tell it was going to be difficult to maneuver once she got tired. She thought about her decision and considered waiting. Then she thought about Caitlin and what she was probably going through. Megan resolved to deal with the discomfort if it meant saving her little girl.

She knew Wyatt would be furious with her after everything they'd been through together, but he'd already done so much to try to find Caitlin. Wyatt was needed here. She couldn't have him traipsing into what could be a dangerous situation. If Wyatt were to be hurt or captured, she wasn't sure the group would continue to thrive without him. He was their glue and it would destroy the family if they lost Wyatt.

Megan knew she was expendable. If she didn't make it back, the group would still go on. She wasn't stupid. She knew what she was doing was foolish, but she couldn't let Wyatt put his life in jeopardy. She was the one who strayed too far and didn't pay attention to the weather. She was the one who had lost Caitlin. This was her mess and she needed to clean it up.

17

Wyatt slammed his fist against the bedroom wall in fury. When he returned to the lodge, he'd been told that Megan had left. He couldn't believe she actually thought she could make it to the other side of the mountain with her ankle in such bad shape. The woman drove him absolutely bonkers with her constant need to prove herself.

Checking the nightstand drawer, he was relieved to see that the gun was missing along with some ammunition. At least she had the sense to realize the danger she was putting herself in.

"Stupid!" he shouted to no one in particular.

He should have known she would do this. She had made it quite clear she wasn't okay with waiting another week. He had thought she was coping. His mom had told him Megan had been staying very busy, putting together supplies and helping around the house.

When Wyatt got home at night, she was perfectly normal. They talked, they laughed a little, and she seemed to be looking forward to the day when Wyatt and the other men would make the trip to Evan's camp.

She should have trusted him. She could have talked to him and he could have forced the issue a bit more with Jack and Chase. The fact that she didn't think she could tell him what she was really thinking stung.

They each had their own issues, but she had to learn to trust him. He would never do her wrong and would never do anything that would jeopardize Caitlin. After all this time, why was she so insistent that her way was best?

The more he thought about it, the madder he got.

"Dammit!"

Rosie appeared at the door. "Sorry, dear. I didn't even hear her leave. I just assumed she was sleeping in. When I couldn't find Duke, I had a feeling something was up."

Wyatt shook his head. "It's not your fault, Mom. I think we all know by now the woman is the most stubborn, hardheaded person on this planet!"

His mom smiled. "And that is one of the main reasons why you love her. It's why we all love her. She doesn't give up. She's tenacious. She would walk through fire for any one of us, which is why I think she decided to do this on her own."

"What do you mean?"

Rosie sat on the bed, patting the space next to her. He sat down.

"I'm sure she thinks that we weren't acting fast enough. I know if one of you boys had been missing for more than a week, I'd be going out of my mind with worry and you're both adults."

"She understands we're doing the best we can," Wyatt interjected. "How could she not?"

"If you were in her place, stuck in bed and forced to convalesce, would you be cooperative?" Rosie questioned.

"Of course not, but I'm a—"

"Don't you dare say, 'man', son. It's been a long time but I would be more than happy to take you over my knee and show you exactly how strong a woman can be when her children are in danger," Rosie vowed.

Wyatt rolled his eyes. "You are probably right, but it still ticks me off."

She laughed. "Maybe it wasn't the best decision to make, but it is *her* way. We all know that by now."

"I'm not going to let her do this alone."

"I think she probably knows that, too. She knows you will come save her."

Wyatt stood. "If I leave right now, I could catch her before she gets there."

"Dear, you could leave first thing in the morning and manage to catch up to her. She isn't exactly swift on her feet these days. Maybe that was her plan all along." Rosie winked.

That idea made sense. Megan wanted to go, but knew he would never let her. Now, she had sped up the timeline and got to go along. He smiled. Megan was full of surprises. He was secretly a little proud that she had managed to get out of the house without anyone noticing. He loved that she was so dedicated to saving her daughter.

"I'm coming, Megan, and you are *so* gonna be in trouble!"

Megan sensed the animals, even though she couldn't see them.

Duke had been very uneasy for a while too. The closer it got to sundown, the more worried she got. They had heard wolves in the area these past few months, but had never been too concerned with them coming around the lodge.

Now that she was out in the woods alone, she could easily be prey. Or worse, bears! They were preparing to hibernate and were busy fattening themselves up. What would happen if one came upon them while they were sleeping? There was no way they could defend themselves against more than one predator.

There weren't that many people living on the mountain and without some sort of refrigeration, they were careful only to hunt what they needed. So long as the animal population continued to grow, Megan was confident they would have a consistent food source as long as they didn't hunt in the same area every time or kill too many does.

They had to make sure the deer could repopulate. Killing all the does would not only devastate the population, but it would also leave the fawns to fend for themselves and they would die too. It was the circle of life and if that delicate balance were upset, they would all starve.

Realizing she was dead on her feet, she looked down at the dog. "You ready to call it a day, Duke?"

The dog had his nose in the air.

She was convinced they were more than halfway to the area she believed Evan's camp to be.

"Okay, buddy. Let's make camp here. I need to get off my foot."

She found a place that provided some natural shelter under the trees. It didn't take long to find some small twigs and branches for a fire. She made sure to collect wood that wasn't directly on the ground. With all the rain, it would be soaked and difficult to burn.

There were plenty of branches that were propped up against other trees and she hoped this meant the wood would be fairly dry between the wind and the sun drying it out.

Once Megan got her fire going, she built a small nest to sleep on using pine needles and one of the Mylar blankets as a sheet to protect herself against the prickly makeshift bedding, which kept her off the ground. She added a few sticks to the fire before stretching out and pulling the second blanket over the top of her.

It was cold. Duke seemed to know what to do and laid behind her with his back pressed into hers. The warmth of the dog's body helped take away the chill almost instantly. It was times like this she remembered how appreciative she was for her warm bed under a roof at night.

Megan started to doze when she felt Duke tense. Reaching her hand around to pet the dog, she felt tremors rolling through him. Sitting up cautiously, she tried to peer out into the dark but couldn't see anything.

Duke's ears snapped up to attention and his hackles went up right before she heard it.

Twigs snapped from somewhere on her far right.

Reaching for her gun, she held it at the ready while she added some small twigs and branches to the fire, being careful not to look directly into it.

She didn't hear anything else.

"It's okay, Duke, maybe it was just the wind," she told him quietly.

Duke growled quietly, which made her hands shake as she looked down at the tense dog who stared off into the night.

Just then, she heard what sounded like chuffing followed by scratching but it was still at a distance.

She knew that sound.

Bear!

Megan quickly extinguished the fire and backed up until her back hit the tree, dragging the dog with her.

Not good. Not good. Not good!

Holding on to Duke's collar, she stared into the dark praying she wouldn't have to use her gun.

She spent the rest of the night shivering and on high alert, tensing up every time she heard a noise or Duke shifted, but thankfully no predators entered their camp. Megan decided to get up and moving when it became obvious she wasn't going to get any sleep. The sun was peeking through the trees, which gave her just enough light to see. She poured some water into the collapsible bowl she carried in her pack and Duke quickly lapped it up. She ate a piece of the jerky before giving some to the dog.

Cleaning up her camp, she made sure to leave nothing behind, and together they headed out. When they walked past where they'd heard the noises last night, Duke stopped to sniff at one of the trees. Megan's hand shook as she reached out and plucked a small tuft of hair from the heavily scratched tree trunk.

It had been a bear!

Grateful the bear never came any closer, Megan vowed that she would never again go out alone like this. It was just plain stupid, especially with her injury.

"Okay, Megan, you've done this twice now. Let's not go for a third."

Suddenly, Duke barked and bolted ahead of her, wagging his tail as he sniffed at the bushes and then raised his leg. Megan took that to mean the predator was long gone as the dog happily marked his own territory while they walked.

Megan did her best to keep up with the energetic dog but after yesterday's walking, her ankle was extremely sore.

About midday, they stopped near a stream and Duke drank his fill while Megan munched on more jerky before giving the rest to the hungry dog.

It was late afternoon when Megan came to a barbed wire fence that had been haphazardly strung around some trees. This had to be Evan's camp!

"We found it, Duke! We found it."

Duke's tail began to wag and he looked ready to take off towards the camp.

"We need to do some checking first. Shh," she told the dog before putting her pack down.

She carefully walked along the fence line. She could see a cabin in the distance. It was very small and there were tents positioned all over the area beyond the fence.

Megan shook her head. "Those are not going to hold up this winter," she told the dog, who was sticking close to her side.

She saw a woman building a fire outside one of the tents. A few men looked to be building a cabin with some logs. In total, she saw ten people. She had to assume there were more. The property looked to be completely fenced in with barbed wire.

"This isn't going to stop much," she said, grabbing some of the barbed wire. "It's spaced too far apart, a person can easily get through with very little damage."

Megan made her way back to where she had left her bag. She was debating her next move. Did she go in, playing dumb and needy or did she sneak in and try to go undetected while she looked for Caitlin? She watched the people working. They seemed normal, doing things she and her own group of people did on a typical day.

"What do you think? Should we go for it?"

Duke appeared uneasy. Megan looked around, trying to see what had him nervous. She didn't see or hear anything.

"Okay, let's play up the injured leg and poor woman all alone."

Duke didn't move. Megan instantly knew something was wrong. Someone was out here! She should have known they would have better security than barbed wire!

Before she could move, a hand clamped over her mouth. An arm wrapped around her chest and pulled her backward into the trees. Megan bit down on the hand.

18

"Ow, dammit, stop it, Megan!"

"Wyatt?"

Megan spun around and saw Rosie and Jack trying to hold back a laugh. Wyatt was standing there with his brow furrowed and looking at his hand where she had just bit him.

"Why would you do that? You don't sneak up on a person and then do that," she said, frantically waving her hands at his injured hand. "That wasn't very smart. Why would you do that?" she asked again.

Wyatt glared at her. "Because you were about to alert those two men holding very big guns to your presence. I didn't want you ending up being held captive as well."

Rosie and Jack pretended to be busy whispering, but Megan knew they could hear the exchange.

Wyatt continued. "You want to talk stupid? Stupid is a one-legged woman walking twenty miles by herself to go into an enemy camp and demand they give back a little girl they may or may not have kidnapped."

Megan jerked back as if she had been slapped.

He was angry. No, furious. She had known he would be upset, but she didn't count on him being this angry. In fact, she'd never seen him this angry.

"I am about sick of you thinking you're Wonder Woman and running off on your own to save the world all the time. I am tired of having to worry about you and wondering what kind of danger you're in." Wyatt stepped close to her, grabbed her face between his hands. "STOP running away, dammit! Let us help."

Before she could say a word, he kissed her.

Wyatt stepped away from Megan wondering if he should apologize but then decided he was still too angry. After they'd discovered that Megan had set off on her own, Jack and Rosie had decided to make the trek with Wyatt while the rest of the group stayed at the cabin. They didn't want to appear too threatening and hoped that with Rosie and Megan, it would help soften the approach. So long as Megan didn't go off half-cocked; otherwise they were all in trouble.

Fortunately, they made good time and managed to catch up with Megan before she did anything foolish. Well, more so than heading off into the forest all alone and already injured.

Megan actually seemed relieved to see him as she jumped into his arms, hugging him tightly. When he set her down, she smiled and waved at Jack and Rosie. Rosie grinned. Jack shook his head at her and waggled his finger. She shrugged her shoulders sheepishly.

"I don't want to get into it all now but believe me, Megan, this isn't over. We are going to have a long talk when we get home."

Megan met his eyes. He thought she was going to give some flippant response, but instead she said she was sorry. Her voice cracked as she spoke.

"Fine. But still not over it," he said, grabbing her hand and gently pulling her back into the trees a bit more.

"We brought along as much of the stuff to barter with that the three of us could carry," he explained.

Megan frowned, staring at the straps straining against Wyatt's shoulders. "I don't recall seeing the kitchen sink on the list of things to barter."

Wyatt knew she was making an attempt at humor but he wasn't in the mood for it. Leveling her with a stare, he adjusted the pack. "It would have been a much easier load if Chase had come along as we'd originally intended but as it is, we made do with our revised options."

He could tell from the way Megan visibly winced that she understood his meaning.

"Our plan is to go to the front gates there." Wyatt pointed to an area off to the left.

"Oh, I was going to go under the fence there and sneak into the camp to take a look around. I figured if anyone caught me, I'd play the injured woman card."

Megan's declaration earned another glare from Wyatt. "Which is why you should have waited for us or let us do it like we had planned."

Wyatt's firm tone came across a little harsher than he had wanted based on the warning look his mom gave him.

When he had discovered she had set off on her own, he had been scared to death and mad as hell. This morning, they had covered a lot of ground in a short amount of time. When they came across what they assumed was her camp and saw the bear markings, his anger had turned to terror. She had put her life and Duke's in serious jeopardy and it scared him to death.

He didn't want to live without her. The idea of something happening to her made his nerves feel raw. Wyatt was convinced he couldn't possibly go on if she were to be seriously hurt or killed. He loved Megan and Caitlin and those feelings helped him to empathize but he still wasn't happy with her choices. She had to learn to trust him and lean on him and on the rest of the group.

"We need to approach like we are friends and not here to tear their camp apart," Wyatt explained.

"That works but what if they decide to shoot us?" Megan asked in all seriousness.

Wyatt rolled his eyes, "I don't think they want to shoot us, Megan. They probably would have already done that if that were their plan. It isn't like they didn't know where to find us."

"Fine, let's go." Megan was anxious to get inside and find Caitlin. She just knew her daughter was in there somewhere.

The foursome slowly walked to what appeared to be the entrance into the camp. Several men carrying semiautomatic rifles stood in front of the makeshift gate. They raised their rifles when they saw them approach.

Wyatt held up one of the backpacks. "We would like to make some trades if you are interested."

A short, stocky man looked Wyatt up and down before turning his gaze to Megan.

"You're the ones that killed Kyle." When he said that, the others shifted the barrels so they pointed directly at them.

Wyatt winced and he felt Megan and Jack tense beside him. He was hoping that had all been forgotten. Clearly not.

Another of the men stepped forward. Wyatt remembered him from that fateful day on the hill. He was the one who demanded Evan walk away.

He looked weary, but didn't appear to be set on revenge. At least, that's what Wyatt hoped since he was the only one not pointing a gun at them.

"I'm Bryan. I'm sure you remember me," he said extending his hand to Wyatt.

Wyatt shook his hand and he felt Jack relax his stance. "I do. I'm Wyatt. This is Megan, my brother, Jack, and my mom, Rosie. We wanted to see if we could exchange some goods. We brought what we could carry."

A small crowd of people gathered behind the gated entrance. People were clearly interested to see the newcomers. Megan smiled down at a little boy clutching his mother's leg. Wyatt watched her scan the area knowing that she was looking for Caitlin.

They were invited inside the camp and Bryan led them to a picnic table that sat next to a large fire pit where both Megan and Rosie gratefully sat down. There were several tents set up not too far from the fire pit, as if they thought the heat from the fire would actually keep them warm through the cold winter.

He did his best to study the camp without looking too obvious. They didn't want to offend their hosts.

Evan emerged from the small cabin that was tucked between some trees. He held Wyatt's stare as he approached the table.

"What are you doing here?" His tone was harsh as he stared at the group, his hands balling into fists.

Megan spoke up. "We wanted to see if we could exchange some things before winter sets in."

Evan looked at her, focusing on her outstretched leg.

"What happened?"

She looked to Wyatt and he debated how to answer, but decided she'd better tell the truth if they wanted to make friends and find her daughter. Giving her a reassuring nod, she turned back to Evan.

"Hunting accident. I fell down a hill," she said sheepishly.

Bryan focused on her. "You hunt?" His voice revealed his surprise.

Megan nodded. "Yes."

"We need food and guns," Bryan quickly stated before Evan could say another word.

Evan glared at Bryan.

Wyatt and Megan looked at each other. The last time they had encountered these two, it was a similar situation. Bryan was the voice of reason. Evan was clearly the leader of the group now, but he didn't seem in control.

Thinking it would be better if he did the talking, Wyatt reached his hand out to grab Megan's, giving it a little squeeze. If they were going to find out anything, they needed to get on Bryan's good side. Evan may have thought he was in charge, but Bryan was the one who called the shots.

"We can probably work out a deal," Wyatt said, looking directly at Bryan, cutting Evan out of the conversation. "What do you have to trade?"

Bryan turned to a boy who looked to be in his late teens.

"Daniel, will you please go get Sharon and tell her to bring the stuff we have to barter."

"Do you barter with others?" Jack asked.

The revelation took Wyatt and the group by surprise. If they could expand their trade market so-to-speak, it would really help. However, it could also put them at risk. If they went around flaunting everything they had, the other groups may try to take it. They could band together and overpower Wyatt's family.

"We do, sometimes," Bryan answered slowly, seeming reluctant to answer.

No one spoke after that and there was a tense silence as the men chose to stand around the picnic table rather than sit.

"Maybe we should all sit?" Wyatt asked, hoping to break the tension a little.

"Oh, yes, sorry, pardon my lack of manners," Bryan said, gesturing for everyone else to sit. He looked at Megan. "You walked all the way here on that bum leg?"

"Yes, I—"

Wyatt cut her off. "She was going a little stir-crazy so she demanded she come along."

Daniel came back with another woman, each carrying a box.

Sharon smiled and introduced herself as she set the box she was carrying on the table and Daniel followed. Wyatt quickly looked them over.

Much like his own group, it was evident from the clothes they wore that they'd all lost weight. A few of the men were sporting beards in various stages from long and scraggly to trimmed short. Evan was the only one who was clean-shaven and he had a few nicks on his chin for the trouble. Of the women standing there, one had opted to cut her hair short while the others were wearing what he'd come to refer to as the traditional, post-apocalyptic hairstyle; a ponytail.

"We don't have a lot, but I'm guessing you don't need a lot," Sharon told them as she looked from one to the other. Wyatt decided the woman wasn't quite as naive as she looked but he also had to admit that, based on appearance, they were definitely the better off of the two groups.

"So, we have some toothpaste," Sharon said, reaching into the box and pulling out a couple boxes of Crest. "We also have some tomato seeds and lots of herbs."

Rosie perked up. "Oh, yes. I would love some of those herb seeds."

Wyatt looked at his mom, but she was all business now.

"We have some moonshine, home brewed, and it is sure either to peel paint or get a person fabulously drunk," Rosie offered.

Everyone laughed, and some of the tension of the exchange dissolved. Humor was always a great way to oil the wheels of any deal.

Rosie opened her backpack and pulled out several pairs of wool socks.

Bryan reached out to touch them before withdrawing his hand. "Oh yes, we really need some clothing, especially socks. It's been harder than expected."

Wyatt looked at the wistful look on his face. There was no way these people would survive the winter if they were sleeping in tents. He had no idea what Kyle was doing when he was in charge, but it was clear they needed help.

Megan stayed quiet as they all talked about what they needed, missed the most, and what they had to trade, chatting as if they'd bumped into old friends in line at the grocery store. She scrutinized them as they talked and none of them seemed suspicious. Hungry, tired, definitely on the lean side, maybe they were simply hiding it well. As they talked, Megan caught Evan casting his eyes off to the side and she followed his gaze to a large outbuilding set farther back behind the cabin where he came out.

Well that's interesting. He didn't seem to notice her watching him as he turned his attention back to the conversation. She tried to pay attention to what they talked about, but that wasn't why she was here. Her eyes kept going back to that building. Why was it so interesting to him? It would be a very good place to hide a little girl or possibly something bad. With images of Kyle in her head, she didn't want to think of what might be bad.

Megan casually stood. Duke watched her. When Evan looked at her in question, she thought fast.

"Bathroom?"

He motioned to an area where a couple of old shower curtains hung.

She hid her cringe. Oh boy had she become spoiled with the outhouse and compost toilet. "Thanks. Come on, Duke."

Evan turned his attention back to the conversation. The others were exchanging goods and listing out what they would like to trade next time. Evan's group had ammunition, but was lacking in guns. The guns the guards had were actually all they had. The semiautomatics were not the best for hunting when accuracy was at stake, which was their priority as well.

They worked out a deal to exchange a gun for three boxes of .22s. The .22s were running low at the lodge and were preferred when hunting small game. It would be a win-win for both groups.

The conversation faded in the distance as Megan focused her attention on the barn. She was going to have to go behind the curtain and into the trees to stay out of sight.

"Let's go see if we can find our girl, Duke."

19

Megan slowly opened the main door that led into the barn, squinting as she stepped into the darkened interior. The barn was old, dilapidated and the roof looked like it would cave in at any time. Loft windows shed some light inside, but given how dirty they were it wasn't much.

"This isn't creepy at all, is it, Duke?"

She doubted the dog understood sarcasm but she felt better that he was with her.

"Do you smell her, boy? Is she in here?"

It was eerily quiet. Megan wished she had brought along her head-lamp. Instead, she was forced to rely on the windows high above that did little to illuminate the dark corners of the barn. The smell of old straw almost made her gag. Clearly, they weren't using this building to sleep in. If she had the choice between a tent and a barn, she would definitely choose the barn. They had a valuable resource that they were ignoring, making her wonder what they were doing out here.

Megan carefully walked down the center walkway, checking each stall. Spotting something in the back of a stall, she scurried in, expecting to find Caitlin cowering inside. Carefully lifting the old horse blanket, she sneezed loudly as a cloud of dust flew up in the air. Throwing the blanket back, she was disappointed to find an old cardboard box with what looked like rusted tools.

The next stalls were completely empty.

Caitlin wasn't in here. Megan wanted to cry in frustration even though she was relieved to know Caitlin hadn't been held prisoner in this dark, stinky, barn.

"No luck, Duke. Maybe she is in one of those tents."

Looking up, a beam of sunlight hit the wall in front of her and Megan's breath hitched when she saw Caitlin's hunting rifle mounted to the wall above the door she had come in.

Reaching her hand up, she traced her fingers along the barrel, making sure it was real.

Spinning around, she quickly searched each of the stalls a second time. This time, she used her foot to kick the straw around, just in case she was hidden underneath. When she didn't find her the second time through, her mind started to race.

There was no loft. Maybe there was a trapdoor. Usually barns had some kind of storage space. Megan dropped to her hands and knees, crawling along the floor, looking for a secret door.

"Caitlin! Caitlin, answer me, baby!"

Duke started barking in response to Megan's shouting.

Wyatt froze when he heard Megan shouting. Looking around, he suddenly realized that she'd never returned from using the toilet. What was she up to now? He looked at Jack, who was about ready to spring up as well.

"What's going on?" Evan demanded.

"Let me explain," Wyatt began but Megan shouted again.

Evan glared at him before jumping up from the table and running towards the barn with Wyatt in hot pursuit. Everyone that had been at the table quickly followed. Something was wrong.

They arrived in the barn to find Megan standing in the center of the walkway, shouting Caitlin's name. Evan grabbed her arm and started to drag her out of the barn and Wyatt saw red.

He lunged at him. Evan fell backward without releasing his grip on Megan's arm and all three went down like a pile of bricks.

Megan cried out in pain, bringing Wyatt to a dead stop.

"What is it? What happened? Are you okay?" Wyatt asked when he realized she was hurt.

Megan was lying on her side, curled into a ball rubbing her ankle. She was groaning, but not speaking.

Rosie ran in moments later. "What happened, dear? Point to where it hurts."

Megan hissed and pointed to the injured ankle.

"I knocked her down, Mom," Wyatt admitted.

"You did what? Why would you do that?"

Wyatt rolled his eyes. "I didn't do it on purpose, Mom."

Megan rolled into a sitting position. "I'm okay. The fall twisted my foot. It will be okay. It just kind of hurts."

Rosie made a tisking sound. "Well, I imagine it does. We need to get you off that leg for a bit. With all that walking you've done the last two days, it's any wonder you can move at all."

Wyatt helped Megan stand up, keeping his arm around her waist to support her.

She drew her shoulders back, pointed a finger at Evan and gave him a look that would send anyone running.

"Where is she?"

Her voice was low, but there was no hiding the anger bubbling beneath the surface.

Wyatt tried to calm her down. She pushed him away, advancing towards Evan.

"Where is my daughter, you creep!"

Evan held up his hands. Bryan stepped in front of Evan. "Megan, I don't know what you are talking about. We don't know where your daughter is."

"Liar!" she screamed the word.

Rosie touched Megan on the arm. "Hon, I don't think she's here."

Megan looked at her, tears in her eyes. "Really? Then why is that here?" She pointed to the rifle on the wall.

Looking up, Wyatt stiffened when he saw the Crickett rifle with Caitlin's initials. Stepping around Megan, Wyatt grabbed Evan by the shirt and pushed him into a wall.

"You better start talking real fast, man."

Bryan grabbed Wyatt's shoulder, which resulted in Jack grabbing Bryan.

Sharon stepped into the barn waving a rifle. "Everyone put your hands down and keep them to yourselves." When Wyatt refused to let go of Evan, she turned to point the gun at him. "Now."

Her voice was firm and left no room for argument.

Wyatt let go of Evan and went back to Megan's side. The two groups ended up lining up facing each other. It was a standoff similar to what they had done that day on the hill.

Bryan spoke first. "We don't have your daughter. Why would we kidnap a little girl? We can barely feed the kids we have. The last thing we need is another mouth to feed."

Evan jumped in to explain the gun. "I found it when we were out hunting. It was at the bottom of a steep hill in the meadow between our two camps." Taking it down off the wall, he handed it to Megan, who clutched it to her chest.

Megan and Wyatt looked at each other. The story was plausible and would explain why they hadn't found it.

"It was covered in mud. I figured it had been out there for a while and would probably need to be taken apart and cleaned," he explained. "I swear. I know now about the things my brother did. Some of them." Evan closed his eyes and swallowed hard. "I am not my brother. I would never do the things he did much less hurt a little girl," Evan pleaded with Megan.

Megan believed him. Caitlin wasn't here. Looking at the gun she held, how could it be that her daughter felt so close, yet seemed so very far away?

Wyatt looked to her, silently asking her what she wanted to do next.

"She's been gone close to two weeks and I'm just so worried about her," Megan explained to the people who seemed now very wary of her. "Since no one was paying attention, I decided to take a look around and when I saw her gun, I thought I'd finally found her."

Sharon stepped forward and hugged her tight. "You poor thing. I can't imagine what you're going through. Let's get you back to the cabin and we will let you rest that ankle." She turned to Rosie. "Would you like to go with me and help get her settled?"

Rosie smiled, stepping forward. "She makes the worst patient."

"Uh, *she's* right here and I am not a patient. I'm fine. Really," Megan responded, looking at the two women in frustration.

"Okay, dear. Wyatt, help us get her back down there without her falling on her face," Rosie ordered.

"Hey," Megan protested. "It wasn't me who fell on my face. It was him." She poked Wyatt in the side.

Wyatt grunted. "Stop it. You have done enough for one day. Can we please get you somewhere you don't move for at least five minutes? I need a break."

Megan stared at him, seeing the anger roll off him. Anger directed at her. Deciding it was best to say nothing, she nodded her head. This was the second time she'd seen him this angry and both times were directed at her.

Between Wyatt and Rosie, they managed to get Megan back to the cabin where Evan was staying. It was clearly an old hunter's cabin and not meant for actual permanent residency. It was maybe the size of a shed. Megan estimated that it was maybe two hundred square feet. The single room had nothing more than an old chair, a bed and a small countertop inside.

Her opinion of Evan and the rest of the people at the camp changed immediately. They didn't have Caitlin. They weren't intent on revenge, which explained why they hadn't seen them all summer. She was convinced they were good people doing what they could to get by although she had no idea why they would have wanted Kyle as their leader. That man…Megan couldn't stop the shiver.

As they walked, Wyatt asked Evan about the larger cabin that was being built.

"We lucked out on finding lumber, so we've been using that to build but we've yet to put the roof on. None of us here has any construction experience and we're stuck on how to build it so it won't collapse under the weight of the snow."

She caught Jack and Wyatt exchanging a look. She could already see their wheels turning. "Maybe we can help you there," Wyatt offered. "My brother has a head for design and we can probably draw up a plan to show you how."

Evan stopped to look at them. "You would do that?" he asked, his surprise evident in his tone. "Yes, yes, we accept." He laughed, clapping Wyatt on the back. "I can't even begin to tell you how helpful that would be."

Megan couldn't imagine leaving them alone to suffer all winter. She worried about the children. They needed a sturdy roof over their heads and a warm place to sleep.

Rosie had insisted that Megan take off her boot so she could look at the damage and Megan wanted to argue with her but the older woman put a stop to that immediately.

Untying her boot, Megan hissed as Rosie and Sharon tried to gently pull it off. "Ow! Oh boy! I think you might have to pull harder."

Sharon squeezed her arm. "Hold tight, this will hurt. Now, on the count of three. One. Two." Sharon pulled the boot away from the heel and with a firm tug, the boot came free.

Megan collapsed back, gasping. "I thought you were going on three."

"I lied." Sharon gave her a smirk as Rosie inspected her ankle.

Poking at it, "Well, it doesn't look like you've done any new damage, but it's definitely irritated and the swelling is getting worse. You're going to need to rest it and that means staying off it for several hours," Rosie told her.

Rosie and Sharon sat with Megan while she elevated her foot. She didn't want to admit how bad it hurt. She had overdone it walking all the way over here and with the added injury, her foot was throbbing in complaint. Megan told herself that things could be worse.

Wyatt knocked on the door of the cabin. When Sharon invited him in, he sat on the bed next to Megan.

"You aren't doing so hot, huh?"

Megan shrugged. "I'll be okay after a rest. I can make it back."

Wyatt grabbed her hand. "It's raining. Evan and Bryan have invited us to stay overnight. You can rest your ankle and we won't risk catching pneumonia or injuring ourselves trying to get back in this rain."

Megan raised an eyebrow. "Really?"

He smiled. "Is this okay with you, Sharon?"

Sharon stood up from the single chair in the room. "It isn't as if we get company too often. At least the kind that isn't trying to steal from us or kill us." Moving toward the door, "I'll head to the pantry and see what I can find for dinner."

Rosie perked up when she heard that. "Would it be okay if I joined you? With the extra mouths to feed, I'm sure you could use a bit of help with the work."

Sharon smiled, holding the cabin door open. "We are always in need of help around here. I appreciate the offer."

"And thank you so much for hosting us."

The two women left, chatting as if they were old friends. Megan shook her head as they walked out the door. Apparently, group matriarchs were the same all over.

Once the women were gone, Wyatt and Megan sat alone in the cabin, neither speaking. Unable to take the silence, Megan spoke up.

"We're staying the night here?" She couldn't keep the nervousness out of her voice. It wasn't as though she'd been nice to them.

"I think it will be okay. I don't think anyone is going to be murdering us in our sleep," Wyatt assured her. "We will be in a tent, though."

Megan crinkled her nose. "That'll be fun."

He shrugged. "Well, better than sleeping under a tree. It's already late and with the overcast sky, it's going to be dark much sooner than normal."

"So, what do you think?"

She knew Wyatt would understand what she was referring to. "I think they are basically just like us. Evan is nothing like Kyle and Bryan is actually a decent guy. I'm not sure of the dynamics of this group, but I did meet a couple of other guys. There is a woman with two kids around as well. I guess they picked her up on their travels north."

Megan thought about what he said. If they were willing to take in survivors, they couldn't be all bad.

"There was a much larger group originally. Evidently Kyle had plans to build some grand new kingdom with him on the throne as ruler. After he was killed, more than half of them left. Of the ones who remained, there were disagreements on how best to do things. Evan and Bryan both thought it was a good idea if they moved on and they were escorted out of the camp with only the clothes on their backs."

Megan covered her mouth in shock. "That's horrible."

"When the two had stopped to make camp for the night, the others joined them. They'd managed to sneak out of the camp with some additional supplies. So they've been trying to make a go of it ever since. Bryan had said the others were not the kind of people they wanted to live with and they were glad when they decided to move on."

"Well, if they were anything like Kyle, I can understand that." Reaching her hand out for him, she grasped it, holding it tight. "Wyatt, where could she be? I was so sure that she was here and now…I'm lost without her."

Wyatt dipped his head down to kiss her on the forehead. "I don't know, but we won't stop looking. They mentioned that they trade with others, so I'll find out who else is on this mountain and if they've seen any little girls around in the other groups. I have to say, it's kind of weird no one has come to the lodge to trade."

Megan laughed. "Well, we did kill one of their people, even if he did deserve it so, it isn't as though we rolled out the welcome wagon for them. Maybe they warned others away."

Wyatt agreed. "That's true and it's probably for the best. If we want to start bartering, we will go to them. That way, we can avoid having people stop by for a surprise visit. It's too risky."

"Definitely. Will you help me go to wherever it is everyone else is? I don't want to be in here alone. It feels weird and I want to be with you when you talk with the others."

Wyatt reached for her boot and helped her put it on. He stood and helped her to a standing position, then waited while she took a few deep breaths. The rush of blood to her ankle took her breath away.

"They have a gazebo-type thing where they all gather behind that new cabin so we didn't see it when we came in. I'll help you over there."

He half carried her to the gazebo, which had been haphazardly covered with wood to serve as a windbreak. The cabin that was being built blocked the wind on the other side. It wasn't exactly a cozy spot and she couldn't imagine trying to eat a meal out there when it was snowing.

Megan was impressed by the large outdoor wood-fired oven that had been built under the gazebo. It was a really good idea and she was going to talk to Wyatt about building one back at the lodge. An oven to cook in would be amazing and she was sure both Rosie and Willow would agree.

She studied the construction to see how it was made. They had used cinder blocks to create a box on the bottom. From her perch on the bench, she could see red bricks lined along the inside of the box. She knew from friends who'd had an outdoor pizza oven that the red bricks were called firebricks. The cinder blocks would crack in the heat but the firebricks would keep them from overheating and the oven from collapsing.

A small fire was burning in the cinder box below. On top of the box, more bricks were used to create the oven. There was a crude door on the front that looked to be some sort of metal. It wasn't the prettiest outdoor oven but she imagined it made cooking casseroles, breads, and even cakes a lot easier. And if they could get a decent crop of tomatoes and peppers, they could make pizza just without the cheese.

The warmth from the fire and the heated bricks helped take the chill off. It was a lot like having a patio heater. Now she understood how they managed to eat meals in the gazebo.

The woman she had seen earlier came over and introduced herself as Tara. Her two children were Amy and Donavan. They chatted for a few minutes before the young woman left to go take care of chores.

Megan sat at the picnic table by herself with her bad leg stretched out across the bench. She watched as Wyatt and Jack spoke with Bryan. She could tell they were talking about the roof on the new cabin by the hand gestures. Jack had become an excellent builder over the past few months and Willow had told her that he enjoyed the challenge.

She was content to watch everyone for the next hour. Every once in a while, someone would come over and introduce themselves. They were actually very nice people who'd been hit just as hard, or possibly harder, than her group had. At least with Wyatt's group, they'd been prepping in anticipation of something bad happening. These guys had been forced to make do without any sort of advantage.

The smell of baking bread made her stomach growl. She was thrilled to know there was real yeast bread in that oven. She hoped they planned on sharing.

Megan was a little sad they lived so far away from the lodge. She could imagine becoming good friends with Tara and Amy was a year younger than Caitlin. They could have sleepovers and have some sort of a normal life.

Rosie and Sharon were chatting near the other large firepit in the center of camp. There was a large pot sitting on a grate over the fire and every so often, a whiff of herbs and spices floated over. Megan was really hungry now.

Rosie carried the large pot of bean soup to the table while Sharon opened the oven and pulled out two loaves of bread that had been baking. They were big and fluffy. Megan was going to make a point to ask if they could trade some of what they had for a little bit of yeast. The baking powder they had in their pantry worked well enough, but there was something about the smell and taste of baked goods made with yeast.

Before the meal started, Evan stood up.

"I want to thank you for helping us out with the roof situation," he started looking at Jack and Wyatt, "and thank you, Rosie, for helping prepare this meal. We haven't had a lot of variety and any new dish is always welcome. I know you didn't come here with the intention of breaking bread with us and you have every right to hate us but I think I speak for everyone when I say, we're glad you're here."

Everyone in Evan's group looked a little embarrassed. Even guilty.

Evan started to speak again. "On behalf of everyone here, I want to say I'm sorry for how things went down. Kyle was my brother, but he was always, well, for lack of a better word, a bad egg. I think we always knew he was different, but I didn't realize the extent of it until recently. He'd distanced himself from my family years ago and it had only been since the EMP that we were back in contact with each other."

Megan believed him. She could tell Wyatt did as well.

"I was a little out of my head that day." Evan closed his eyes and took a few deep breaths. "I have no desire to exact revenge. Quite frankly, you did us all a favor. We probably would be dead by now if my brother had lived. He didn't have our best interests in mind. He manipulated everyone he came in contact with for his own selfish desires and we were so desperate to survive, we blindly followed."

Evan sat down. Tara reached out and rubbed his back. It was then Megan realized they were a couple. Subtle, but she could see the emotion in Tara's eyes.

Wyatt stood. "Thank you and I am truly sorry the way that all went down. Thank you for your hospitality and the food we are about to eat. I hope we can continue to trade and lean on each other in the future."

He sat down. There was silence for a few seconds before Bryan let out a loud whoop.

"Let's toast to new beginnings—and a new roof!"

Sharon poured small bits of the moonshine they'd brought into everyone's cups. Once the toast was over, they all dug into the bean soup Rosie and Sharon had put together. Conversation began to pick up, and once again everyone was laughing as if they were old friends. Megan smiled as she was drawn into the conversations. She definitely could get used to this.

20

The conversation was easy and they all shared stories about how they were getting by. An older man, John, who appeared to be an American Indian, held up an arrow tip. He explained they were prepared to use bows and arrows to hunt this winter in order to conserve their ammunition.

The man knew the art of flint knapping.

"You should see the stuff he's made," Evan said excitedly. "He has taken rocks and made them into ax heads, spearheads and arrowheads. We have been trying to depend on the old ways for hunting. So far, we've managed to catch some fish and other small game like grouse and rabbits by spearing them."

Wyatt was intrigued. He knew they had to consider bow hunting. They had a lot of ammunition but what if this was how they had to live for decades? Not only were they not set up to reload their own ammunition, but they also didn't have the necessary supplies. He wanted to make sure Ryland and Caitlin had what they needed when they grew up, which meant finding alternate ways to hunt.

As they sat, eating, talking and having small sips of Albert's moonshine, a gust of wind tore through the gazebo. The tablecloth that had been spread out was caught in the wind and the bread went flying. Duke barked and ran for the bread.

"Oh my!" Sharon grabbed a rock and put it on the tablecloth. "I guess we're in for another storm."

Duke found a quiet spot to enjoy the bread he had scavenged off the ground. He positioned himself in a way he could still watch the group in case something else was dropped, but wouldn't be disturbed.

Everyone sat back down and finished eating their meal. The wind gusted but the conversation was rolling along. Evan mentioned a group of guys that Wyatt and his family wanted to avoid at all costs.

"They call themselves the Raiders and they're a destructive bunch; preferring to terrorize people and steal supplies than hunt and scavenge like the rest of us," Evan told them.

"They have working ATVs and they come out of nowhere," Bryan added.

"Has anyone gotten hurt?" Jack asked. He flexed his hand as he sat there and Wyatt knew he was thinking about his wife and son.

"Not us, no," Bryan answered. "But as you can see, we don't have much to offer and that's intentional. We realized that if we get too big, we'll attract their attention and we have so little as it is."

Wyatt glanced around. He was right. If he was in some sort of raiding or scavenging group, he'd probably walk on by, not expecting to gain anything for the effort. It was what they'd tried to do by making the lodge look looted when no one was around. What might have worked before the EMP wouldn't now. Especially if these raiders came through.

"Are they armed?" Wyatt asked.

"To the teeth," Evan answered.

A shiver ran down Megan's spine and she leaned into him, grabbing his hand. Wyatt knew exactly what she was thinking. Knowing there was a group of men roaming around the mountain, armed and dangerous, made her nervous. It terrified him.

"How have you managed to avoid them?" Jack asked next.

Evan shook his head. "Oh, we haven't avoided them, but we've done a very good job at looking destitute. When we see them coming, we hide the weapons. We have some secret caches. You'll forgive me if I don't tell you where they're hidden."

"Not a problem. We would do the same," Wyatt answered. "So, has anyone tried to track them down? Do they have a camp on the mountain?"

Bryan shrugged. "We honestly don't know. There is a group in town who are excellent trackers, but they've never been able to find the Raiders. Once they raid, they vanish. There are a lot of people who would really like them to disappear if you know what I mean. The Raiders are big on making enemies, not friends."

Megan sounded uneasy. "How do you fight off an enemy you can't see and didn't know anything about? More importantly, would they take a little girl?"

No one answered for several long moments.

"I honestly don't know," Bryan finally said. "I can't imagine them taking care of a kid. They look like something out of a dystopian nightmare and they're organized. They carry enough guns and ammunition to take on a small army. I can't see them wanting to deal with a kid. It would slow them down."

"Well great, that description is only slightly terrifying," Megan told them. "On the plus side, hopefully they'll ignore Caitlin."

Evan nodded and then lifted his hand, pointing his finger toward the woods. "What about the Green Woman?" Evan asked no one in particular.

"The Green Woman?" Megan asked. "What is that? Like an actual person?"

Sharon quickly explained. "We call her the Green Woman because she is always dressed in Army green. She never says a word, but she draws her gun quicker than any person I have ever met. She has never actually said she was going to hurt one of us, but she makes it clear she doesn't want you near her."

"We've seen her a few times, but we keep our distance. I'm pretty sure she has a home near that big meadow, which is where we usually run into her," Evan explained. "She seems harmless, just a little on the odd side. Always alone."

Megan reached into the leg pocket of her cargo pants and pulled out the map she had used to find Evan's camp.

"Where? Can you show us where you've seen her most often?"

The meadow was huge and considering it was a giant square, the Green Woman could live anywhere.

Evan walked around the table and stood over Megan, he pointed to a section.

"That's the area where we fell!"

Wyatt jumped up to study the map as well.

"Are you sure? We covered that area during our initial search for Caitlin."

Wyatt couldn't believe he could have walked right past this Green Woman.

"We'll check there on our way back tomorrow," he told Megan.

"Even if she isn't there, she may know what happened. She can stay out of sight. You wouldn't even know she was there if she didn't come out and make herself known," Bryan explained.

"Thanks for the tip."

There was a pause in the conversation as another gust blew through. Wyatt looked around at the tents.

"So, I have to ask, what's your plan for winter? I mean, tents don't seem like a real good option. The two cabins aren't going to cut it either. Are you moving into town?"

Bryan answered. "We will stay here. Town has become too dangerous and food is scarce. We think we'll be better off up here. We had to weigh the two options; live in houses with limited access to food and water or live basically on top of each other with plenty of resources around us."

Wyatt nodded. It made sense. In town, they would have to walk a lot farther to hunt for food, and then run the risk of being attacked for what they caught. In the mountains, meat was plentiful if you knew how to hunt. The snow could be used for water. He understood their reasoning but was still concerned about their shelter situation.

"What about that barn?" Jack asked. "Why don't you stay in it?"

It was Sharon's turn to explain, "The roof is not in good shape. We can't risk a heavy snowfall causing it to collapse. Thanks to the plans you helped draw up, next spring we will fix the roof but we didn't have the time or materials to do it before winter this year."

"So, you will all stay in these two cabins?" Megan asked.

Wyatt had counted fifteen people in the group. There may have been more in town, scavenging for supplies. Evan's tiny little cabin would certainly be cozy and the woodstove would keep it warm, but they would be sitting on top of each other.

Wyatt looked at Megan and he could see the doubt in her eyes. She silently agreed with him. They had to have another shelter somewhere. Their reason for secrecy was understandable. They weren't going to press the issue.

The silence held some tension. The other group had secrets they wanted to hold onto. Wyatt quickly tried to change the subject. "Tara, I saw you carrying some snowshoes earlier. Did you make them?"

"Yep and I really hope they work!"

"Can you show us how you did it? We have a couple pairs, but it would be nice to have a pair for each of us. We have no idea how much snow we will get up here but I imagine it will be more than we want to try to walk through."

"I read an article years ago about making your own and just did my best to copy it from memory. Unfortunately, I don't have any more willow branches here but I can tell you how I did it. I'm sure there are other ways and other materials you can use. You can certainly fine tune the shoes based on what works best for you," Tara explained.

"Willow branches, about two inches around, are the best choice. They are nice and flexible. You could use other branches, but you would need to slowly steam the wood to get it nice and bendy."

She sent her daughter to grab the snowshoes she had finished earlier.

"Basically, each shoe should kind of look like a tennis racket with a rounded toe and a pointed heel. The width needs to be a few inches wider than the boot you will fasten to the shoe. I like to make mine about thirty to forty inches long. They are easier to manage and provide the support you need to walk on the snow."

Her daughter returned with the snowshoes. Tara held one up. "I stripped similarly sized branches to make the frame and used smaller branches to create crossbars where the ball of the foot will go. You'll definitely want the toe hole so you can drag your feet across the ground. Without it, you'll have to pick your feet up each time you take a step and that gets exhausting. Since we don't have a lot of para-cord or leather to spare, I mixed strips of bark with the paracord in a weave pattern across the shoe frame. I used leather straps to tie them on, but you could use anything, even duct tape if you had to. Now, technically, you could use them at this point. The key is making sure you tie your boot to the shoe really well."

Tara handed Wyatt the snowshoes. "And well, that's it! I don't know how durable these will be, but I figure they will last through this winter at least. Bit of trial and error, so we will see where we went wrong and go from there."

"This is really impressive, Tara," Wyatt said, carefully examining the shoes. "Thank you."

The wind and rain really started to pick up. Megan involuntarily yawned and quickly covered her mouth. Wyatt knew she had to be exhausted. He stood, indicating they were ready to turn in for the night.

Sharon, Bryan and Evan all exchanged a look that confirmed Wyatt's suspicions that something was up. He began to feel uneasy. Whatever it was they were hiding couldn't be good. He second-guessed his deci-sion to stay at the camp overnight.

He wasn't about to put his family in danger and figured if someone's feelings got hurt, too bad. You couldn't trust anyone and while these guys appeared to be all nice and hospitable, maybe that was their plan. Maybe they were lulling them into a false sense of comfort and *would* attack when they were asleep.

Wyatt put his hands on his hips and stared directly at Bryan and then Evan.

"What's the deal? Something is up. I would appreciate you being straight with us."

Megan tensed. Jack moved to stand beside his brother. Rosie casually moved behind her sons and rested a hand on Megan's shoulder.

There was a very long, tense silence as the other group looked at each other, seeming to have a silent conversation. Wyatt's heart raced as he considered the possibility they had walked right into a trap.

Tara looked incredibly nervous. She motioned for her kids to leave the gazebo, which increased the feeling of doom.

"We'll go. Just keep what we gave you." Wyatt reached down to grab Megan's elbow. He would take his chances in the forest with a storm brewing. These people weren't being straight and he didn't know what they were hiding. He didn't like it one bit.

Megan stood, with the help of Wyatt and Rosie. Wyatt kept his arm around her, prepared to shelter her if things got ugly.

Jack moved to grab the packs that had been propped in the corner of the gazebo and whistled for Duke who'd finished his treat and trotted over to join them.

The foursome backed out of the gazebo. The others stood and watched, not making a move to stop them. They turned and Wyatt held onto Megan as they covered the distance to the fence line. With every step, Wyatt expected to be shot in the back or ordered to stop.

Megan leaned into his side. "It's okay. None of us could have known."

He looked down at her. "I should have known. We need to get as far from here as possible. Can you make it?"

"I have to. I'll be fine. Just get us out of here."

They reached the makeshift gates that led out of the camp. The two guards they encountered earlier stood at the gates.

"We're leaving," Wyatt said. He kept moving forward.

One of the guards held up his hand. "Doesn't look like it. Evan wants to have a word with you."

Wyatt turned enough to look behind him. Evan was walking towards them with long, purposeful strides.

He turned back and whispered in Megan's ear. "When I say run, grab my mom and push your way through those guards. Do whatever it takes to get out of here."

Megan froze. "We can't just leave you and Jack."

Wyatt gave her a look that made it clear he wasn't in the mood for a discussion. He had decided and she had better obey.

Evan approached, his gaze never leaving Wyatt's face.

"You aren't leaving."

21

Wyatt pushed Megan behind him. He stepped towards Evan, using his size to intimidate the smaller man. It wasn't exactly working. Evan had a smirk on his face that irritated and worried Wyatt.

"You aren't leaving," Evan repeated. "There is no reason for you to head out in the dark in this storm. We have shelter for you. And no, we aren't going to kill you in your sleep."

"Why would we trust you?"

"Because we are your only friends," Evan stated. He said it in a way that Wyatt couldn't tell if it was a joke or a threat.

Wyatt could see Bryan approaching behind Evan. He debated ordering Megan to run, but something made him hesitate.

Bryan had an easy gait. Not the walk of a man who was about to execute the people he had just shared a meal with. He walked as if he hadn't a care in the world. Wyatt didn't know if that was a good thing or a sign of trouble.

He walked up, slapped Wyatt on the shoulder and chuckled. "You are one intuitive guy, man. Seriously. Are you ex-military or special forces or what?"

Wyatt eyed him. "Something like that."

"Well, Mr. Paranoid, we would like to show you something. And it isn't anything crazy or evil." Bryan looked at Jack. "Please, come with us."

Wyatt wasn't getting any bad vibes. He looked past the fence line, into the dark forest. He thought about what it would be like trying to walk through the rocky, uneven terrain in complete darkness. With his mom with them, Megan's injury *and* the pending storm, Evan and his people seemed to be the lesser of two evils, and he didn't like the odds either way.

Jack looked at Wyatt and nodded his head, giving his agreement to see what it was they had been hiding. Wyatt hoped he wasn't leading his family to their doom.

"Okay. Any funny moves and I will break your neck," Wyatt told Bryan. It could have been taken as a joke but Wyatt was very serious.

Bryan laughed. "Got it."

They made their way back to the gazebo, walked past the two tents that were set up next to Evan's small cabin and kept going. They were headed into the forest the camp backed up to. The area didn't look very inviting. It was heavily treed and the undergrowth grew wild. Evan pressed on, telling the others to watch their step as he took what looked to be a familiar path to him but Wyatt couldn't tell since there didn't appear to be many footprints.

Wyatt brought Megan up beside him again so he could help her navigate the uneven terrain. They walked about one hundred feet when they saw what the big secret was. There was a large cabin with another small outbuilding not too far away.

Wyatt smiled. He knew they had been hiding something, but he didn't suspect it would be this. This was amazing.

He looked at Megan. His arm was wrapped around her waist, supporting her. She had gone completely stiff.

"What's wrong?" he asked so quietly that only she could hear.

"What if she's here?"

Wyatt shook his head. "They would have told us. This was their big secret and not anything to do with Caitlin."

Evan walked to the cabin. "It's an old forest ranger station. We don't want anyone to know it's here. The tents are a decoy. The Raiders haven't discovered this yet. If they knew it was here, they may decide they want it and the supplies we have inside."

"Smart. Very smart." Wyatt nodded in approval.

"We make sure to take a different route through the woods each time to avoid making a trail. Walking through the heavy brush and trees isn't fun but it helps maintain the natural barrier between the camp and the cabin," Bryan explained.

Wyatt looked at the cabin. He would personally add some more defenses to it but the simple fact that it was completely out of sight was a very good offensive move.

Evan opened the door. "Come on in. We have two rooms we will give you guys, if that works?"

They walked in the door to find a very cozy setup inside. Two couches in an L-shape designated the living area with a potbelly stove putting off plenty of heat. There was a pot on the woodstove with steam rising out of it.

The cabin had a full kitchen with a small dining table and chairs in the middle. Evan opened a door, indicating one of the rooms they would occupy. There were two twin beds on either wall with a small window between. The door next to it was a bathroom, which wasn't functional.

"We think it was some sort of composting toilet that drained to a septic system buried on the property, but there's something wrong with it," Evan told them.

"Our composting system is a bit more rudimentary, but it also means fewer things going wrong," Wyatt told him.

Another door led to the second room with two more beds with bright quilts on each.

Megan stayed on the ground floor as the rest of the group walked up a flight of steep narrow stairs to a loft area. Duke stood beside her, leaning into her good leg. Upstairs was a third bedroom. There were two twin beds in the room along with a couple of mattresses on the floor. The area could easily sleep another six to eight people.

"Most of us sleep in here," Evan explained. "Whoever is on guard duty sleeps in the small cabin in the main camp. During the summer, we did use the tents but it's too cold to do that anymore. We could in a pinch but why would we when we have this." He smiled as he spread his arms wide.

Jack laughed. "You guys really had me convinced you were going to hole up in those tents all winter. I have to admit I was really worried about you."

They made their way back down the stairs.

"I'm sorry we were so shady, but we weren't sure how much we could trust you. This is our livelihood. We can't afford to lose it," Bryan explained.

"I understand and appreciate you trusting us with your secret," Wyatt answered. "But what made you decide to trust us?"

Evan and Bryan looked at each other and seemed to have another silent conversation. Finally, Evan spoke up. "What went down with Kyle was bad. Not just everything that happened to you guys. There was more, so much more. After my brother was gone, we decided that we need allies, not enemies, if we're going to survive. The things he did..." Evan's voice trailed off as he stared off looking at some unseen horror.

Before he could continue, Bryan added, "We know there are hard feelings but we figured if we put our cards on the table you'd see that we're sincere and have something to offer this partnership. More importantly, understand once and for all that we don't have Caitlin."

When he finished speaking, he was looking directly at Megan and frowning.

"Megan, maybe you should sit down before you fall down." Bryan pointed to one of the couches.

She hadn't realized exactly how much effort she was putting into standing up until Bryan said something. Without speaking, Wyatt took her elbow and guided her over to the couches where she sank gratefully down and leaned her head back. As soon as she did, other parts of her body began to point out small pains and areas of exhaustion. Closing her eyes, she felt Wyatt sit down next to her, wrapping his arm around her shoulders and letting her lean against his chest.

Opening her eyes, she watched Evan, Bryan, Jack and Rosie settle in the living room area.

The conversation dropped to a lull as Megan felt herself falling asleep. She hadn't slept much the night before and the day's intense activities took its toll on her; she was falling fast. She roused when a middle-aged man with a full beard stopped by. He looked like he might have been a biker once upon a time based on the leather cut he wore with various patches sewn on it. Despite his gruff appearance, the man was very soft-spoken. Megan couldn't help smiling as she imagined him playing Santa Claus.

The man, Greg, offered to radio back to the lodge on his HAM radio. Albert had one set up in a corner of his room, but rarely used it since they'd not been able to reach anyone for months.

Wyatt took him up on his offer to radio back to the lodge first thing in the morning.

"That'd be great, man," Wyatt said quietly. "I'm sure the others are worried and I'd love it if we could let them know we're okay here. All of us," he finished as he stroked Megan's hair.

Forcing herself to wake up, Megan shifted into her position and smiled at the others. She had to admire everything they'd managed to accomplish with what they had. She'd also come to realize that Evan and Bryan's group was much larger than they'd first suspected. They'd made it appear they were small in number, just like they kept this cabin a secret. It was smart. If the Raiders were as bad as they claimed, they didn't want to appear too capable. That might attract more attackers.

Appearing to be much smaller and less prepared would benefit them as well. Wyatt and his family had sort of done that already be keeping things well hidden, but given the size of the lodge, eventually a group like the Raiders would head their way.

Tara and her two children had come in and headed for the loft room upstairs. Evan excused himself to join them.

As the conversation wound down, Bryan asked if there was anything else they needed.

"No, we're good here," Jack assured him. "I suspect we're ready for bed as well."

Rosie and Megan took one room and Jack and Wyatt took the other. As they made their way to their rooms, Bryan tossed a blanket on the couch and made himself comfortable.

Megan lay in the small twin bed, thinking about her little girl. So far, they'd been unable to find her but she refused to give up hope. If this Green Woman could be found, maybe she could talk to her and find out if she'd seen Caitlin or even better, maybe her daughter was safe with her. But if that were true, how come no one had seen Caitlin? She prayed her daughter wasn't seriously injured.

Duke made himself comfortable beside Megan's bed. She drifted off to sleep, anxious to get started in the morning. She was going to find this Green Woman and hopefully Caitlin.

22

Megan woke up feeling as bad as she had the first morning after her accident. The fall in the barn had done more damage than she first thought. She laid perfectly still, breathing through the pain.

"I think you may have re-sprained it or maybe tore the tendons that had started to heal," Rosie said from the bed across the room.

"I hope not. It doesn't feel like that. More of a throbbing pain."

Rosie got out of bed and pulled the blanket off Megan's leg. She gasped when she saw the exposed foot.

"Oh sweetie, I should have checked this last night before we went to bed. I need to get this bandage off. We need to get some circulation to those toes."

Rosie quickly unwound the bandage and Megan sighed in relief. The bandage had been restricting her ankle for so long, it felt as if it had been let out of a small box.

"With the bandage off, you need to stay right here in this bed." She grabbed the pillow and blanket off her bed and used them to elevate Megan's leg.

"Not again," Megan groaned.

Rosie put her hands on her hips and looked down at Megan. "You shouldn't have made the journey in the first place. Your ankle wasn't healed. I don't think it's that bad though. It looks good and is already pinking up. Yesterday was simply too much. Relax for an hour or so and then we will get you up."

"Okay. Thanks, Rosie."

Megan lay in the room all alone listening to the wind howling outside. The rain was beating against the window so hard she worried it would actually shatter it. The thought of trying to walk home in a storm that seemed as bad as the one that caused her original injury filled her with dread. What if someone else became injured?

She was really glad that Evan and Bryan had shared their cabin with them. While she was prepared to sleep in a tent, it would have been a very wet and cold night.

She heard a knock on the door before Wyatt popped his head in.

"Hey, heard your ankle is giving you some trouble," he said, sitting next to her on the small bed.

"Yeah, but Rosie doesn't think it's all that bad. Just need to stay off it for a bit."

He nodded. "I radioed back to Chase. All is good there."

When she looked at him in question, he shook his head no. "No, she didn't come home."

"I am hoping we can find that green lady they were talking about," Megan said excitedly.

Wyatt hesitated. "Well, we will."

When he paused, Megan scowled at him. "But?"

"But it is really nasty outside. Like tree branches coming down and muddy. Evan has offered to let us stay another night." When she started to protest, he held up a hand "You need to rest the ankle. Jack is going to help them get that roof on in exchange for a couple of bows and some of the arrows John has made."

Megan sighed, feeling her frustration mounting at the lack of activity. "Wyatt, we need to talk to this Green Woman."

"I know and we will; but not today. We can't risk you getting hurt again and what if one of us slips or a tree branch takes us out? It isn't safe out there right now."

"I know. I was thinking that same thing. Mother Nature is conspiring against me finding my daughter." Struggling to sit up, "There's no way I can sit in here by myself all day stuck in my own thoughts. Will you help me up please?"

He waggled his eyebrows. "Or I could join you and we could stay in bed all day. Just the two of us."

She slapped his arm. "Wyatt! We are guests. Besides, I'm betting these walls aren't very soundproof and oh no, what if your mom walks in. Nope. Help me up."

Wyatt laughed and scooped her up from the bed and carried her to the couch. She complained about it, but he told her it was more efficient and to deal with it.

The door opened, bringing in a huge gust of cold air along with Rosie, which made the both of them chuckle.

"Wow! It is nasty out there. Megan, would you mind hanging out with Tara's kids for a bit. I am going to help her clean up the other cabin. It's too small for four people to be in and it isn't safe for the kids to be roaming about."

"Sure. It will give me something to do."

Megan realized she had no idea how she was going to entertain the kids. Without TV, video games or the ability to go outside, she imagined it would get pretty boring. She suddenly felt anxious. Caitlin was easy to entertain. She loved to read, draw or hang out with Duke.

Megan looked at Duke. "You better help me out today, buddy. I hope you are ready to be the star of this show."

He barked and wagged his tail. Megan hoped that was a yes.

The day passed by quickly. People were in and out of the cabin for different reasons. Megan was convinced it was Wyatt and Rosie who were making sure she stayed off her leg.

The kids, Donavan and Amy, looked bored. Megan had a feeling they were here to babysit her and not the other way around.

"Do you guys like to play Scrabble? I saw the game sitting on the shelf."

Donavan didn't look interested. "Amy doesn't spell. She's seven."

Megan wanted to tell him it was a great way to learn, but let it go. She scanned the shelf and saw Candy Land.

"How about Candy Land?"

Donavan rolled his eyes. "Fine."

He grabbed the game off the shelf and they set it up on the floor in the living room area.

"Amy doesn't get to win just because she's the baby," Donavan stated with authority.

"I would never do such a thing," Megan told him. This kid was nothing like Ryland even though they were probably very close in age.

"Donavan, what do you like to do?"

He shrugged. "I don't like to play baby games."

Megan gritted her teeth. "Okay, so what do you like, then? Do you like to play ball, go hunting, drawing?"

The boy perked up when she mentioned ball. She was quite proud of herself for finally finding the little chink in his armor.

"Well, I used to play basketball a lot but now I can't."

Megan understood the kid's frustration.

"Maybe Evan can find a basketball. It wouldn't be hard to make a hoop," Megan offered.

Donavan thought about it for a few seconds. "But the ball won't bounce on the dirt."

Oh this kid, Megan thought.

"Well, you could practice your shooting at least."

That seemed to appease him.

They played three rounds of Candy Land before the kids decided they'd had enough of her company. Donavan came up with an excuse to go check on his mom and they both left without looking back.

Megan was thankful for the silence, but kind of missed their company, even if Donavan was a bit surly. Amy was fun and reminded Megan a lot of Caitlin, which had her missing her daughter.

She kept waiting for Wyatt to show up and say they were leaving to search for the Green Woman. When lunchtime came and went and they were still there, Megan had a sneaking feeling they weren't going anywhere.

She became frustrated and antsy. Every minute they sat around here was another minute Caitlin was out there doing who knows what.

"What do you think, boy?" she asked Duke. The kids had left to go help with chores, leaving her and the dog alone in the cabin.

Duke was sprawled out on another couch, his head propped up on the armrest. He barely wagged his tail. Clearly, he didn't feel like being disturbed.

"Well, I am tired of waiting around. I'm going to see what's going on." She stood and waited a few seconds to see if the rush of pain would hit. When it didn't, she hobbled to the bedroom to put her boot back on. The swelling was definitely down because she was able to pull the boot on. She left it loosely tied and stood up slowly, waiting to see if her foot would start throbbing.

"So far, so good." Moving carefully, she made her way to the door, being careful not to put too much weight on her ankle.

Megan carefully made her way through the thick trees. The ground was wet and slippery from all the rain. She assumed that was why Wyatt had decided not to come get her.

The main camp area was a flurry of activity. There was a small group in the gazebo and she could see smoke rising from the brick oven. Her mouth watered at the thought of fresh baked bread again. Bread with yeast just didn't compare to what they'd been eating the last few months. Rosie had been able to perform miracles with different bread recipes consisting mostly of flour, salt, water and some sort of fat. But Megan missed the deliciousness of bread made with yeast.

There were two men—Megan couldn't remember their names—using small shovels to rub mud into the cracks between the logs that made up the cabin wall. She knew this was called chinking. She had loved history in school and had always thought it was very cool how the pioneers had built their homes with things they found in the environment.

The mud had a bit of a reddish tint, which told Megan there was some clay in it. She watched as they slapped scoops of mud on a log and then used the shovel to push it in the cracks. In the old days, pioneers often used dried corncobs to help fill in the gaps. They had quite a few of those cobs back at their own camp. They were saving them, but none of them knew exactly for what. They just knew they would be useful.

She spotted Wyatt almost instantly. He was holding a ladder for Jack, who was standing close to the top, working on the roof of the new cabin. From what she could see, they'd made good progress. She knew a lot more about the construction process than she did before the EMP thanks to Albert, Chase and especially Jack, who was happy to share his calculations with anyone who would listen.

Jack had used long poles made from branches to create trusses. The trusses looked like triangles sitting on top of the cabin frame. He was obviously building it extra sturdy to handle the snow load. She knew by looking that the trusses would be exactly two feet apart. That was the way he built. He said it kept things easy and gave all the support they needed.

When Wyatt noticed her, he smiled. She gave him a look that let him know she wasn't pleased.

Megan hobbled over to the cabin area. Jack had come down off the ladder and told Wyatt he didn't need him for now.

Wyatt and Megan walked a few feet away from the beehive of activity at the cabin to get some privacy. He held her around the waist, which she didn't want to admit was a huge help. It took a lot of the pressure off her one good foot.

"Hey, I was just going to see how you were doing. Is the ankle feeling better?"

"It's better." He gave her a hug in response. Leaning back to look up at him, "I take it we aren't going to search for the Green Woman today?"

He sucked in a breath through his teeth. "Well, I was going to talk to you about that."

Megan glared. "Wyatt, if there's any chance she's seen Caitlin, we need to find out what she knows." She could feel herself getting upset and she tried to rein it in.

Loosening his hold on her, he told her honestly, "Jack wanted to get them going on the roof and my mom was adamant that you really needed to give that ankle a rest. We all know how important it is to get Caitlin back, but with all the rain, walking will be dangerous for those of us with two good legs. If you get hurt worse, or if someone else were to—Jack or my mom or Duke...."

She stopped him from continuing. "I get it. I do. I just wish you would have told me instead of leaving me hanging like that." Gesturing to the roof, "It looks like you guys are making progress. How's it going?"

"Yep, just finished the trusses. Jack is going to get them started on placing the horizontal logs across the trusses. I don't think we need to stick around to help with the completion. He only wanted to get them started," Wyatt explained.

"Got it. I'm going to go back to the big cabin and chill, I guess." She was pouting and she could tell from the look on his face that he knew it.

"Think of it as a learning experience. Jack is getting to practice here. In the spring, we want to build a new cabin on the property for Jack, Willow and Ryland. Maybe we can build one for us as well."

Megan nodded. The idea was appealing. They had talked about having their own place, but it was always just talk. What if they could actually do it?

The group had also talked about more people joining them. It was inevitable. Chase needed companionship. One day he would fall in love and want to bring that person into the group. They needed more space. More private, individual space. So far, things had been okay but with that many people living in one house, it was bound to get tense.

"Megan?"

"What?"

"Jack isn't doing all this work for nothing."

She raised an eyebrow. Her arms were crossed over her chest. He had told her before she looked just like Caitlin when she didn't get her way.

"Evan regularly trades with a group farther east. It wouldn't make a lot of sense for us to trade with them, because it would be about a two-day hike one way for us. But for Evan, it's only one."

"Yeah," she huffed, getting more frustrated.

"That group has goats. Like a whole herd."

Megan's eyes lit up. She dropped her arms.

"Really?"

Wyatt smiled. "Yep. They have agreed to get us a nanny and a billy in exchange for building this roof. Two of the nannies in the tribe just had babies and they will get them once they have been weaned from their mothers. So, we'll trek back here in a few weeks and we'll need to bring them more socks as well."

Megan clapped her hands together like a little kid. "Are they the kind Willow was talking about? The kind for milking?"

"Yep, Nubians."

Megan hobbled back to him and kissed him on the lips. "Thank you. Sorry for being a brat."

He laughed. "You are always a brat. Never apologize. The kids are going to be thrilled, huh?"

Mentioning the kids brought Megan right back to Caitlin.

"Yes, which is why you need to get this done so we can get out there and find Caitlin."

"I know, Megan." He leaned down to kiss her. "And we will."

She turned to walk away. He swatted her on the backside. "Go rest that leg so you'll be ready to do some walking."

Megan turned back, rolled her eyes. "I'll be resting my leg and jotting down all the things I want Willow to make with that goat milk."

He laughed. "I'm sure you will."

Megan was stretched out on the couch, with her leg propped up like a good patient, when she heard a knock on the cabin door.

"Come in," she shouted. It was way too much hassle to get up and answer the door.

It was Greg, the radio guy.

"Hi," she said, not sure what else to say.

He handed her a dark blue walking boot.

"Here. I had found this a few months back and figured if one of us ever got hurt, it would come in handy."

Megan had to wear one of these years ago when she had sprained her ankle in a softball game.

"This is great! I really appreciate it. Thank you so much, Greg. I'm not sure how I can repay you."

"Don't even worry about it. I'm sure there are plenty more of these things around. Most people ignore the medical equipment stuff. To tell you the truth, I have slings, knee braces and even a few back braces. These guys all thought I was crazy, but injuries are going to happen. I figure these braces and whatnot can help make it better.

"You have a knee brace?" she asked. Her mind instantly went to Albert.

Greg chuckled. "I have several. You need one?"

"Actually, there is a guy at our camp. He has a bum knee. It only acts up every now and again, but I'm wondering if a brace would help."

Greg smiled. "I will get it to you before you leave tomorrow. Tell him I know what it's like. I would love to meet him one of these days. Us old codgers gotta stick together."

Megan laughed. "Old codger is right. He is the sweetest, kindest, grumpiest man I have met in a long time."

Greg laughed again. "That pretty much describes all of us OGs. I better get back to it. I just wanted you to have this. I know you're tough, but you have a long journey back and a little support will help."

"I really appreciate it and I have no problem taking help, especially if it means that I can walk semi-normally."

23

Megan was restless. Her body was not used to being so inactive. The past couple of weeks had been tough but now that her ankle was feeling better, it was even harder. She wanted to get up and move. She wanted to look for her daughter.

Thanks to the new walking boot, she could comfortably walk and now that the throbbing was gone, she almost felt normal. So long as she didn't overdo it, she was ready to find Caitlin.

Rosie was softly snoring in the bed across from her and Megan envied her. She wished she were able to fall asleep so fast and sleep so peacefully. While she'd always been a light sleeper, ever since Caitlin had disappeared, Megan hadn't been able to sleep well at all.

The lack of sleep was taking its toll. She was grumpy, and despite how tired she was it made it more difficult for her to sleep. She had battled insomnia in the past but this was worse. Now, she lay in bed imagining what Caitlin was doing. She thought about whether her little girl was warm or scared. Was she being fed?

Megan was staring at the ceiling when she saw movement out of the corner of her eye. She quickly sat up and stared out the dark window. The storm had passed earlier in the day and the almost full moon acted as a nightlight of sorts. The trees surrounding the cabin filtered the light, but she could still see a little.

She watched the window, not moving a muscle. There! There it was again! Someone was out there!

Megan quietly got out of bed and stood to one side of the window. She didn't want to alert whoever was out there that she was up. She strained her eyes. A figure emerged from the shed that was beside the cabin and they weren't walking as if they were on patrol.

"Just a little more," she whispered in the darkness. The figure was nothing more than a shadow. A beam of moonlight cut through the trees. Once the shadow entered the moonlight, she would be able to see who it was.

She got her answer within seconds. It was a woman wearing dark green clothes. It was the Green Woman! Had she been nearby the whole time? How had no one seen her?

She watched the woman, carrying a large bag, walk towards the line of brush and trees that concealed the larger cabin. Megan decided to follow her. That was the only way she was going to find out if she knew anything about her daughter.

Megan quickly strapped on the walking boot, told Duke to stay, and left the cabin, hoping she hadn't lost the woman's trail. She crossed the cold, hard ground at a quick pace, finding the spot she thought the Green Woman had entered the trees and carefully made her way through.

Her goal was to be quiet and sneak up on the woman, but tree branches were snapping under her feet and the boot made a heavy thumping sound with each step. Megan slowed down in order to control her breathing as well as the noise she was making.

She broke through the trees into the clearing of the main camp area. It was eerily quiet. Where was their security?

Megan stood completely still, standing just inside the tree line. Her eyes scanned the area, looking for movement. Her ears were tuned to pick up any noise that didn't belong in the still night. Nothing.

There was no way she dreamed this.

Megan waited for a few seconds before slowly moving forward. She looked down at the ground, but it was impossible to see any clear tracks. She made her way to the small cabin. She waited, expecting the woman to come out of the cabin or at least show herself in some way.

She waited several long minutes. There was no movement in the camp. No sound to indicate anyone was skulking around. Megan's frustration made her want to scream. She decided to go to Wyatt and tell him what she saw. He would take it seriously.

Megan slowly made her way back through the trees. Something caught her eye. It was a little box of gauze on the ground. She looked around. The path back to the large cabin was different from the one she had taken the first time. This must be where the Green Woman had come through. She definitely wasn't imagining anything. Not with proof.

She picked up the gauze and turned around, heading back to the main camp. She walked slowly, looking for any more signs the woman had come through here. There was a very faint path visible. Megan looked for signs of branches being broken or plants being pushed down. She scanned the area until she found it.

Instead of cutting directly across and into the main camp, the woman had walked parallel, staying in the trees. Megan followed the path and found herself at the barn. She'd been in the barn already, what could she possibly want in there?

A movement behind her had her spinning around so fast she nearly lost her balance. She saw nothing, but her ears told her something was moving in the opposite direction back to the shed and large cabin.

"What game is she playing?" Megan hissed under her breath. She was torn between going into the barn to find out what was potentially so important or following the Green Woman. It only took a second for Megan to make her decision. She didn't have a flashlight and she had already searched the barn in the middle of the day and come up empty. She needed to speak to her.

Megan walked as fast as she could, trying to catch up to the woman. She stayed on the edge of the tree line facing the secret cabin area. There! Megan spotted the woman going back into the small shed. She decided to sneak up and ambush her there. It would be easier to corner her in the small space than in the wide-open forest.

The woman was inside the small shed. Megan could hear her moving around. She took a deep breath and pushed the door open.

"Don't move."

The words were said with an authority that even surprised Megan.

The woman froze with her back to Megan.

"Turn around."

After a brief pause, the Green Woman slowly turned around. She was holding a green canvas bag with one hand and a small pen light in the other.

"Where's my daughter!"

Megan's voice was calm, which surprised her considering her heart was racing, her palms were sweaty, and every nerve ending in her body was telling her to attack.

The woman refused to make eye contact. Megan took a side step with the intent to block the exit but she wasn't looking where she was stepping and managed to kick a large container with her booted foot. She hissed in pain, trying to mask how much it hurt as pain shot up her leg and into her hip. The woman took advantage, catching Megan off guard as she tried to barrel past her. Megan lost her balance and landed hard on her butt.

She shouted in frustration. The Green Woman jumped over her and ran for the door. Megan was not about to let her get away. She reached up, grabbed the woman's pant leg and yanked, bringing the other woman to her knees with a grunt.

Megan tried to stand up, but the boot made her clumsy. The Green Woman kicked back, her booted foot landing square in Megan's chest, barely missing her face. The blow was powerful enough to cause Megan to lose her grip on the pants.

"Stop! Stop! Where is she? Give me my daughter!" Megan scrambled up, but by the time she got to the door, the Green Woman was gone.

Megan wasn't going to give up; she awkwardly ran and walked at the same time, dragging her booted leg. She made it to the trees before all hell broke loose. Her shouting woke the whole camp. Wyatt was racing across the rough terrain, wearing nothing but his jeans.

He caught up to Megan and grabbed her arm.

"What the hell happened? What are you doing out here?"

Megan pulled him, trying to encourage him to enter the trees. He refused to go in with his bare feet.

Evan burst through the trees a few feet away from Megan and Wyatt.

"What's going on?"

"She was here!" Megan shouted. "Let's go. We have to follow her!"

"Who?"

Megan groaned. "The Green Woman. Wyatt, let's go. She is getting away."

Just then, there was another shout. It was Bryan and another one of the men from the camp.

"We've been raided, again!" Bryan said, storming towards Megan. "What did you take?"

Wyatt stepped in front of Megan and put his hand up, silently telling Bryan to back off. Evan moved to stand next to Bryan.

Jack appeared out of nowhere and stood next to Wyatt. It was another standoff.

Bryan angrily looked at them. "We took you in. We thought you were our friends. And then you rob us while we are sleeping?"

Wyatt spoke calmly but Megan could hear him gritting his teeth. "We didn't rob anyone. We were sleeping. You don't want to start accusing people—" His sentence was cut short.

Megan pushed him out of the way. She stepped forward and got right in Bryan's face.

"Really? Robbing you? I'm sorry, do you not consider stealing children a crime?"

Bryan looked confused.

"What are you talking about, Megan?" Wyatt asked. The anger in his voice was palpable.

She spun around. "The Green Woman has been nearby the whole time, which means Caitlin could be here! I watched that woman skulk through this camp like she'd been here a lot, which means she's camped close by. My daughter might be close by."

Wyatt pulled Megan behind him again. "You want to tell me what that's all about?" he seethed.

Evan sighed and held up a hand. "We aren't hiding the Green Woman. Obviously, she was here, but it isn't because we invited her. She raids us on occasion. When we've tried to stop her, someone usually ends up with a knock to the head."

Megan watched Evan, trying to gauge whether he was being honest or giving them another story. She didn't believe him. Why wouldn't they mention that little tidbit earlier?

"I'm telling the truth," Evan reiterated. "You can search this area, top to bottom again. I guarantee that your daughter isn't here. The Green Woman is probably long gone as well. She's like a damn ghost the way she comes and goes."

Megan was pulling on Wyatt's arm.

"What?"

"We have to follow her. If she isn't staying here, we have to follow her to her camp. She might have Caitlin!"

Wyatt looked down at his bare chest. He noticed his jeans weren't buttoned and quickly fixed the problem.

"Megan, I need to get some clothes and shoes on first."

She looked down, realizing how little he had on.

"Fine! Hurry up and get dressed. I need to get my flashlight anyway."

Evan stopped them. "I will grab my gear and look for her trail. Catch up to me when you can, but please don't go in front of me. If I am going to find her tracks, I don't need you stomping all over them."

Megan waved her arm in acknowledgment as she limp-ran back to the cabin. She didn't trust Evan but if he proved to be a better tracker than she was, then she would take all the help she could get.

Wyatt watched as she limped off with determination. His mom had been quietly standing off to the side, watching the scene unfold.

When he got close to her, she stopped him. "Do you think it was really her?"

"I believe her. She is pretty shaken up. Can you try talking to her while I throw some clothes on?"

Rosie nodded and walked with him to the cabin.

Wyatt dressed in less than three minutes, but Megan had still managed to beat him out the door.

Bryan was waiting for Wyatt when he emerged from the cabin.

"She took a lot of first aid stuff," he said in a grim tone.

"Thanks, man; I'll let Megan know."

"Hey, uh, sorry about, well you know, getting all crazy about the theft and whatnot. We have barely enough for us, so every time stuff disappears I get enraged."

The tension was still there but Wyatt gave him a tight smile.

"I get it. It's cool but I will tell you we aren't raiders. We are exactly who we say we are. You can trust us."

Bryan didn't return the smile. "Can any of us really trust anyone?"

"No, I guess not." And that statement right there really bothered Wyatt. This was what life had come to. There would always be lines drawn and "us versus them" situations.

Wyatt caught up to Megan who was rubbing a hand across her chest. "You okay?" he asked.

"Yes. She got in a good kick. I will definitely have a bruise."

"You fought her?" Wyatt asked incredulously.

She chuckled. "Not exactly fought. She knocked me down. I grabbed her pant leg. She kicked me in the chest. End of fight."

Megan could see Evan up ahead. He had made his way to the edge of camp and was staring into the trees.

"Do you trust them? Believe they don't know the Green Woman?" Megan asked.

"I don't know. All I know is it's time to get out of here."

They walked up behind Evan, being careful not to disturb any tracks or other signs that the Green Woman may have left behind.

Evan turned to face them. "Well, I followed her tracks to this point and then they disappear into the heavy brush. This is the third time I have seen her around here. Every time she leaves the camp in a different area, but almost always the same direction."

Wyatt nodded. "She's smart. She knows how to keep us off her trail."

"Yep, but I have a pretty good idea of where she may be. With your map," he pointed to Megan, "I think we can pinpoint an area to do a thorough search."

"I think we could probably find her on our own," Wyatt said.

"Wyatt, I swear we had nothing to do with any of this and certainly not with taking Caitlin," Evan reiterated.

Megan wasn't in the mood to hash out what they did or didn't do. She needed to find her daughter and that meant they needed to get moving.

"Fine," Megan said, giving Wyatt a look to let it go for now.

Evan looked at Wyatt. "She is clearly an expert in wilderness survival. I suspect she is a former military specialist of some sort. That means she knows how to stay hidden. We probably all walked right by or over her home on several occasions."

"Wow," Wyatt said with plain admiration in his voice.

Megan shot him a dirty look.

"She isn't a hero. She is a potential kidnapper," Megan pointed out.

Wyatt looked properly chastised.

"No matter what she is, the goal is to find her. We will worry about who she is or isn't once we get Caitlin home," he said.

"So what's the plan? We leave now?" Megan asked impatiently.

Evan looked to Wyatt.

Wyatt took a deep breath.

"We need to get a plan together. We need supplies."

"Fine, let's grab our bags and go," Megan said, turning back around and heading towards the cabin.

Wyatt watched her go.

"She is determined," Evan commented, coming to stand beside him.

"Yep. Especially when it comes to her daughter."

"Well, I can lead you guys to where I suspect she is. We'll look for tracks and other clues to confirm her location."

"That would be great. I guess we better hurry up and get our stuff together before she leaves without us."

Evan laughed. "Do you think she will at least wait until the sun comes up?"

It was Wyatt's turn to laugh. "Nope. She will risk breaking her other leg and both of ours. I say we stall another hour. By then the sun should be making its way up and we'll have better visibility."

Evan shook his head. "I cannot believe we are about to head into the forest in the middle of the night."

"Come on, where's your sense of adventure?" Wyatt chided, punching him on the arm.

Turning to give him a serious look, "This new life is an adventure, and a dangerous one. So, if given the option, I much prefer to experience it in daylight," Evan answered solemnly.

Wyatt agreed with his reasoning. Now if only he could get Megan to comply.

24

Megan impatiently waited for Evan and Wyatt to get their stuff together. When it became clear that they were intentionally delaying to wait for sunrise, she decided to start walking towards the spot where Evan had lost the Green Woman's tracks on her own. She was eager to get going. If the two men didn't hurry up, she would continue without them. Even under the trees, with all the rain and mud, tracks could be lost and subtle signs could disappear—they didn't have any time to waste.

Shouldering her pack, she was heading out the door when Wyatt announced he was ready. She smiled at him over her shoulder and he actually looked sheepish. Yep. He was delaying things.

By the time they finally made their way out of the cabin, the sun had broken over the horizon, washing the area in a pretty pink glow. There was a chill in the air and the dampness from the past couple of days of rain made the air smell a little putrid but lush at the same time, reminding her of her fall down the ravine. She hoped it didn't set the tone for a bad day.

The mist hovering above the ground would make it difficult for them to see very far ahead but she wasn't worried. It was a clear sky and the sun would help burn it off. It didn't matter if it was so foggy she couldn't see ten feet in front of her or if it was pouring rain. She was going to find that Green Woman today. Her dad would say, "Come hell or high water." The phrase applied here. She wasn't leaving the area until she found her daughter. They were so close now.

Megan watched as Evan and Wyatt walked towards her. They were discussing something important. Each had a serious look on his face.

"What?" she asked as soon as they got close enough. "What's wrong?"

Wyatt grimaced. "Nothing. We just wanted to make sure we were prepared for anything. Jack and my mom are going to be heading out shortly to return to the lodge with Duke."

Megan nodded. "And?"

She wasn't going to let Wyatt off the hook. In the time they'd been together, Megan knew when he wasn't telling her something. She started walking, so he kept pace beside her.

"Did you happen to see what the Green Woman stole from the shed?"

Megan shook her head. "It was in a green bag. I didn't exactly have time to ask for an inventory."

"It was medical supplies," Wyatt stated.

What did it matter what the woman stole, a thief is a thief. "Okay. And?"

Evan enlightened her to their suspicions. "She usually only takes food and supplies. She has never taken any medical supplies in the past. We think Caitlin is injured and that is why she was here."

Even once it was spelled out for her, Megan kept her cool. She was not going to panic. Not yet. First things first.

"As much as it hurts me to say, Caitlin definitely could have gotten hurt in that mudslide. Look at me," she said, gesturing to her leg. "I didn't make it out unscathed. Assuming this woman has her and the supplies are intended for Caitlin, then I'm glad she is taking care of her. That is a good sign. If she came all this way and went through the trouble of stealing medical supplies, she can't be all that bad, right?"

At least that's what Megan kept telling herself because if she, for one moment, imagined anything horrible happening to her daughter, whenever she found that person she would be the only one walking away alive.

Wyatt hadn't really thought of it quite like that. He had a feeling Megan was acting cool with it all, but as soon as she laid eyes on Caitlin, she would probably claw out the Green Woman's eyes. If her daughter was seriously injured, he had a feeling he and Evan wouldn't be able to stop Megan from hurting the woman.

They didn't spend a lot of time talking as they navigated the uneven terrain. Each was lost in thought. Wyatt knew Megan was envisioning the reunion with her daughter. He couldn't help but wonder if they were on another wild goose chase. They had been searching for Caitlin for nearly two weeks and each time he was convinced they would find her, they came up empty-handed.

Evan was walking ahead. In some areas, they had to walk single file through the dense trees. The route was different than the one Wyatt had used to get to Evan's camp in the first place.

"I know this is a search and potential recovery mission, but I can't risk using the main trails. We can't make it too easy for strangers to find our camp," Evan explained.

Wyatt agreed. "Staying in the cover of the trees should help mask our path and could give us an advantage if someone is watching the main trails." The Green Woman may not be that far ahead or she could be lying in wait, just in case someone did come after her.

"You sound like you know what you're talking about. Military?" Evan asked him. His eyes were continually moving as he scanned the ground.

"SEAL."

Evan popped his head up to look at him. "Then you should be doing this, not me."

Wyatt held his hand up. "You're doing a good job, plus you know the area. Best if you lead."

Evan stopped occasionally to gauge direction and look for signs the Green Woman had passed through the area. Watching Evan work made Wyatt feel as though his own tracking skills were rusty. Granted he spent the majority of his time in the desert as a SEAL, he knew from his buddies who'd been assigned to more tropical climates that tracking in this type of environment took a great deal of patience and attention to details. With the dense brush, finding actual footprints on the ground was impossible if you were trying not to disturb the area around them. Some of the depressions they found were only partials and difficult to gauge the size of the footprints let alone what type of shoe made them. It was like looking for a needle in a very wet haystack.

Evan was using many of the same tricks Megan used when hunting. Even so, Wyatt was glad Evan was doing the tracking. Despite how coolheaded Megan appeared to be, he knew that her biggest concern was her daughter and Wyatt didn't want her blundering through the forest blazing a path obvious enough for anyone to find.

The silence between the three allowed them to remain alert. Idle chitchat was never a good idea in this type of situation. They needed to be able to hear every little sound in the forest. It could be the Green Woman preparing to attack or it could be a bear out looking for a last meal before hibernation. The Raiders could also be around, which was another worry for Wyatt if they decided to venture farther up the mountain. Would his family be able to protect themselves? So far, the Raiders hadn't made it up their side of the mountain, which was why he'd been okay with his mom and Jack heading back to the lodge. If there'd been any sign of strangers up their way, he would have insisted they wait. At the same time, he knew that both Willow and Ryland would be worried and they were needed back home. They all were.

Evan put up a hand signaling them to stop. "Listen," he whispered.

Wyatt and Megan both cocked their heads to the side, as if that would improve their hearing. No one breathed or moved.

Wyatt waited. "What? The birds?"

Evan nodded. "You hear them? Someone or something just disturbed them. It's coming from over there." He pointed off to the right.

They had been skirting around the meadow, not wanting to risk exposure out in the open. It made the route a little tougher and it was taking longer but it gave them the protection they needed.

"Do you think it's her?" Megan asked.

Evan shrugged. "It makes sense if it is. That is the general direction I think her camp is in; we've just never been able to spot it."

"Let's go," Megan said, giving Evan a small push on his shoulder.

She had been put in the middle between the two men. If Evan didn't move, Wyatt knew Megan would go right over the top of him.

The trio was making good time. It was late morning. If they found Caitlin, they could still get to the lodge well before dark.

Wyatt had moved off to one side, looking for any signs of a cabin or even a hut. He took a step and before he knew what was happening, his leg was encompassed in excruciating pain. The surprise attack made him shout out in agony.

Megan and Evan both stopped and ran to him. Wyatt had dropped to the ground and was writhing around unable to hold still. He frantically tried to pry open the rusty jaws of the bear trap that had gripped his lower leg.

"Oh my God!" Megan shouted, dropping to her knees. "Evan, help me!"

Slipping his pack off his shoulders, he left it where it fell and got on the other side of Wyatt.

"Wyatt, listen to me," he stated very calmly. "You have to stop moving around. You are making it worse. I know, man, I know it hurts, but you have to stop so I can open the trap."

Megan moved to the top of his body and put his head in her lap. "Shh, Wyatt. Stop. Let Evan release the jaws."

Evan positioned himself at the end of Wyatt's outstretched leg. He quickly moved the pine needles and brush that were hiding the trap.

"It's a spring trap, which is a good thing," Evan told them. Using his body weight, Evan pressed down on each side, loosening the spring and making it possible for the jaws to open.

Unfortunately, the trap was old and rusty. It wasn't cooperating. Someone had modified the trap and lined it with small teeth. Wyatt's pant leg was hiding the damage but he could tell it was a serious injury by the amount of blood pooling on the ground and how much it hurt.

"Megan, I need you to pry open the jaws. Grab a stick."

She quickly found a branch and stuck it in the jaws while Evan pushed down.

"Now, Wyatt," Evan told him. "Turn your foot and pull back. Quickly!"

Megan and Evan used all of their weight and energy to open the jaws. They waited for Wyatt to comply but he couldn't seem to shift his leg.

"I can't move it," he groaned.

Megan removed her right hand from the stick that she was using to hold the jaws open.

"Megan, don't! You could lose your arm." Evan shouted, knowing exactly what she was going to do.

She ignored him and stuck her hand into the trap to turn Wyatt's foot just enough for him to scoot back and pull it from the sharp teeth.

As soon as Wyatt's foot and Megan's hand were clear, Evan released the stick, jumping back at the same time. The trap's mouth slammed together, creating a horrible, screeching metal on metal sound that sent the nearby birds swooping out of the trees amidst angry chattering.

Megan rushed to Wyatt, who had collapsed back on the ground. He was breathing fast and she could see perspiration on his forehead. She'd never seen him this pale before as his breath rasped against lungs that sounded constricted from pain.

"Hold on, baby, hold on," she soothed while carefully pulling the shredded pant leg up. She gasped when she saw the injury.

Evan was standing over her, looking down at the leg. They both froze. Bone was exposed and the leg was bleeding profusely.

Megan took a deep breath. She felt a calm wash over her. She closed her eyes and envisioned the medical books she had read over the summer.

When Megan opened her eyes, she was ready. "Evan, I need a bandage. A large bandage."

He quickly opened his own pack. "Here, use this." He handed Megan a small package. She knew exactly what it was—an Israeli bandage. It was what soldiers carried into war. The gauze pad included a pressure bar.

Evan opened it, being careful not to touch the sterile pad. She put the nonstick pad against the nasty gash. The pressure bar was positioned over the pad covering the wound. She wrapped the leg, making sure the pressure bar stayed in position. The bandage would then apply pressure to the wound to stop the bleeding.

The gauze would help protect the wound until they could get it cleaned, stitched and dressed. Megan had read about the Israeli bandages in one of the first aid books at the lodge but had never seen one in person. They needed to get their hands on more of these.

Wyatt started to shake. Megan knew he was in bad shape. The bandage was quickly turning red. The blood flow wasn't stopping. He was going into shock and they were miles from anybody that could help. Regardless, she refused to do nothing.

"I need a blanket," she instructed Evan, much like a doctor would demand a surgical tool from a nurse.

Evan quickly grabbed one of the Mylar blankets from his own bag and tore open the packaging. He left it folded in half and covered Wyatt.

"We need to elevate his feet." Evan leapt up on a search for something they could use to do just that.

He came back with a short log. "Will this work?"

"Yes. I will hold up the injured leg while you lift the other and push the log under."

They quickly got Wyatt's feet on the log. Megan was repeating soothing words of comfort the entire time.

She moved to his head and lay down next to him, holding his face in her hands. "You're going to be okay. Just hang in there. We need to get you to the lodge."

"Megan, look," Evan said, pointing through a clearing in the trees. "We couldn't see it when we were walking." A small trail of smoke was rising in the air. "It's definitely a wood fire. I can smell the fir."

"Do you think it's her? How close are we?"

Evan nodded. "I'm guessing this trap is one of her defense systems. We must be very close. I'm surprised with all the noise we're making that she didn't come out to investigate or shoot us."

Megan looked at Wyatt. His eyes were closed and she could see the pain etched on his face. He was suffering. She looked back at the smoke that acted like a beacon to Caitlin's position.

"Go," Wyatt whispered. "Go get her. I'll stay here."

Megan laughed. It wasn't like a funny laugh, but more of an ironic laugh. She managed to get this close to her daughter only to potentially lose the man she loved. She was forced to make an impossible decision. Did she stay with Wyatt and get him to the lodge or go get her daughter?

If the Green Woman checked the area, she would see the sprung trap and the blood. She would know someone had been close. She may move, taking Caitlin with her. Megan wanted to scream in frustration.

Evan was looking to her, waiting for her to make a decision. Could she leave Wyatt? Could she actually leave her daughter?

The answer was no to both. But she couldn't possibly walk away from Caitlin. She was her everything.

"I'll get him to the lodge. If you help me make a stretcher, I can get him there," Evan said, helping her make up her mind.

Wyatt propped himself up on his elbows. "You need to go get her, Megan. Don't you dare leave without her. Shoot the damn woman if you have to."

Megan looked at Wyatt, cupping the side of his face with her hand. "Are you sure?"

"Megan, I'll be fine. It doesn't hurt nearly as bad as it did. The pressure actually makes it feel a little better," Wyatt said through gritted teeth. "You need to get moving."

Evan was already up and gathering the supplies needed to build a stretcher. It was all eerily similar to what had happened two weeks ago. Instead of Megan being injured, it was Wyatt. This Green Woman had a lot to answer for but she wasn't sure she wanted to ask any questions.

Megan helped Evan put the stretcher together and it took both of them to get Wyatt loaded on. The movement caused the leg to start bleeding again, fresh blood oozing out the side of the bandage. She rewrapped the injury, putting more pressure on the wound, and added a layer of gauze over the top of the Israeli bandage. The last thing Wyatt and Evan needed was a predator following the blood trail he was sure to leave if they didn't bandage that wound.

Her gaze happened to land on his holster. It was empty. "Wyatt, where's your gun?"

He lifted his head and looked down as if he wasn't quite sure. Laying back, "I gave it to my mom. Jack was the only one armed, and given everything going on I felt better knowing she had a gun too."

Dropping her pack, she pulled the gun from the nightstand out and handed it to him. "Here, take this."

Wyatt shook his head. "No, you'll need it."

"I'm armed, Megan, it will be okay," Evan told her.

She shook her head and pressed the gun into Wyatt's hand. "Nope, not good enough. If a predator gets a whiff of you, you'll need the extra protection."

"What about you?" Wyatt tried to hand her the gun back but she took a step back.

"I'm good, I've got Caitlin's rifle. Besides, as angry as I am, I probably won't need it."

Wyatt huffed out a breath that was part laugh and part acquiescence. "See you at the lodge." Wyatt tried to pretend as if everything was totally normal. He tucked the gun under his good leg, not bothering to holster it. His voice was strained and she could see him squeezing the sides of the stretcher, knuckles white. He was in serious pain.

Megan nodded and tried to smile. She was unable to speak. Tears were forming in her eyes and her throat felt like it would close up altogether. Watching Evan drag him away was hard, but she knew what had to be done. Caitlin needed her.

She shook off the fear, which threatened to engulf her. It was time to bring her daughter home. From here, Evan would get Wyatt back to the lodge ahead of Rosie and Jack, but she knew Willow could help Wyatt. She hoped. The leg had looked terrible. Megan shuddered. It was very serious and if they didn't get the bleeding to stop, Wyatt was in real trouble. They all were. He was the head of their family. They couldn't lose him.

She quickly checked to make sure the Crickett was loaded and set off in the direction of the smoke. She was prepared to shoot to kill if it came to it. No one was keeping her daughter away from her. No one.

25

Megan picked her way carefully toward the plume of smoke, shifting slowly through the pine needles to make sure she didn't trigger an alarm or step on a bear trap. The boot felt like dragging a weighted ball around. No matter how careful she was, it was heavy and bulky and crushed everything underneath it. The vision of a bull in a china shop came to mind. Assuming that bull was wearing cement shoes.

The trees blocked the plume of smoke from time to time, but she kept going in the direction she last saw it, sometimes dropping down into a squat to keep it in her general path. She could smell the fire and knew she was getting closer. The fog had started to roll back in, which helped trap the smoke in the air working to her advantage.

She knew she was close. The trees were super thick in the area and it was hazardous walking. There were stumps, large rocks and all kinds of prickly bushes springing up from the ground. It was almost impossible to see through the trees at this point and the fog had greatly reduced her visibility. Her main goal was to stay on her feet as she carefully put one foot in front of the other, reminding Megan of her initial trek to the lodge. She couldn't afford to injure herself. There would be no rescue this time. Not with Wyatt injured.

She bit back a sob. "You will not fall apart now, Megan. Not yet."

The trees were starting to disorient her. When they had seen the smoke, it felt like they had been so close. She had been walking for close to thirty minutes and hadn't found the cabin or hut she was looking for. Everything started to blend. All the trees looked the same. The terrain looked the same and she was worried she was walking in circles rather than towards the smoke.

It was time to stop and think for a second before she ended up completely lost. Megan used an old trick her dad had taught her. She closed her eyes, opened them and then kind of let them go out of focus. She didn't see each individual tree or the pine needles scattered over the ground. The fallen logs blurred.

There! She saw it. There was the faintest trail through the woods. The grass and bushes were slightly depressed. It was a very thin trail that zigzagged, making it difficult to identify. To the untrained eye, it didn't appear to be anything more than a part of the natural environment. Except it wasn't.

She followed the trail and nearly whooped when she spotted it. Not fifteen feet away was what she had been looking for. A very tiny cabin, barely visible through the trees that had grown very close together, almost creating a wall.

It was very rustic and with the thick trees surrounding it, it was easily missed and she'd bet that Evan's group may have easily walked past it when hunting and not even noticed it. The roof was covered in moss, branches and pine needles. The cabin itself was an A-Frame with the sides extending nearly to the ground. There were small windows on each side. It looked like some sort of fairy cottage.

A small fire pit was shrouded by the trees. Megan spotted a large green barrel set up at the corner of the cabin. Clearly a rain barrel. The woman was smart and resourceful. They had suspected it, but now Megan knew it. She could probably survive up here for years, all by herself, and no one would notice.

Off to the back side of the cabin, she could see a shed of some sort. Maybe a barn? She didn't know, but she hoped she didn't have to search in there. It looked like it would collapse at any minute.

The cabin looked very ramshackle as well. Megan imagined it had probably been here for several decades or more. With the amount of growth around the cabin, it was clear it had been relatively untouched.

It was probably an old hunting cabin, she mused, or maybe some old hermit lived in it back in the seventies or something. She realized the previous residents didn't matter. Nor did it matter how long the cabin had been here. What mattered was the woman who had claimed it. Megan was about to meet the person who had taken Caitlin.

It was then a horrible thought crossed her mind. What if this woman didn't have Caitlin at all? She had already been wrong before. Megan had to hold back the panic that threatened to take over. If Caitlin wasn't here, Megan knew she was truly lost. No Caitlin and what if Wyatt…? She shook her head. She wasn't going there.

No need to borrow trouble, she reminded herself. She could panic after she determined Caitlin wasn't here. For now, it was all about getting inside. The woman was a fighter and wouldn't go down easy. Megan was ready. She owed the woman a good kick after what had happened at Evan's place.

Obviously, finding a back door was unlikely, so her only chance was to barge in through the front. She doubted knocking would really get her far. It would only alert the woman inside that she was coming. Nope. She was going to rely on the element of surprise.

She stared at the door covered by heavy growth and vines, which were meant to conceal it, she was sure. This was it. She was convinced Caitlin was beyond the door. It was the only thing keeping her from her baby girl. Her mother's instinct was pulling her to this spot. It gave her strength and the resolve needed to go through the door, not knowing what was on the other side.

Megan used her left hand to feel around the door, trying to figure out how to open it and hoping she didn't trigger some sort of booby trap. She found a knob hidden under some branches. Taking a deep breath and holding Caitlin's rifle in one hand she pushed the door in. It took her eyes a few seconds to adjust to the dim interior.

The ceiling was incredibly low, barely six feet high if that, and a lantern hung in the center. The ceiling height threw her off for a second. The pitch of the roof was misleading. Her eyes finally focused and she could see another door along the back wall.

There was a ladder against the wall as well. She assumed it must lead to a loft, explaining the low ceiling height in the main room. Megan didn't waste any time looking around the small space. She walked directly to the door, once again turning the knob and kicking it open, with the rifle at the ready.

Her eyes quickly found Caitlin lying on a bed in a dim room. The tiny window above the bed let in very little light. The woman she had fought with at Evan's camp was leaning over her daughter.

No one moved. Megan stared at the woman dressed in green. The woman stared back at her, her eyes wide with shock. Caitlin's eyes darted back and forth between the two. Megan debated tackling the woman, but worried Caitlin would be injured in the fight that was sure to ensue; nor could she simply shoot the woman and risk hitting her daughter.

"Step away from my daughter."

26

The woman stood, holding her hands up. Her eyes appeared huge behind the thick lenses of the glasses she was wearing.

Megan stepped forward, keeping the barrel of the gun pointed at the woman.

"Get back. Don't touch her," Megan commanded.

"Mom?" Caitlin called out. Her voice was hoarse.

Megan looked at her daughter. Her breath caught in her lungs. She felt as if she couldn't breathe. Her daughter looked so frail on the bed. There was a candle burning on a small table next to the bed. It cast an eerie glow over Caitlin's pale face.

She spent several seconds drinking in the sight of the little girl she had been missing so much. It was that small pause in her guard that the Green Woman took advantage of. She sprang forward, knocking the rifle out of Megan's hands.

The woman kicked the gun away and attempted to tackle Megan to the ground. Megan pushed back, knocking the woman into the open doorway. Her glasses flew off her head. Before she had a chance to regain her footing, Megan rushed to the bedside and pulled Caitlin to her, shouting at the Green Woman to stay away from her daughter.

Her adrenaline was pumping. She would fight this woman to the death if it meant saving her daughter. She was squeezing Caitlin tight, afraid to let go for fear she would never get the chance to hold her again.

It was the sound of Caitlin's quiet voice that yanked her back from the brink of a rage attack. Caitlin was crying. Sobbing.

"What's wrong? What's wrong, baby?"

Megan pulled back a little and saw the oversized white t-shirt Caitlin was wearing was quickly being stained with blood.

"Oh no! What happened? Did I hurt you?" Megan was frantic, trying to find where the blood was coming from.

"It's the stitches," the woman in the corner said calmly. "Her wound must have opened up again."

The woman was on her knees, using one hand to feel in front and around her. Megan realized she was looking for her glasses. She wasn't about to tell the woman she was a few inches from the things. She wanted every advantage she could get. If that meant keeping the woman blind, so be it.

Megan was confused. "Stitches?"

Her one advantage was over. The woman found her glasses and quickly put them on, blinking several times to focus. She held up her hands and slowly walked forward.

"She had a pretty deep gash. I stitched it up. It healed for the most part, but she developed an infection and it opened again. I was just cleaning it and reapplying a fresh bandage when you came in," she explained.

"Stay back," Megan said. Her mind needed a minute to process what was happening. The woman had stitched her up?

The woman, who Megan guessed to be in her forties, stood still, kept her hands up, and waited. Megan understood why Evan and his group called her the Green Woman. She was wearing Army green pants and the standard issue t-shirt tucked in tight. Her brown belt accentuated her tiny figure. The woman looked like a soldier, complete with combat boots.

Despite the military garb, she looked very unassuming. Her brown hair was pulled back into a tight bun, which made the black-framed glasses on her face really stand out. She was very thin, but Megan knew the woman wasn't weak. She was all muscle.

"Who are you and why have you been keeping my daughter here?"

"My name is Brenda Clarke. I am a doctor, well, a former Army doctor that is. I found Caitlin in the woods. She was badly injured. I brought her here to take care of her injuries."

Megan eyed her, unsure if she was really buying the story.

"Why wouldn't you bring her home?"

Brenda looked ashamed. She looked down at the ground, not meeting Megan's eyes.

"I should have. I know who you are and where your lodge is. I just, well, at first, I was busy tending her wounds. Then, well, I guess I kept making excuses to keep her here. She is a good girl and… it gets really lonely out here."

Megan shook her head. "You knew where we lived but you thought you would keep her here? In the real world we call that kidnapping."

Brenda clasped her hands in front of her, squeezing them. "I'm sorry, truly, but she needed to heal. She couldn't walk out of here and I certainly couldn't carry her out. Even the small distance I carried her when I first found her was dangerous. Was I supposed to knock on the door and let you all know I had the injured little girl at my house? I have lived out here a long time without anyone knowing I was here. I wanted to keep it that way. Plus, I couldn't leave her alone that long. At least not initially and definitely not once the infection developed," she explained.

"Mom, she has been taking care of me," Caitlin said. "After we fell down the hill, I couldn't wake you up. You were bleeding a lot and I got scared. I was going to go back and get Wyatt, but I think I got lost. Everything sort of looked the same and I wasn't feeling well."

Brenda nodded. "She was wandering farther away from the cabin. There was a deep cut across her chest and stomach that looked like she'd been impaled. I wanted to get it cleaned and stitched right away before she lost any more blood."

Caitlin nodded in agreement with Brenda's version of events.

"Caitlin told me what had happened to you guys. The storm was still raging when I found her. I was more concerned about getting her to safety than trekking to your cabin. By the time I got her back here and was able to go back and look for you, you were gone."

The doctor took a step forward, holding her hands up. "I need to look at that wound. I am not going to hurt her, I promise."

Megan looked down at Caitlin; the blood had made a small circle on the shirt. She didn't trust this woman but with her daughter actively bleeding, she needed help. Giving the woman a curt nod, she scooted over on the bed, but didn't get up.

"Lay back, Caitlin, let me see." Caitlin lay back down and lifted the shirt up, exposing the injury on her stomach. Parts of it were pink and puffy and appeared to be healing but the other looked as though she'd reinjured it. Megan could see where the delicate skin had pulled apart.

Megan hissed. "What happened, honey?"

"A tree branch cut me when I fell down," she explained. "It was bleeding a lot. It didn't hurt nearly as much as my foot, though."

Megan looked at Brenda. "Her foot?"

Brenda once again looked away. Megan saw the guilt cross her face before she had a chance to try to hide her expression.

"What happened to her foot?" Megan said again, louder and with more force.

"It got caught in a trap, Mom," Caitlin explained.

Megan instantly thought of what Wyatt had just endured. Caitlin's tiny little leg would have been crushed! She pulled the covers off and saw the bandage around Caitlin's right ankle and foot. The foot seemed to be intact and there wasn't any blood on the bandage.

"How bad?" she demanded of Brenda.

"It wasn't that bad. It did require a few stitches but it was a small trap." Brenda quietly explained. "I was able to get her foot out without any problems. Nothing was broken. It was bruised and tender for a few days, which is another reason I didn't want to move her immediately."

Megan considered telling her about Wyatt's own injury. Evan was convinced the Green Woman was the one who set the traps in the first place. She was responsible for Wyatt's injury and Caitlin's. Megan looked at her, realizing why she had gone to such great lengths to help Caitlin. Guilt.

Brenda carefully felt around the area on Caitlin's stomach.

"Megan," Brenda started. When Megan raised an eyebrow in question, she quickly explained how she knew her name. "Caitlin told me your name. She has been telling me about everyone at the lodge. I feel like I know you all so well."

"Oh," Megan said. She didn't know what else *to* say. Her daughter knew not to talk to strangers or share personal information but for her, these were different circumstances and she couldn't be upset with her for oversharing. She only hoped it wouldn't cause problems.

"Can you hand me that bag over there?" she said, pointing in the corner of the room.

Megan recognized it right away. It was the one she had at Evan's cabin. She grabbed the bag and handed it to Brenda.

"Actually, I need a gauze pad if you could get it for me. I know I put a bunch in there somewhere."

Megan dug through the bag and found a box of small square packages. This is why she had been looting? She had made the long trip to Evan's place to get medical supplies to treat Caitlin? Megan was thankful, but she also wondered why she didn't simply ask for help.

Brenda cleaned the area and used some medical tape to create a butterfly stitch. Once she was happy with the way the wound looked, she put a fresh bandage over it. She explained everything she was doing.

"All good," she declared.

"Thank you," Megan said. "We need to get going now."

Brenda looked surprised. "You're leaving?"

"We have been looking for Caitlin for nearly two weeks. The family has been worried sick." Megan stopped. She didn't want to alarm Caitlin by revealing how seriously Wyatt was injured. "And one of my group was hurt. The others took him back to the lodge. I would really like to get there and see how he is doing."

"Who got hurt, Mom?" Caitlin asked.

Megan hesitated. "Wyatt did, honey."

"What happened?" she asked.

"He stepped in a *trap*." She said it more to Brenda than her daughter, emphasizing the word trap. She knew Brenda had set that trap and it wasn't put there in the hopes of actually getting a bear. It was a booby trap meant to keep people away.

Brenda apologized. "I'm sorry one of your group was injured but I'm alone out here. There are dangerous people out here who want what little I have. I need to protect myself."

Megan was furious over everything that happened but she didn't want to make things worse. "I understand your concern. The meadow looks to be fertile hunting. I hope we can work out some kind of arrangement, like you tell us where the traps are or what areas you want us to stay out of. Then we won't have to worry about any more injuries."

The tension in the room amplified.

"I only recently set the larger traps. Those men are getting closer each time they come through. I wasn't trying to hurt anyone but trust me; those traps may help you out as well."

"How could they possibly help us?" Megan asked. Her irritation was growing.

Brenda chuckled. "You guys live up there and have your nice little barbed wire fence around the property and think you are safe. There is a group of bad men, very bad men, who aren't going to be stopped by a little fence. They have a lot of firepower and love to waste it."

"We've heard all about the Raiders or whatever you want to call them. So far, we've been left alone. We don't go looking for trouble or stealing from other people."

The last was said with more vehemence than Megan intended, but she was offended by Brenda's remarks. They'd done their best to keep the lodge and everything they had safe and this woman was picking it apart as if they were nothing more than children at play.

"We aren't trying to kill or maim anyone. We only want to establish a boundary. We know it isn't going to stop anyone from coming in if they really want to. In fact, we've already been down that road and guess what? We're all still here."

Brenda shrugged. "You have your way and I have mine. There's only one of me. I have to go on the offensive. I can't wait and see or wait for someone to rescue me. My traps could very well stop them from continuing on to your camp."

Megan was a little surprised at how cold and calculating the woman was. She was so gentle when she was talking to Caitlin and tending her wound.

"Why are you so willing to jeopardize innocent people?" Megan asked.

27

From experience, Megan knew this new life came with hard decisions. She'd already made some, but what this woman was doing? Was she truly prepared to go there herself?

Brenda sighed. At first, Megan didn't think she would answer. "Look, I am not trying to be mean or purposely hurt anyone. This new world will kill those who don't know how to survive in it, which is what we are all trying to do."

She shrugged her shoulders as if it was such an obvious answer there was no reason to question it.

Megan just stared at her in amazement.

"I am career Army. There isn't any gray area. When there is a mission, you do what it takes to fulfill the mission. I don't get hung up on what other people may or may not do or how they feel about my actions. I can't control them. I can only control me."

"But why not tell us? You said you have been watching us. Why not talk to one of us?"

Brenda looked embarrassed. "I am not really a people person. Before all of this happened, I was completely dedicated to my job. My focus was the wounded soldiers coming in, some with catastrophic injuries. I fixed them or they died. It was as basic as that. Some of their injuries," Brenda shook her head. "Let's just say, I learned a lot about booby traps."

Megan shook her head, trying to understand how a person could be so cold, so unattached from humanity and yet, be a doctor.

"Well, I am not going to say I understand but I don't think you need to live alone, completely cut off from the world."

"Isn't that what you did?" Brenda asked her.

"What are you talking about? I don't live alone."

"Caitlin told me about leaving your home and heading for the mountains by yourselves. How after she woke up, you left again. Something about only being able to rely on yourself." Brenda stared at her through her thick lenses, making her feel as though she were under a microscope.

"That was different!" Why was Megan trying to defend herself with this woman? "Besides, I've learned the benefits of working with others."

"You have your way, I have mine." Again, Brenda's comment was made with no emotion.

Megan didn't want to get into a big argument. The woman *did* have a point. In fact, Chase had been talking about doing more to be proactive against potential raiders in recent months. It must be a military thing. Chase wanted to set up more booby traps around the perimeter and not the kind that only alerted them to an intruder's presence. He wanted to step it up a notch and send a clear message. Just like

Brenda.

She decided to back down a bit. She had no right to judge this woman. "Listen, thank you for taking care of Caitlin."

"I really enjoyed having her. Maybe too much. I've been alone since the EMP. Like alone, alone. I haven't had a conversation with another person until Caitlin. When I found her, she was hurt and in and out of consciousness. I was focused on getting her better. It felt good to have a purpose again."

Megan nodded. Despite their differences, they did have things in common. Megan had been climbing the walls those two weeks she was stuck at the lodge. She needed to do something. She had to have a purpose to get out of bed every morning. If she had been completely alone, with no one to take care of or nothing to do, she imagined it would be tough to keep going too. Thankfully Rosie knew that and had kept her busy. Brenda didn't have a Rosie on her side, or anyone else for that matter.

Megan also had to agree with Brenda's decision to take Caitlin to her home. Her little cabin was definitely closer to where the accident had happened. She imagined she would have done the same thing had the roles been reversed. Well, she would have made contact with the girl's family and that's where they differed.

"I am truly sorry. I know I shouldn't have kept her here or hid her away from you all. I was being selfish. It was so nice having another person around. Someone to take care of. You don't realize how lonely life is until you are alone, day in and day out."

A little voice in Megan's head pointed out that was exactly what she'd been wishing for. Some place where it was her against the world and she would thrive. Except she wouldn't have been truly alone. Even though she had been lacking in adult friendship and conversation before she found Wyatt and his family, she had Caitlin. Having her daughter had given her purpose and the will to keep going during some of those really hard days but she would never in a million years have kept a child longer than absolutely necessary.

"I can't say I understand but I will say I know a little about being alone. You know, you could come back with us. I realize it isn't easy relying on others. Believe me when I say it was a hard lesson for me to learn, but you've no idea how much easier it is when you're working as a team. To know that someone has your back and you have theirs. And maybe, you could take a look at my friend, Wyatt?"

Brenda looked like she would say no, but then asked about Wyatt.

Without saying the words, Megan conveyed the severity of the injury. Brenda looked mortified.

"I will go with you two and see what I can do to help your friend, but no more. My home is here. I am a doctor or I was a doctor, I guess. Can you be a doctor if you don't have medicine?"

Megan laughed. "Oh yes. My friend Rosie has all the medicine in the world right in our backyard."

When Brenda looked at her quizzically, she explained Rosie's knack for using herbs and plants to heal.

"That's amazing," Brenda said. "I know very little about plants, but I do know a lot about field medicine. Meaning I can use a pen to do an emergency tracheotomy, but not a lot about natural medicine. My years in Iraq taught me far more than I ever wanted to know about practicing medicine in some of the worst conditions you can imagine."

Megan realized how important it would be to the group if they could have an actual doctor in the house. Rosie's medicines were great but for serious injuries, a doctor could mean the difference between life and death. She knew she should have probably consulted the rest of the group before inviting the woman back to the lodge. She only hoped everyone would be okay with it. At the very least, she could help Wyatt before they sent her packing.

Brenda's field training and general knowledge of survival in enemy territory would be a huge help, and given that she's been on her own, clearly she wasn't adverse to hard work.

Megan knew Albert would be the toughest one to sell on the idea. That was just his way. If she could get Wyatt on board, the rest of the group would eventually agree with the decision to bring Brenda into their little community. Maybe she could visit from time to time.

With the decision made, Megan asked if Caitlin's boots and coat were around. She wanted to get going before it got any later. As it was, they were going to be walking home in the dark. It was then she realized how spartan the place was. It was also incredibly clean.

"How did you end up out here, anyway?" Megan asked as she got Caitlin dressed.

"I was stationed at Lewis-McChord. I happened to be in Spokane to get some additional training when the EMP happened. I stuck around for a bit, before things got really bad. Originally, I was with a group of doctors and other military personnel, but things got ugly. We had some very different ideas about what we would do to survive."

Brenda didn't have to say the words. Megan had been around the city when things started to get bad. She had seen good people turn into murderers and thieves. Good people who had probably never gotten a speeding ticket were suddenly willing to kill another human to take a can of corn. It was an ugly world.

As she tossed some things into her bag, Brenda continued her story. "I knew there was no way I could get back to base, to the people I knew and trusted. So, I headed for the hills. I wanted to get as far away from the city as possible. I wandered around for weeks before I found this little cabin. I decided it was my best chance at survival and claimed it as my own."

Megan could imagine the chaos so many people felt the moment that EMP struck. She had been fortunate enough to be able to get home with her daughter. People like Brenda were stranded and completely alone. She thought about those who were visiting the area or just passing through and found themselves in a strange area with no supplies, no shelter and no friends.

She hoped they had the common sense to carry emergency bags in their vehicles. Megan had heard of keeping an emergency kit at home, at work and in the car but she had to admit, she wasn't one of those to buy into it. She always assumed she would go buy what she needed if there was ever some kind of emergency.

This was a situation where the entire world changed in an instant. There was no time to prepare and no time to run to the store. Megan had ventured out of her house on the second day, to try to get some food and batteries for their flashlights. What she saw had terrified her. Store windows were shattered. There were carts strewn about the streets where people had used them to get their goods home and then abandoned them.

She had witnessed people fighting over loaves of bread. A woman with a baby had been hit in the head with a rock. Megan had rushed to help her. The woman had been carrying diapers when she was beaten and robbed. The woman had nearly been killed over a pack of diapers.

That was when Megan decided to stay put. Going out in the streets was far too dangerous. It wasn't worth the risk, and judging by the empty shelves in the stores she did see, it was a risk with little chance of reward.

It had been life altering. Every time she met someone new, that moment came rushing back. She had been so fortunate to have what she did at home, and finding Wyatt had truly been a blessing. One she would always be grateful for, even if she sometimes found herself questioning her dependency on them.

Brenda and Megan heard the noise at the same time. They both froze. It was an engine. The sound of it completely shocked Megan. She hadn't heard an engine in months. The foreign noise had taken a second for her brain to register what it was.

It wasn't a car engine. It was much higher pitched. Megan realized it was an ATV. Not one ATV, but several!

"It's them!" Brenda shouted, dropping the bag of supplies she had been putting together. "Help me, Megan!"

28

Megan had no idea what she was expected to do. Brenda had sprung into action, moving with a speed that shocked Megan.

"Pull that cord." Brenda indicated a rope hanging above the small window. "Tie the cord to the bolt below the window."

Megan did as she was told. A piece of wood dropped over the window. She quickly tied the cord to the bolt screwed into the wall. The wood would help keep out trespassers but not for long.

"Do the other two windows in the living room while I barricade the door," Brenda ordered.

Brenda raced for the front door. There was a long piece of wood propped up next to the door. She grabbed it and laid it across the door. Each side of the door had a bracket for the wood to slide into. Megan hoped it would be enough to slow anyone down, but given the age of the wood and the dry rot, she didn't think it would keep anyone out.

Megan slammed the wood over the windows and asked what to do next. Brenda ordered her into the back bedroom with Caitlin again. Megan watched as Brenda placed another one of those horrible bear traps in front of the door. She was going to have to talk to her about those traps, but right now it could be the thing that saved their lives.

Brenda pushed the single chair in the tiny room in front of the door. Megan wasn't sure why until she saw her stand on top of the chair. Above the door was an old coffee can mounted to the wall. Brenda grabbed what appeared to be fishing line that was attached to the top of the can. She ran the fishing line to the doorknob and wrapped it around several times.

When she realized Megan was watching, she explained, "The can is attached to the wall with a screw. When the door opens, it will pull the can over and dump the old cooking oil on top of whoever came through the door."

Megan was impressed. It was very medieval. If the oil would have been hot, it would have been far more effective, but they didn't have that kind of time.

When Brenda realized Megan was still standing there, she yelled at her. "The drawer in the kitchen. Grab that leather bag. Dump the marbles on the floor," Brenda ordered, grabbing a knife that had been strapped to the underside of the chair.

Megan quickly dumped the marbles. What Brenda really needed was some LEGOs. Those were every parent's worst nightmare to step on. Of course, these guys wouldn't have bare feet but if they did, it would be the perfect deterrent. She spotted a box of .22s in the drawer and grabbed it. She was going to need those.

"Get in the room and close the door," Brenda instructed. "I will be in the loft. If they get to this point, I will take them out. Get to the farthest corner of the room and stay put. Pull the mattress over the two of you."

Megan grabbed Caitlin's rifle. "I will shoot if need be."

Brenda nodded. "Just stay away from the door. They have guns and they shoot; these flimsy wood doors are not going to deter them. Get into a position where you can see the doorway, but stay out of sight." She climbed up the ladder, stopping at the top. "Take care of Caitlin."

The words were unnecessary, but Megan was moved by them. Brenda had grown to care for her daughter. If they got out of this, she was definitely going to fight to get her accepted as one of their own.

"Be careful," Megan said before closing the door.

Brenda crawled into the loft and looked out the tiny window. She could see four men wandering around outside. They found her cold boxes where she had been growing lettuce, spinach and radishes. She cringed as they ripped her vegetables out of the ground. That was her food for the winter!

Were they only interested in being destructive? Didn't they care about food? If it had been her, she'd have kept the vegetables. In this region, winters are cold and having a steady supply of fresh produce could mean the difference in how healthy you stayed.

She checked out her adversaries. The men were all dressed like something out of a dystopian movie where only the most intimidating survived.

"I get it. You think you're a bunch of bad asses. Bullies are more like it."

She quietly fumed as they walked around kicking at the stalks of corn she was hoping to harvest this week.

Her garden had been difficult to grow with no tools. All of the seeds had been looted from other camps around the area. Watching them destroy everything without even thinking about taking it for themselves was alarming. They weren't looters. They were menaces out to damage and destroy for the fun of it.

She had worked long and hard to build up this little cabin and make it into a home. Watching these men destroy all of it in a matter of minutes was hard to take. The thought of starting over was daunting. Brenda rolled her shoulders. She couldn't dwell on that or the complete mess they were making. Right now she needed to focus on getting them all out alive.

She scooted back to the edge of the loft. "There are four men," she said just above a whisper. She knew Megan would be able to hear her through the thin walls. "If they come through, I can take out at least one, maybe two, but that means the other two will be yours."

"Got it," was the very calm reply.

She didn't want to contemplate what Caitlin's mom had been through that she wasn't panicking at what was about to happen.

The sounds of the men talking and shattering glass made Megan's heart race. This situation was different from any other she had been in. She knew they would come into the cabin. The rifle was a single shot .22 LR. It was great for hunting, but in this situation the time it took to reload could be too long.

She should have kept Wyatt's semiautomatic handgun instead of insisting he take it with him. At the time, she'd been more concerned about them being attacked by a bear or a mountain lion. She never once thought marauders would show up. The very idea that guys would be riding around on ATVs terrorizing people sounded ridiculous.

Caitlin was on the floor, against the wall with the top mattress over her. It would do very little to actually protect her, but at least it was something. There wasn't anywhere to hide or shelter. Megan briefly thought about grabbing Caitlin and the two of them escaping through the bedroom window into the woods behind the cabin. With her daughter safe in the woods, she could circle around and come up behind the men, potentially boxing them in. Assuming there wasn't anyone else hiding in the woods waiting for exactly that.

Megan didn't know which was worse—not knowing or possibly knowing too much. Did she want to know what they were doing out there? From the sounds of things, she could guess and it made her cringe at the wanton destruction they were doing.

There was a lot of shouting, cursing and more smashing of glass. Megan could hear Brenda groaning in frustration. They were destroying her home. If they lived through this, Brenda would have to figure out how to live through the winter. Megan hoped she would see the benefit of learning to rely on others for assistance like she had.

A loud thud on the door nearly caused Megan to have a heart attack. Her hands were sweaty and she could feel the grip on the rifle slipping. She had to get her nerves under control. Another thud and more cursing. So far, Brenda's barricade was holding.

Just when Megan thought that maybe she should take Caitlin out the window, leaving Brenda behind, glass tinkled to the floor in the bedroom. One of them had broken the bedroom window. The wooden barrier was flimsy and it wouldn't be long before one or all of them came through.

"Johnny!" a deep voice from the front of the cabin could be heard.

"What?" shouted the man who was a few feet away from Megan and Caitlin. Megan could see the board bouncing as the man pushed against it. One good push and it would be off. Megan and Caitlin would be trapped. Running out the door would lead them to the men in front.

"Get up here and help me bust in this door!"

There was a pause; Megan prayed the man would go to the front. The wood slapped back against the wall as the man gave up and obeyed the other man's instructions. Megan jumped up and stood to the left of the door. It wouldn't be long before the men got through the front. She was going to have to shoot to kill. Again.

"I'm ready," she said in a quiet, steady tone.

"Mom, I'm scared," Caitlin said from her position on the floor.

"I know, hon, I know. Grab that blanket and cover up. Be sure to cover your head and if things get too scary, plug your ears." Megan hoped the extra layer would offer some protection from wood that was sure to splinter when the bullets started flying. Megan silently promised herself to fight to the death.

Megan had no idea what was about to happen, but she didn't want Caitlin to be any more traumatized than she had to be. If there was blood, glass or a horrible scene played out, she didn't want Caitlin to witness it.

It had been hard enough with her daughter being forced to grow up so quickly, she didn't want her to see what was about to unfold. This wasn't the movies where she could soothe her fears by telling her it was all make believe. This was very real.

Brenda's voice could be heard over the pounding against the front door. "I am going to try to get them all, but experience and training tells me I'll only get two before I'm hit. You *have* to take out the others, Megan. Do you hear me?"

"I will. We can do this, Brenda." Megan was relying on Brenda's military training. She would listen to the woman and follow her orders.

A gunshot reverberated through the room. Caitlin screamed. Megan quickly shushed her and told her it would be okay. Inside, she was terrified. Her hands were trembling as well as her knees. She felt like she was going to drop the gun, making her grip it even tighter.

There was a loud banging noise as the door was thrown open. They had shot off the lock and broken the barricade. A man yelled out. Megan assumed he just got oil dumped on him. While it certainly wouldn't hurt him, it could slow him down. She waited.

A shot rang through the air. Megan hoped that was Brenda shooting.

"Get her!"

The man's voice nearly paralyzed Megan with fear. She pleaded for her survivor's instinct to show up. Right now she felt like screaming and running in the opposite direction but she knew she was going to have to fight. Megan prayed for the strength and courage.

There was a loud crash and a shout of pain. One of them had just found the trap. Megan smiled. Okay so they did have their uses.

Another shot split the air. This time one of the men cursed. He had been hit. It was what Megan needed to hear. They had a chance. Brenda had managed to get one; hopefully different from the one who stepped in the trap. Two wounded men were better than four able-bodied men.

Boots pounded across the floor. Megan knew they were coming. She quickly wiped her hand on her pants before putting it back on the trigger. She was ready.

She expected the door to be kicked in. Instead, she heard Brenda yell. It sounded like a warrior's cry. There was a loud thud and the sounds of wrestling. Megan couldn't believe what she was hearing. The small woman was going hand-to-hand with at least one of them, possibly all of them.

"Now, Megan!"

29

Brenda's voice was the only warning she got. The door swung open. Brenda's body had been thrown against it. The woman landed on her back on the floor. She stayed down. Megan knew she was supposed to shoot the man that was standing in the doorway.

The man looked like he hadn't bathed in months. He was glaring down at Brenda, ignoring Megan. She didn't waste another second; she pulled the trigger.

The man looked at Megan in complete shock before grabbing his chest. The close range of the shot had him stepping backward out of the doorway. Brenda scooted forward and kicked the door shut.

"Hurry, Megan. We have to get out of here. Where's Caitlin?"

Brenda was still on the ground, but had flipped to her hands and knees.

She was feeling around on the ground. It was then Megan realized Brenda didn't have her glasses on. She was practically blind.

"Caitlin, we have to go." She reached for her daughter who had her fingers pressed tightly against her ears. Pulling her daughter's hands away, she pointed. "I am going to boost you up through the window," Megan said, grabbing one of the small blankets tossed in a corner. She used it to clear the remaining shards of glass from the window.

It took them less than a minute for all three of them to get through the window. Megan had tossed her pack through the window before crawling through. If any of them had been even ten pounds heavier, they wouldn't have made it. The boot on her leg made it difficult for Megan to maneuver, but she managed to get out the window.

The whole time they could hear the men shouting and trying to save their friend. Megan knew the guy was dead. She had shot him at close range, directly in the heart. There was no saving him.

Megan grabbed Brenda's hand. "We need to get away from here as fast as possible. Stay with me. Caitlin, don't get too far in front of me."

"Head for the barn," Brenda instructed. She automatically started dragging Megan in the opposite direction.

Megan knew the men would discover they weren't in the bedroom anymore. She was hoping to buy as much time as possible. They would likely be afraid to come through the door for fear they would be next, which they would be if she had stuck around.

The barn wasn't Megan's first choice. She wanted to get as far away, as fast as they could.

"They have ATVs," Brenda said. She clearly understood Megan's hesitation.

Megan had forgotten about the machines. They could run them down within seconds.

Brenda was holding onto Megan's shirt as they quickly crossed the distance between the house and barn. It was a very small barn, not big enough for livestock like cows and horses.

The girls rushed inside. Brenda dropped another barricade bar across the single door entrance. It was incredibly dark, with only a small sliver of light coming through a hole in the side of the barn. Megan held on to Caitlin. The rifle was slung over her shoulder. She figured she better reload it.

She dropped to the ground and felt around in her pack. She found the small box of ammunition and grabbed out a handful. Megan wanted the bullets easily accessible and stuck the extras in her pants pocket. If she had to take more than one shot, she didn't want to be digging around in the pack. Every second would count.

Megan felt Brenda shuffle by her. Seconds later the room had a steady bit of light coming from a small window. It was one of the old, single-pane windows that opened out. Brenda opened it and a small breeze filtered in, which Megan realized was needed. The barn stunk to high heaven. She hadn't noticed it at first, but now that the fresh air was mingling with the stagnant air, it was obvious.

"We can watch through here. Megan, you may need to take out the rest," Brenda said with such a lack of emotion it disturbed Megan.

She remembered the woman had spent years in war zones. This wasn't anything completely new to her. She was cool under fire and didn't seem bothered by the situation. Megan envied her. She was not so calm. Every nerve felt like it was bared. Her skin was crawling and her insides felt like Jell-O.

This situation was nothing like fighting with Kyle. He had been a single attacker and it had all been over within seconds. These men were unknowns. She had no idea what they were capable of. She envisioned rape, torture and horrible murders. The panic threatened to take over.

"Megan, take a deep breath. We are good here. You can see them coming. Take one shot, reload and take another. With that rifle, you can take them out before they get close. You can do this," Brenda assured her.

She had to do this. There was no other choice. Brenda was essentially blind and couldn't hit the broad side of a barn. Caitlin wasn't an option. There was no cavalry coming. It was all on her.

Megan put the barrel of the rifle on the windowsill to help keep it steady. The gun was loaded and she was watching the house. She expected the men to come around the backside and follow the same path they did.

When she saw movement, she took a deep breath and prepared to shoot.

All three men were carrying assault rifles. She could see magazines already loaded in each gun. These guys were coming in hot. Megan didn't hesitate. She focused on the man closest to the barn, aimed, and pulled the trigger. Nothing.

"Oh no!" she wailed.

"Crap," Brenda said, standing from her position of towering over Caitlin.

Megan was thankful Brenda was willing to sacrifice herself for her daughter.

"It didn't fire," Megan said, trying not to panic.

"Give it to me," Brenda demanded.

Megan wasn't sure what the woman was going to do. She couldn't possibly see the weapon in daylight. With the filtered light, she would be blind.

It didn't stop Brenda. She ran her hands over the barrel, opened the bolt action and quickly took the gun apart with a speed that amazed Megan.

"I grew up with this gun. I can take it apart and reassemble it with my eyes closed," she joked. "Plus, in the Army, you are trained to know your gun inside and out; although I can't say we used Cricketts."

Megan watched out the window. The men were walking away from the barn. She hoped they assumed they had run into the forest and would head in that direction. If she didn't have to shoot anyone, she would be happy but she would do it, if it came to that.

The sliding of the bolt action drew her attention back to Brenda.

"Hand me a bullet," she commanded.

Megan reached into her pocket and gave her one of the bullets. Brenda loaded it, slid the bolt into place and handed the gun back to Megan.

"It was jammed. It's all good now. After this is all done, I will show you how to make sure that doesn't happen again."

Megan couldn't believe Brenda had just lectured her about taking care of the gun at a time like this. She wanted to laugh at the absurdity of the situation. The gun had been in a storm, left exposed to the elements, and then stuck on a wall. It had probably not been dried or cleaned and was already rusting.

A shout from outside got Megan's attention. The men were headed towards the barn. She didn't hesitate. It was a quick shot. The man leading the charge to the barn dropped like a rock. Megan reached into her pocket and quickly loaded another round.

The men were moving fast. There was no way she could take out both men.

"They are fifty feet away. Brenda, get Caitlin out of here!" she shouted as she watched the man on the far left raise his gun. The .223 caliber bullets would tear through the flimsy wood barn as if it was toilet paper. Megan took a second shot and the man closest to her dropped.

Caitlin screamed when the last man standing opened fire. Megan dropped to the ground and belly crawled to the back corner where Caitlin and Brenda were huddling. The sound of the rapid firing gun made her ears ring.

"What do we do?" Megan asked over the gunfire.

Brenda didn't answer right away.

"We need a distraction," she answered. "If we can get him to stop shooting, you can get off a shot. You will only get one chance. You seem to be a good shot. Can you do it?"

Megan froze. One shot. One chance to save their lives. It was a lot of pressure but when she looked at her terrified little girl, she knew she had to. There wasn't any other choice.

Megan nodded. "Yes. But how are we going to distract him long enough for me to get to the window and get a shot? What if he isn't in view?"

She was trying to hide the panic in her voice but there were so many variables. Replacing a magazine only took a few seconds but she suggested getting in position and shooting while he was reloading.

Brenda didn't like the idea at all. There was a good chance Megan would be shot trying to get to the window.

"I can distract him," Caitlin said. Her small voice was difficult to hear over the gunfire.

"No, Caitlin!" Brenda and Megan said in unison.

"Mom, I can make a wolf sound. Me and Brenda hear wolves out here all the time. If he thinks I am a wolf, he might get scared and run away."

Brenda put her hand on Megan's arm when she started to object.

"It's a good idea. I have heard Caitlin's wolf impression. She is really good. You taught her well."

Megan knew Caitlin was an expert at making animal noises. Kids were like sponges, and thanks to working with the others on her wilderness skills, her immersion into the forest had given her an advantage at a young age.

"Fine. But how is he going to hear you?"

Brenda pointed to the wall directly behind them. "There is a small opening back here. It isn't big enough for us, but I think Caitlin can squeeze through. I think whoever lived here had chickens and that was their way in and out. I put a board over it when I first got here. I can pry it off."

"I don't want her out there alone!" Megan couldn't believe what Brenda was suggesting.

"Megan, this is our best shot. She can make it to the trees, make the wolf call, and then run if it doesn't work."

It was then Megan realized they were trapped. If she didn't kill this man, they would all be at his mercy and he could pick them off at his leisure. Caitlin would likely be killed or kidnapped. She didn't want to imagine what he would do with her baby. Caitlin had a chance if she could get away. It would take the man minutes or longer to realize she had escaped.

If Caitlin could get back to the lodge, she would be safe. Wyatt and the family would protect her. Megan's heart skipped a beat at the thought of her daughter in the forest alone, running for her life but she knew it had to be this way.

Megan hugged Caitlin. "I love you, baby. You be safe. Don't you stop. You keep running until you find Chase or Jack. They will be looking for you."

Brenda was running her hands along the wall, trying to find the thin piece of wood covering the hole. She found it, yanked a few times and pulled the board off.

"Stay against the building until you hear one of us tell you to go," Megan instructed. "Caitlin, if it has been a minute or you don't hear anything, you start running anyway. Do you hear me? You run as fast and as far as you can."

"I hear you, Mom. I will."

Caitlin crawled through the hole, tapping lightly on the wall to tell them she was pressed to the outside wall of the barn. Brenda had her hand out the hole to signal Caitlin when to make the wolf call and when to run. Megan belly crawled as close as she dared to the window. The bullets were still flying, but most seemed to be concentrated to the window and door area at standing height.

There had been a few close calls, but fortunately the man was aiming pretty high or was more interested in terrorizing them than hitting them.

Finally! There was a pause in the firing. Within seconds, Megan heard Caitlin's wolf call. It was amazing how much it sounded like the real thing. She didn't hesitate. She jumped to her feet and ran for the window.

She prayed the rifle wouldn't jam. She got the barrel into the windowsill, scanned the area and quickly saw the man. He had his gun barrel pointed to the ground and was staring into the trees. Caitlin's wolf howl echoed through the area again.

Megan didn't wait to see what he would do next; she took a breath, exhaled and fired. It only took a split second for the man to drop. He fell backward as the bullet entered his skull, killing him instantly.

She couldn't breathe. Megan stared at the man lying on the ground, the AR-15 still in one hand. A magazine had dropped beside him as he fell. The eerie sound of the wolf call cut through the air again.

"Is he down?" Brenda asked in a hushed voice.

Megan couldn't immediately speak.

"Megan? Are you okay? Are you hit?" Brenda's voice was calm, but the panic was bubbling to the surface.

"Yes. I mean no. Yes, he's down. No, I'm not hit."

She looked around. There was no movement. Did they get them all? Megan was disgusted by the carnage that lay outside the barn. Three bodies littered the once pristine area.

"Tell Caitlin to stay put. We need to get out of here. Can you make your way back here?"

Brenda was already moving towards her.

"I have to have my glasses, Megan. I can't possibly live without them in this world."

Megan knew what she was saying. They had to go back to the cabin. Did she dare take Caitlin past the dead men? Did she dare leave her daughter out here by herself?

"You stay with Caitlin. I'll go. I don't want her near those men and there is no way I am leaving her out here alone. I'll be right back."

The two women went in opposite directions once they left the barn. Brenda had one arm out, using the barn to guide her around the back to where Caitlin waited. Megan ran as fast as she could with the boot hardly slowing her down. The adrenaline was pumping through her veins, giving her strength and speed. She knew she would regret it later, but regrets weren't an option at the moment. They had to get out of there before more of them came looking for their buddies.

She skirted the men, hoping they were truly dead. She went in the front door of the cabin, being careful not to slide in the oil that had been dumped on the floor. Megan scanned the floor, looking for the glasses that enabled Brenda to see.

She made her way back to the bedroom, stepping over the man lying dead on the floor. She kept waiting for him to reach out and grab her ankle like she had seen so many times in the movies. He didn't. She found the glasses in the corner, just outside the room. Megan grabbed them and rushed towards the front door.

The bag of medical supplies may be needed to help treat Wyatt she realized and quickly ran back to the room to grab them. On her way back to the door, she heard men's voices. She nearly puked. It was like a punch to the gut.

She hadn't gotten out in time! More men were on their way and once they saw the bodies, all hell would break loose. She prayed Brenda and Caitlin were already on the move. Megan reached into her pocket, grabbed another round, loaded it into the gun, and slid the bolt into place. If she only got one shot, she was going to make sure she took out at least one of them.

Megan popped her head out the door, looked left and right and saw nothing. She could hear the voices coming through the trees to the right of the cabin. The sounds were coming from the meadow area. The barn was on the opposite side. She could use the cabin as cover and get to the barn. She hoped.

She didn't hesitate and ran, once again as fast as her legs would carry her.

30

"Megan, stop!"

It was Chase's voice. Megan froze and spun around, the sudden shift in her momentum almost sending her sprawling to the ground. Chase, Jack and Ryland were all racing through the trees.

"Oh my gosh. Please tell me there are no other men out there?" Megan shouted. Even she could hear the hysteria in her voice.

"No. Not that we saw. Are you okay? Did you find Caitlin?"

Megan nodded. She couldn't stop the tears from flowing down her face. Jack hugged her before Chase pushed him out of the way and wrapped his arms around her.

"We need to get you back. Where is she?" Jack asked, looking around. He looked inside the cabin. His eyes stopped on the first man Megan had killed.

"What the hell happened here, Megan? We heard a lot of gunfire. It sounded like a war zone!"

Chase pulled away from Megan and looked her over.

"Dad, look over there!" Ryland shouted, pointing to the area where the other three men lay.

"Megan, where is Caitlin?" Chase asked. His voice was calm. He spoke slowly, enunciating each word.

Megan rolled her eyes. "I'm fine. She's fine. She's with Brenda behind the barn. I came to get her glasses."

"Who's Brenda?" both men and Ryland asked in unison.

"Come on, I'll introduce you. Jack, Brenda is the Green Woman. It's a long story, but she is a doctor. We need to get her to Wyatt."

The men walked behind her. She knew the moment they saw the side of the barn, riddled with holes.

"You were in there?" Chase asked. Megan could tell by how tense he was that he knew the answer but still didn't believe it.

"Yes. We're all fine."

She called out to Brenda and Caitlin. It was Brenda who came around the side of the barn first. Megan knew she couldn't see anything. Probably just four giant blobs moving towards her.

"Brenda, it's me. Jack, Chase and Ryland are here." She knew she didn't have to explain who they were. Caitlin had probably told her plenty of stories.

Caitlin burst around the corner. "Ryland!" she screamed and ran towards them.

Ryland ran towards her. When they met in the middle, they both started talking so fast it was impossible to hear what the other was saying.

Chase and Jack waited a few moments before interrupting the exuberant reunion. They each grabbed Caitlin and showered her with love. Brenda had her glasses back on and was watching it all unfold. Megan knew the woman felt horrible for keeping Caitlin from the people that loved her so deeply.

"Jack, Chase, this is Brenda. Brenda, this is Jack, Chase, and as you probably figured out, Ryland."

Brenda extended her hand. All three of the guys shook her hand in return. Megan could tell they were holding back. They were being polite but she knew they weren't entirely on board with her plan to take Brenda back to the lodge to help Wyatt.

Caitlin and Ryland were in their own world. Talking so fast it was impossible for the adults to keep up.

"How's Wyatt?" Megan asked.

Jack looked away. Chase, always the one to tell her straight, looked her directly in the eyes. "It's pretty bad. He insisted we come back for you. The man is stubborn, even with his leg nearly cut off."

Megan cringed. She knew Chase was angry with Brenda for setting the trap, and she didn't blame him. Right now, it was about getting Brenda to Wyatt.

"I'll grab my supplies," Brenda said, rushing back to the cabin.

Chase and Jack waited until she was out of hearing distance before they peppered Megan with questions.

She held up a hand. "She was an Army doctor, like a real doctor. She spent a lot of time in war zones and she saved Caitlin. Let her help Wyatt and we can go from there."

"Fine," Chase said. "But she isn't leaving my sight."

Brenda was back within minutes, carrying a medical bag along with the weapons from the dead men, which she handed to the guys. She had a pack on her back as well.

"I'm ready. Let's get moving. The longer that wound is open and untended, the higher the risk of infection. We don't want it to go beyond twelve hours."

As they moved through the thick trees, Brenda asked questions about the injury. Megan could see her formulating a plan as they walked.

"Chase, can you please take Brenda on ahead. I'm slowing you guys down. The kids can stay with Jack and me. Just get her there, please," Megan pleaded.

She was trying to move as fast as she could, but there was no way she could go as fast as Brenda and Chase. They were both light on their feet. Brenda was extremely athletic and could move faster than any of them.

Caitlin's ankle was still bandaged and Megan didn't want to risk injuring it any further. The little girl was still weak. She just didn't have the strength to move as fast as the rest. There was no reason to make Wyatt suffer any longer than he had to.

Jack backed her up. "Go. We'll be behind you the whole way."

Chase nodded and the two of them jogged out of sight. Megan figured it would be a good chance for Chase to see what Brenda was capable of. He needed to see she could be an asset to their group even if she didn't stay. Brenda needed to realize they could help each other.

Megan couldn't help but laugh at the irony of her trying to convince another person to depend on others. Been there, done that, she thought to herself. Hopefully, Brenda would see the benefit, like she had, and decide to give the group a chance.

31

By the time the rest of the group made it back to the lodge, it was well after sunset. Megan went straight to the room she shared with Wyatt. Brenda was just finishing up.

"How is he?"

"Good. I know it looked bad, but it was a clean cut and you did a great job stopping the bleeding. Thankfully, he didn't hit an artery or he wouldn't have survived the trip back here. I cleaned and stitched it and reset the bone but it's going to be painful for a while. Rosie is already preparing herbals to fight any infection, which is going to be our biggest concern."

Wyatt sat up a little more in the bed. Brenda had given him an abbreviated version of what had happened.

Megan smiled at him. "I got her back."

He nodded. "Yes, you did. There was never any doubt."

Brenda carefully pulled the covers over Wyatt's legs and excused herself shutting the door behind her.

Megan practically pounced on the bed, snuggling up beside him. The past couple weeks had been extremely difficult. She missed holding him, spending time with him, and simply being together.

Caitlin's absence had nearly torn her apart and she had no idea what she would have done if she hadn't found her. Now she was home. Megan and Caitlin were both healing and Wyatt would quickly heal thanks to Brenda. Life could get back to normal. At least she was praying it would.

"How ya doing?" Wyatt asked as he stroked her hair. Megan pressed herself against his chest and wrapped her arms around him.

Suddenly, all the weeks of pent-up fear, anger, pain and finally, happiness all collided at once and the tears just came. It took her several minutes to respond and she hiccupped, trying to will herself to stop crying.

Drawing in ragged breaths, she finally managed to answer him. "Better now. So much better."

"If you're not ready to talk about what happened at Brenda's cabin, let me know. It had to have been terrifying."

She nodded against his chest. "It was. They came out of nowhere on ATVs and just destroyed everything because they could. It was frightening listening to the damage they were doing and knowing they were coming in the cabin."

She shuddered. "I cannot believe I shot and killed those men. Never in my wildest dreams would I have imagined myself doing something so horrific. I don't want to ever take another life."

Wyatt could understand what she was going through. His first few kills on his first tour had been devastating. Even though he knew it was a matter of his life and the lives of his men, it was still hard to wrap your head around.

His commanding officer had told him when it stopped bothering him, he better get out before all of his humanity was gone. While it never got easier, he was able to compartmentalize the killings a little faster. He didn't dwell on what he did. It was always in an effort to make the world a little safer.

Megan was not used to death or evil in general. Those men would have killed her, Caitlin and Brenda or worse. He knew it was only a matter of time before they encountered the group Evan had warned them about. Wyatt was just sad it was Megan that had to do it.

They sat in silence a while longer.

Wyatt needed to talk to her about Brenda. Chase had briefly told him about her plans to bring Brenda into the group. While Wyatt trusted Megan's judgment, it was still a decision that deserved some thought and the whole group needed to be on board.

"So, tell me more about Brenda," he started.

She wiped her face before sitting up to look at him.

"I know what you guys are all thinking but she isn't Kyle. She isn't like that at all." Megan quickly gave him all the information she knew about Brenda and how she ended up with Caitlin.

Wyatt hadn't gotten any weird or dangerous vibes from the woman but they still had to be leery. They truly could not trust anyone.

Megan told him all about what had happened at the barn and how Brenda had used her body to shield Caitlin when the bullets were flying. The three of them working together had enabled them to survive.

Wyatt was convinced but they still would have to convince the others.

"We need to talk to the group but I really don't see an issue with it. However, does she want to be here? She sounds pretty independent," he commented.

"Honestly, she was hesitant at first, but Wyatt, she won't make it by herself all winter. Those men destroyed her home. Maybe she can live here through the winter and take breaks throughout the summer if she really wants to be alone. She seems to prefer it, or at least that's what she said."

Wyatt nodded. "It would be nice to have a doctor around here. My mom is great but nothing can compare to the knowledge and experience Brenda could bring to the group. She's more than smart and with her military background, I can see her being a huge asset."

They laid side by side on the bed for another thirty minutes chatting about everything they had been through over the past few days. Megan seemed to be on edge.

"So, wanna tell me what is bothering you?" Wyatt asked, knowing she probably wouldn't.

She sighed and then actually answered, which surprised him.

"Those men. What if there are more? I mean, the way Evan described the group, there *are* more. A lot more. When they see what happened to their friends, they will want revenge, right? Wyatt, they had AR-15s. They opened fire on two women and a little girl. They have working ATVs. What if they come here or raid Evan's camp? It isn't as if we can outrun them, not if they're on the four-wheelers. I'm sure Chase told you what they did to the barn. What happens if they try to do that here?"

Wyatt was also concerned, but there was no way to predict the future. Everyone in the group was an excellent shot. "Sometimes, it doesn't matter if you have fifty bullets or only one," he explained to her. "It's about taking the shot at the right time. Like you did."

She nodded, but he could tell she wasn't completely comforted. He imagined it would be some time before she was able to relax again. She had been through something traumatic. All summer they had looked over their shoulders waiting for Evan to retaliate for Kyle's death.

Now that *that* threat was resolved, they had to worry about men who were far more menacing than Evan and his group. Wyatt had a sinking feeling it would be like this for the foreseeable future. Things were not going to be easy. People would always be raiding, trying to take what they wanted instead of actually having to work for it.

Even if they were lucky enough to build up allies, how do you fight against the power these guys appeared to have?

They would have to adapt for worst-case scenarios, and raiders on ATVs were moving to the top of the list.

Wyatt made the decision to talk with Chase about making sure their security was their number one priority. Things had to be tighter. They had to make some drastic changes to protect their family. Prepping for winter was now secondary. All the food and firewood would be meaningless if no one was around to enjoy it.

Rosie knocked and then popped her head in the bedroom. "I know it's late but would you two like to join us for a late dinner? It's been a long time since we have all been together and I think we could all use a little normalcy."

Wyatt and Megan looked at each other and nodded.

"Yep, be right out," Wyatt answered.

"I'll grab the crutches for you," Megan said. They were propped up in the corner of the room, right where she had left them.

They made their way out to the long kitchen table where everyone was already seated. Brenda was sitting between Rosie and Chase, with Caitlin directly across from her. Caitlin and Ryland were still talking a mile a minute.

Megan leaned toward him whispering, "I don't think either of them have taken a breath since they were first reunited." She chuckled and Wyatt smiled. It was good to see the two of them back together.

When Duke saw Megan, he barked and trotted over to greet her. She dropped down into a squat to rub the dog's head. "I missed you too, big guy. Are you happy Caitlin is back?"

As if he understood her, he turned to look at her daughter, his tail wagging. "I'll take that as a yes."

Evan was seated at the table next to Jack who had a notepad out and was busy making sketches. Their heads were together as they talked more about building new cabins and potential defense options to set up around the cabins and inside. Brenda looked very uneasy. Wyatt had a feeling she would rather be anywhere else. He wasn't convinced she was the type of person who would blend well with others. He had tried talking to her when she was bandaging his foot, but she kept her answers short. He suspected it had been a long time since she'd been around a group of people this large and some of them weren't looking particularly friendly. It didn't help that Duke's hackles were raised when he first sniffed at her. Wyatt suspected he could smell Caitlin on her and since his little friend wasn't with the woman, he was concerned and on the defense.

Brenda was military through and through. He imagined she was extremely regimented and would want things to be done a certain way. That didn't work well when you were trying to blend with others. But he'd bet she'd take orders well.

Wyatt and Megan found their spot at the table and sat down. Dinner was subdued, but there was still plenty of conversation and the kids finally quieted enough to eat. It wasn't until the end of the meal that the elephant in the room was addressed. Brenda.

It was Albert who brought the topic up, as expected.

"We need to have a discussion," he started. "We aren't ready to accept new people in and quite frankly, I don't think it is a good idea."

Chase added his own two cents. "There are definitely some concerns that need to be addressed. Brenda, as you can imagine, we can't simply welcome you with open arms. Some things that happened concern me, and I am sure the others in the group, starting with Caitlin."

Brenda pulled her shoulders back. Wyatt saw a soldier being scolded by a superior officer. She would not talk back or defend herself. She would listen and not show an ounce of emotion. Wyatt knew that would be taken the wrong way by at least a couple in the group.

He put his hand on Megan's leg under the table. She looked at him and understood. Wyatt wanted Megan to get Brenda out of the room. This was not a conversation she needed to be a part of. Megan hesitated. He rubbed her leg, assuring her it would all be okay.

Before Megan could extract Brenda from the situation, things quickly heated up. Everyone was talking at once, grilling Brenda for keeping Caitlin and setting the traps.

Megan stood up. "Brenda, if you would please come with me, we can let them all talk."

Albert objected, of course. "You don't need to be going anywhere alone with her."

Wyatt slapped his palm on the table when Albert's comment sparked more loud conversation.

"Enough!"

The room fell silent. The tension was high. They were not in agreement. Despite what Brenda had done for him, the rest of the group didn't want her around.

Wyatt inwardly groaned. This was going to be a long night.

32

Megan felt terrible for the way the group was treating Brenda but she also remembered that it had been much the same way when she first arrived. Granted, Brenda *did* kidnap her daughter even if her original intentions were more altruistic. Given everything that had happened, Megan was prepared to forgive the woman and she hoped the others would too. In the meantime, she was more than happy to extract the woman from the situation before things really got ugly.

Her opinion had already been established and she trusted Wyatt to speak for her.

Brenda was more than happy to leave the table. Megan could imagine how uncomfortable it must have been listening to people talk about your good points and bad points as if she was up for auction. Been there, done that. She didn't like it then, but she understood their concern now.

The funny thing was, Evan was vying to get her to return to his camp, which she could also understand because it was the same reason why she wanted her to stay. Anyone with a valuable skillset was an asset to any group and truth be told, after their shootout today, she trusted Brenda.

Megan took comfort in knowing Brenda would have somewhere to go if her own group decided not to let her stay. It would give the woman options in case she decided that living with others was a good thing. It had taken a while for Megan to come to appreciate the power of teamwork; she hoped Brenda would too. At the very least, it would be less lonely.

Brenda and Megan grabbed their coats and walked out the front door, both pausing to take a breath of the cool night air. Duke followed them out and wandered off towards the nearest tree. Megan looked upwards and marveled at the stars in the sky.

"I will never get over how beautiful it is out here. Without the streetlights or the lights from a city, the stars seem so much brighter and more vibrant. I know it has to do with the lack of light pollution, but sometimes I just want to enjoy the view without thinking about the science."

Brenda stood beside her, looking up at the sky. "It really is beautiful, isn't it?"

"Yes, it is. I love when it is a clear night and you can see for miles across the sky," Megan replied.

They walked to the bench off to the side of the cabin. Megan had spent all summer cleaning the area up and making it a perfect place to sit and stargaze. It always reminded her of that moment she first showed up at the lodge. It was the moment her life changed forever.

Duke joined them and Megan rubbed his head affectionately. The dog looked towards Brenda and made a sort of grunting noise before he flopped over to demand belly rubs.

"I'm sorry you have to go through this tribunal council type thing," Megan told Brenda, who seemed to be lost in thought. "If it's any consolation, they did it to me too and Caitlin was unconscious at the time."

"Caitlin told me what happened. I'm glad Rosie was able to figure it out. I don't think I would have." She shrugged. "It's okay what they're doing. I mean, it's actually a good thing. It would be more worrisome if you simply invited anyone and everyone to live with you. I understand if they would rather that I didn't stick around. I didn't make the best first impression. I don't even know that I want to stay, to tell you the truth."

Brenda leaned down to pet the dog, but her motions were stiff making Megan wonder if she'd ever had a pet growing up.

"I get it. After the EMP, it was just the two of us. Sometimes I miss the silence." Turning to face Brenda, "I do want to thank you for finding Caitlin when you did. I can't imagine what would have happened had she been stuck out there for hours with her injuries. It could have been much worse."

Brenda gave her a curt nod and Megan felt like her thanks had made her uncomfortable. Or maybe she was still feeling bad for keeping Caitlin to herself.

"So, if you don't stay here, what else are you going to do? You can't go back to your cabin; not yet anyway."

Brenda nodded. "Yeah. That is definitely not a good choice but I refuse to let them run me off either. If I have to, I'll rebuild."

Megan didn't say anything. She thought about the bodies scattered about the area. They would need to dispose of them and clean up the mess they made when they shot the place up.

Brenda interrupted her thoughts. "I really like Rosie and Willow. It has been a long time since I sat around and talked with other women. Men too. You never realize how much you depend on human interaction until it is gone. I have never been a big people person but the isolation plays tricks on your mind."

Megan nodded and listened as Brenda talked about the lonely months she had spent. Despite being alone, she had managed pretty well. She told Megan about her secret caches of food and other supplies that were buried around her cabin as well as all around the forest. She was prepared to bug out of her cabin if it ever came to it.

One of the perks of being alone meant she could pick up and move in a heartbeat. She didn't need to talk it over or worry about moving a large group. She simply grabbed her pack and left.

Megan marveled at how well prepared Brenda truly was. She wasn't going to be completely destitute if she decided to stay on her own or if the group refused to let her stick around. Megan hoped they could come up with some kind of compromise.

Wyatt listened as each person offered their opinion on Brenda and whether it was a good idea for her to join the group. Caitlin and Ryland had excused themselves and gone upstairs. They had more important matters to discuss. Caitlin had put in her two cents. She liked Brenda, she saved her life and she wanted her to stay. Ryland agreed with Caitlin. Anyone who would save his friend's life was okay by him.

Now it was up to the six of them. Megan had already put in her vote.

"How do we make sure we don't have another situation like Kyle on our hands?" Chase asked.

No one answered right away.

It was Rosie who came up with a solution.

"One of us needs to be with her at all times. Like glue. She sleeps with someone and isn't allowed to roam the property alone."

"For how long?" Jack asked.

"Until we are comfortable everything is on the up and up," Chase answered.

"Why don't we have her stay at her own cabin and we just get to know her a little at a time?" Jack ventured.

It was Evan who offered an opinion on that option.

"She can't go back there right away, Chase. Not with the dead bodies still there. You guys have to know the others will be coming to look for their guys. Would you really send her back?"

Chase nodded in agreement. "True, but bringing her here could also invite more trouble."

"Evan, how do you guys go about letting new people into your group?" Wyatt asked. Their group had clearly grown in numbers over the summer and things seemed to be going just fine.

"Well, we do have that one cabin in the main camp. Any newcomers are basically quarantined there. They are not told about the main cabin. We keep a guard with them at all times. If they can't handle being watched like a hawk those first few days to a week, they leave. We all take turns talking to the newcomer. They begin to open up and we get a sense of who they are."

Wyatt nodded his head. It was about the only real option. They didn't have a spare cabin but they could probably figure something out.

"I'm sure Megan will volunteer to do most of the babysitting but I think it would be best if we all took turns. We all need to evaluate her and get a better idea of who she really is," Wyatt explained.

Albert scowled, but nodded in agreement. "We'll give her a week to start and after the week is up, we have another meeting. At that meeting we decide if she stays or goes."

Everyone agreed but Wyatt had one more condition to the trial period. He didn't want Brenda to know she was being tested and watched. If she knew, she could fake it. They needed to see the real her.

The group agreed. Brenda would be allowed to stay at the lodge for a week. After a week, they would make a final decision.

Wyatt wanted to talk to Jack about building a cabin or some kind of shelter they could use as temporary living quarters. It was likely they would come across more people who would want to join their group. They had to have a way to vet them while keeping their own people relatively safe.

Jack agreed that a small, single room cabin like Evan's would be a good idea. They wouldn't have to be too picky with construction. It would only need to be big enough for a person to sleep in. Wyatt and Jack didn't want to refer to it as a jail but it would be somewhere that separated the new person from the group. If they had to, one of their own group would watch the little cabin all night.

It may not appear welcoming and a newcomer may not like it but it would be the way it had to be. If someone wasn't willing to go through a trial period, they would not be welcome in the group.

Wyatt hobbled back to bed. His leg was starting to throb and he was ready to get a good night's sleep in his own bed with his lady tucked in close beside him. Jack agreed to have Caitlin and Ryland have a sleepover in his room.

While no one actually thought Brenda would do anything, they wanted to be safe. Having the kids in the room with Jack and Willow would keep them relatively safe, just in case Brenda turned out to have ulterior motives.

Chase would be sleeping on the couch across from Brenda. He would keep an eye on her all night. Everyone knew Chase was a light sleeper. Brenda was stealthy, but they were confident Chase would hear or sense movement. Evan volunteered to sleep on the floor upstairs as well. Just in case Brenda managed to overpower Chase. He was happy when Jack told him he could use one of the kid's cots instead of sleeping on the floor.

When Brenda and Megan came back into the cabin with Duke, Chase explained the sleeping arrangements. Brenda didn't show any emotion, simply thanked them for their hospitality and quickly spread a blanket on the couch.

Megan went downstairs after getting Caitlin ready for bed and helping Brenda get settled in. Duke had insisted on sleeping with Caitlin and Megan thought that was a good idea. The dog would alert everyone if there were any problems. There was still a lot of tension, but she hoped it would settle down soon. She was convinced everyone in the group would eventually come around and Brenda would be welcome around there.

It wouldn't happen overnight and it would likely take months or longer. Brenda was a bit of an odd duck. Her tendency to hide all her emotions would make it difficult for anyone to judge how she was feeling, but with time that could change.

Brenda had been through a lot. She was going to have to learn to rely on others. Megan didn't know for sure, if this arrangement would work out but they had to try.

As she lay down next to Wyatt for the night, she thought about the way things worked out. Some would call it fate.

Kyle's poisoning of Caitlin had led her here, to the home she loved, her accident had led to peacemaking with Evan's group, and had quite possibly saved the life of a woman who was all alone in the world. Yep, life had a funny way of working things out.

EPILOGUE

Wyatt sat at the kitchen table with his leg elevated on another chair. It had only been a couple weeks since his accident and while he was itching to get back to work, between his mother and Brenda lecturing him, he agreed to convalesce. With Albert hobbling around a bit better thanks to the new knee brace and Megan still wearing the boot, they were down able bodies and Wyatt didn't dare make it worse.

The days were getting shorter and the temperature was dropping. It would be close but he was fairly sure they were ready for winter so long as no one else became injured or sick. With Chase's help, the kids brought down a deer and while they didn't appreciate having to help skin it, everyone was eating well and Albert took it upon himself to cure the skin for later use.

Brenda's skills had become sought after and she was able to barter her services for some additional supplies from some of the neighbors. Come spring, Wyatt imagined expanding their network with other groups in the area, and soon they might have everything they needed.

When Evan had returned to his camp, he'd taken some men to bury the bodies and collect the remaining guns and the ATVs. Except, the equipment was gone and only three bodies remained.

Both Megan and Brenda were sure they'd taken down all four men and Wyatt had yet to tell anyone what Evan found, not wanting to worry anyone else.

Wyatt didn't want to imagine what that could mean or why the Raiders would only pick up one body. With a survivor, revenge was only a matter of time, and unlike Evan's group, Wyatt didn't doubt they would come.

His mom was already making plans for Thanksgiving and he knew they had much to be thankful for this year. They had a roof over their heads, warm beds to sleep in, food on the table, and were making friends and allies.

There was so much more at stake now and Wyatt wasn't prepared to let his guard down for any reason but he couldn't help buying into the growing enthusiasm that maybe things didn't look as bleak as he once thought.

He smiled when he heard Caitlin and Ryland's animated chatter as they came stomping inside followed by Duke. With the new mudroom, they no longer had the cold wind blowing into the lodge every time someone opened the back door.

Shifting uncomfortably in his seat, he nodded absently at something the kids said, not really listening. Looking up at their smiling faces as they trudged up the stairs, he made the decision not to tell anyone about the Raiders. No sense in creating more worry. This was definitely something Wyatt would have to shoulder at least for a little while longer. After all, that's what leaders did.

END OF 'DARK HUNT'

EMP Lodge Series Book Two

Keep reading for an exclusive extract from **Dark Defiance.**

AFTERWORD

Dear Readers,

For the purpose of the story, in chapter 2, I decided to give Caitlin a Crickett rifle. While definitely not the first choice in hunting rifles, it is an excellent starter gun for children. A more common choice for hunting would be a 20-gauge shotgun but given that Caitlin's character is only eight and small for her size, the weight of the gun and length of pull would have been too much for Caitlin, although Ryland probably could have managed it.

Perhaps better choices would have been for Caitlin to use a .223 Remington (think AR-15 or bolt action) and Megan a .308 Winchester or a .30-06 Springfield in case they do encounter a bear. Why? Because a .22 LR does not have enough power to penetrate a deer's skull since all .22 LR cartridges are loaded with either soft lead or lightly jacketed bullets with very little powder behind them due to the lack of case capacity. Most game animals' vitals are located behind the shoulder and the shot should be placed approximately one inch behind the elbow rather than in the neck (an easier target for a child), which depends on hydrostatic shock to incapacitate the animal rather than physical damage to the internal organs.

However, in this post-EMP world, wish lists are longer than easily accessible supplies and my decision in choosing Caitlin's weapon was not based on what would be the best choice but on what I thought might be more readily available.

That said, I hope you enjoy:

Caitlin's Birthday Cake Recipe modified

• 1 cup brown sugar

• 1/2 cup (8 tablespoons) butter (can substitute oil but butter tastes better)

• 2 large eggs

• 1 teaspoon baking soda

• 1/2 teaspoon salt

• 2 teaspoons baking powder

• 1 teaspoon cinnamon

• 1/2 teaspoon ground cloves

• 1 3/4 cups whole-wheat Flour

• 1 cup unsweetened applesauce

• 1/2 cup raisins, golden raisins, or currants

• 1/2 cup chopped walnuts

Ground flax seed can be used as a vegan alternative or if you don't have eggs. Mix a bit with water and stir until you get an egg white type consistency. Rendered squirrel fat can be used in place of the butter or oil. While definitely not ideal when baking a birthday cake, squirrel is surprisingly mild in taste. Sugar can be a bit harder to find natural substitutes for. The Stevia plant can work but you would want to use a much smaller amount, so go by taste until you figure out what works best for you. If there are alder trees nearby, they can be tapped for their syrup, which is similar to maple syrup, but you always want to be careful that you don't permanently harm the trees.

THANK YOU

Thank you for purchasing Dark Hunt
(EMP Lodge Book Two)

Get prepared and sign-up to Grace's mailing list
to be notified of my next release at www.GraceHamiltonBooks.com

Loved this book? Share it with a friend, www.GraceHamil-
tonBooks.com/books

ABOUT GRACE HAMILTON

Grace Hamilton is the prepper pen-name for a bad-ass, survivalist momma-bear of four kids, and wife to a wonderful husband. After being stuck in a mountain cabin for six days following a flash flood, she decided she never wanted to feel so powerless or have to send her kids to bed hungry again. Now she lives the prepper lifestyle and knows that if SHTF or TEOTWAWKI happens, she'll be ready to help protect and provide for her family.

Combine this survivalist mentality with a vivid imagination (as well as a slightly unhealthy day dreaming habit) and you get a prepper fiction author. Grace spends her days thinking about the worst possible survival situations that a person could be thrown into, then throwing her characters into these nightmares while trying to figure out "What SHOULD you do in this situation?"

You will find Grace on:

BLURB

Strength in numbers can make the difference between life and death—but only the right numbers.

Megan Wolford has finally found herself a family she and her young daughter can rely on in these terrifying times. Their group is small, but they trust each other with their lives—and Wyatt is showing her day by day how to love again. With a long winter looming, they'll have to hunker down in the lodge in order to survive, but there are deadlier threats to their safety than harsh conditions.

When a neighboring group is struck by ruthless raiders led by the fearsome McDaniels, they must form an uneasy alliance with Megan's new family. Newcomers mean more mouths to feed and more people to trust, but they will need every pair of hands they can to fight off the raiders.

Get your copy of Dark Defiance here!
www.GraceHamiltonBooks.com

EXTRACT

Megan Wolford stared through the trees, heart pounding.

She wasn't going to leave without her. She'd learned that the hard way and vowed not to let it happen again. As she scanned the area, she wished Wyatt could be here with her, he'd know what to do. Unfortunately, he was still healing after stepping in one of the bear traps Brenda had placed around her little cabin. Megan still shuddered when she thought about how much worse it could have been.

Thankfully, he was sort of walking around—well, hobbling around in the walking boot Greg had given her and using Albert's crutches. He was also a terrible patient. He detested being cooped up more than Megan did. Not that she could blame him, but his injury had been that much more severe and between his mom, Rosie, and Brenda, they could both out-stubborn him and he was mostly behaving.

A noise off to her side snapped her out of her thoughts and she looked over to see Jack sidling over. Megan and Jack had taken on many of

Wyatt's responsibilities over the past month, and together, they had become a formidable team.

"Do you see her?" Megan asked.

"No," Jack said. The frustration in his voice mimicked Megan's own feeling.

"Where in the world could she have wandered off to?"

Megan was tired of scouring the woods looking for her, but they couldn't leave without her. *Wouldn't* leave without her.

"It probably took off, deeper into the forest this time now that it's more familiar with the area."

"Her," Megan corrected, not trying to hide her irritation.

Evan and Bryan tramped through the trees behind them, making their frustration clear with the amount of noise they were making and probably sending her running. Bryan was shaking his head. "I say let it come back when it's ready."

"Her!" Megan shouted.

She stomped away from the three men. How could they be so heartless threatening to leave her out here? It was inhumane and even though he might be frustrated, Megan knew Jack would never leave her alone like that.

Wyatt and Jack were not only brothers, but best friends. Wyatt trusted Jack with his life. Megan trusted Wyatt's judgment and had naturally gravitated towards a friendship with his brother. She wasn't the best at making new friends but Jack had become one of her closest friends and allies.

He was one of the nicest, kindest men she had ever met. She was so thankful she had gotten the chance to know him. Their relationship had evolved into one you could compare to a sister and brother bond.

Megan had developed a strong friendship with both Rosie and Jack's wife, Willow, too. The women managed to keep the lodge running and good food on the table. All of which she would be the first to admit put her in awe. She paid attention when she was with them, but Megan was the first to admit she was more comfortable hunting and working outside with the Morris brothers. She wasn't looking forward to the winter months when she couldn't spend as much time outside. She suspected there were going to be times she felt quite claustrophobic cooped up in the lodge with so many people.

Knowing Megan wouldn't give up and leave her behind, Evan and Bryan went in the opposite direction, eager to get this search over with so they could tackle the other chores at their camp.

Jack caught up with Megan and they fell into an easy stride, walking side by side.

"She couldn't have gotten far," he reassured her. "I hope."

Evan's baritone voice boomed through the trees to the left.

"Over here! Hurry up, Megan! I'm not even going to try to catch her. It's up to you."

Megan and Jack took off running through the trees. Stepping on a small rock, she twisted her ankle, pain shooting up her shin all the way to the hip.

"Ow!" She stopped and leaned against a tree.

Her ankle had healed, but every so often she managed to turn just right and it stretched the weak muscles and healing tendons. While there were days that she wouldn't mind the security of wearing the boot again, she also knew that the longer she wore it, the more at risk she would be for weakened muscles. She needed to build her strength back up, but preferably by not stepping on rocks like that.

Sucking in a deep breath, she took a minute to breathe through the pain as she did a mental check to make sure everything was okay. She tried to be quiet, but the groan came out and Jack was immediately at her side checking on her.

"That's it," Jack said, putting a hand on her shoulder. "Just breathe. It will pass."

Megan closed her eyes and nodded, appreciating Jack's calm guidance. He pushed her when she needed it, but was always there to give her a few kind words when things were especially tough.

Wyatt was still struggling with his injury. He was used to leading the family; he'd been especially grumpy and touchy these last few weeks and had gotten too gruff around his family, which had caused some hurt feelings. When Megan had confronted him with his behavior that night, they'd come to an agreement. She promised that he could vent to her all he wanted, but he wasn't allowed to upset anyone simply because he wasn't able to do everything he needed or wanted to do to help prep for winter.

She completely understood the feeling. Been there, done that, she thought.

The next morning, Wyatt had apologized for his outburst and he'd delegated many of the more strenuous tasks to others. She knew it still bothered him to do so, but he was trying. Things would slow down some once the truly cold weather hit and they would all see more downtime.

Jack stood beside her while Megan leaned against the tree, waiting for the pain to pass. He was a patient man and had helped her through many situations just like this one. Jack and Megan had taken on most of the hunting and scavenging with Wyatt down and had brought Ryland on a couple hunting trips. His excitement when he managed to shoot the wild turkeys was contagious and he always put them in better spirits. Chase generally stayed closer to the lodge working on those chores and functioning as head of security, with Brenda and Albert rotating watch shifts. Willow and Rosie took care of all the chores in the lodge and Rosie was teaching Caitlin about the garden and different medicinal herbs. Her little girl was soaking everything up and was turning into a pro identifying safe plants to forage, which appeased Megan's worry over whether she might eat something poisonous again.

The summer had been stressful with everyone on edge at the lodge, waiting for retaliation after the incident at Brenda's house. Most mornings, Megan woke wondering if today would be the day the Raiders found them and took revenge, but both Wyatt and Jack were quick to reassure her that they were safe, but the worry existed. *For how long?*

Despite the concerns about her, Brenda had proven to be a strong asset. The woman was an expert in everything from her medical knowledge to weapons and she was always willing to lend a hand. The kids both adored her and she remained at the lodge as a permanent resident.

But Brenda was still very standoffish. Megan wasn't sure if it was all the time she spent on her own or simply her way, but she didn't say a lot and when she did, it was nothing personal. While she was grateful for the help Brenda provided, Megan knew very little about the woman who had ultimately saved the lives of both Caitlin and Wyatt.

This trip was supposed to be Jack and Megan's last before the snow started to fall and they would be gone for at least a week. It was the longest she'd been away from the lodge without Wyatt or her daughter, but she was comforted in the fact that Wyatt would remain to keep Caitlin safe. The plan was to scavenge an area of the nearby town that they hadn't fully explored with Evan and Bryan.

When Evan had originally radioed Albert, asking if they wanted to go along on the last trip, it was Wyatt who agreed that it would be a good idea. He was feeling better and had insisted Chase go along to help carry supplies back. They needed to pad their stores before winter. The trip was risky, but Megan had agreed with Wyatt and they'd managed to score big on their trip into town. She couldn't wait to get back to the lodge to show Wyatt the haul they had found and the surprise gift she received from Evan.

Brenda had volunteered to go with them, but Megan convinced her to stay at the lodge. With Chase going, Brenda was needed to help with security. Their numbers were spread thin with Wyatt down. While he could definitely shoot, he couldn't move quickly and Brenda could definitely do both.

"It is going to kill one of us one of these days," Jack said, trying to get a laugh out of Megan.

"You're right. If I don't kill her first," Megan grumbled. She was growing tired of their cat and mouse game and was very ready to get back to the lodge.

They both knew she would never do anything to cause her harm, but she certainly did try Megan's patience.

"You ready? Let's go before it, I mean she, takes off again."

Megan stuck close behind Jack as they ran as fast as possible through the wooded area. She could hear Evan and Bryan shouting ahead. All that would do is scare her and she would run off again. Megan was going to explain, again, how to calm the poor thing down.

When they finally reached the clearing where Evan and Bryan were making a huge fuss, Megan had to hold back a laugh. Both men looked frantic. They were waving their arms in the air, dodging back and forth, as the baby goat bleated in glee and slipped between Bryan's legs.

Megan and Jack watched as the men came up with the plan to divide and conquer. It was decided Evan would capture the doeling, who watched him closely while Bryan served as backup should she run away again. After a moment of hesitation, Evan dove for the goat but she easily moved out of the way. Unable to stop his forward momentum, Evan hit the ground with a loud thump, chest first.

They all laughed. Except Evan, who came slowly to his knees taking painful breaths.

"Megan, I am about sick of that stupid goat. You need to put her on a leash or something," he huffed out, standing and brushing himself off.

"It's a baby, Evan. You don't chain up a baby goat," she chastised.

Megan walked towards the doeling, who was playfully butting her head against a small tree stump. The kid was occupied, allowing Megan to walk right up to her.

It was a game they had played many times in the past few days. The little doeling was far more precocious than her brother, who tended to stick around the pen and didn't try too hard to get out. The same could not be said for his sister, who constantly escaped and ran off, enjoying the merry chase that ensued.

Megan looked at the stump that had caught little Misty's attention. Only now, upon closer inspection, she could see it wasn't a tree stump. It was a cross made from tree branches.

She took a step back with Misty in her arms, now realizing where she stood. There were eight crosses.

Megan couldn't stop the chill that shivered down her spine.

Get your copy of Dark Defiance here!
www.GraceHamiltonBooks.com

Made in the USA
Middletown, DE
13 September 2024

60883522R00179